"NOT MUCH OF A SOULDIER"

"NOT MUCH OF A SOULDIER"

(FROM DRUMCLOG 1679, TO DUNKELD 1689)

by

David Christie

DB

DIADEM BOOKS

"NOT MUCH OF A SOULDIER"
(FROM DRUMCLOG 1679, TO DUNKELD 1689)

Published by Diadem Books
Distribution coordination by Spiderwize

For information, please contact:

Diadem Books
16 Lethen View
Tullibody
ALLOA
FK10 2GE
Scotland UK

www.diadembooks.com

Cover illustration from: *The Cameronian Regiment at Blenheim, August 2, 1704* by Richard Simkin.

ISBN: 978-1-908026-11-8

"A fine resolute man, but not much of a souldier!"

(Gen Hugh Mackay on Lt-Col William Cleland. 1689.)

Dedication

This book is dedicated to Colonel Hugh Mackay,
The Cameronians (Scottish Rifles),
the last father of the Regiment.

TABLE OF CONTENTS

ACKNOWLEDGEMENTS

MOST OF THE SOURCES used in writing this story are contemporaneous, or nearly so, with the events described. Eyewitness accounts have been particularly helpful and, at a remove of over three centuries, still retain their immediate vibrancy. In particular *Col John Blackader's Diary*, (edited by A Crichton, 1824), containing eyewitness accounts of the Battle of Dunkeld, and Blackader's letter immediately thereafter, were particularly useful. John Mackay of Rockfield's biography of Hugh Mackay (1842), has also been of the greatest help, whilst Michael Shields' record of the goings on recorded in the United Societies' minutes *Faithful Contendings Displayed* (1780), is a treasury of detail on Cameronian behaviour during the period.

Some more modern works must be acknowledged. Linklater and Hesketh's *Bonnie Dundee* (1989), and Maurice Grant's biographies of Richard Cameron (*The Lion of the Covenant* 1997), and Donald Cargill (*No King but Christ* 1988) helped to give a deep insight into these personalities. SHF Johnston's History of The Cameronians (Scottish Rifles) Vol I (1957) is a remarkably well researched document and has been the source of much fine detail. Ginny Gardner's *The Scottish Exile Community in the Netherlands 1662-1690* (2004), was a wonderful source of minutae for scenes in the Netherlands, and Hector Macpherson's biography *The Cameronian Philosopher* (1972) remains the only modern biography of Alexander Shields.

I have to thank Ian Martin for his advice on Leven's Regiment, as well as Mark Jardine for his biographical details on the Cameronian order-of-battle 1689 and his involvement in the BBC Dunkeld Walk, wherein Louise Yeoman, Neil Oliver, Allison Reid, and Trish Owen also provided some interesting background on the battle. Thanks also to the National Archives of Scotland and the National Library of Scotland for their unfailingly courteous and helpful attitude.

My appreciation to Bert Kappers for checking the Dutch quotes, and to Michael Bauer for the Gaelic. Also to Peter Gordon Smith for the map, Yolanda Ellis for the diagrams, and Judi Detleefs for her help with the cover.

Thanks are due to the Regimental Trustees of The Cameronians (Scottish Rifles) for permission to quote excerpts from the Disbandment Connventicle in 1968, and to the Dow family for permission to quote Leslie Dow's poem. I also wish to thank many of my old comrades-in-arms for their help and considerable encouragement in writing this book, in particular Hugh Mackay, Philip Grant, Ian Farquharson, Brian Leishman, and Mike Sixsmith. And last, but not least, my patient wife Janet.

LIST OF ILLUSTRATIONS

PRINCIPAL CHARACTERS

Fictitious characters in italics.
(A fuller list of characters is at the end.)

Blackader, Rev John. Covenanting preacher, prisoner on the Bass.
Blackader, Lt John. Cameronian officer, son of the above.
Cameron, Rev Richard. "The Lion of the Covenant."
Cardross, Lord John. Exile and cavalry commander.
Cargill, Rev Donald. Covenanting preacher and martyr
Cleland, Lt-Col William. First commanding officer, Cameronian Regiment
Cleland (née Steel), Margaret. William's wife.
Cleland, Janet. William's sister
Douglas, James. Earl of Angus. First Colonel, Cameronian Regt.
Douglas, James. Marquess of Douglas, father of above.
Douglas, Rev Thomas. Covenanting preacher
Elphinstone, Col Dougie. Despatch rider extraordinaire.
Gordon, Sir Alexander of Earlston. United Societies' emissary.
Graham, John of Claverhouse, Viscount Dundee. Jacobite leader.
Hamilton, Sir Robert, of Preston. Leader of Cameronian extremists.
Henderson, Maj James. Second-in-command, Cameronian Regt.
Hackston, David of Rathillet. Covenanting leader and martyr
Ker, Capt Daniel of Kersland. "Rabbler of the curates."
Learmont, Maj James. Covenanting officer, prisoner on the Bass.
Leven, Earl of. Exile, soldier and statesman.
Mackay, Maj-Gen Hugh of Scoury. Dutch-Scots Brigade and C-in-C Scotland.
Monmouth, Duke of. Variously royalist and rebel leader.
Monroe, Capt George. 18th Coy, Cameronian Regt.
Orange-Nassau, William, Prince of Orange, subsequently King William III & II.
Renwick, Rev James. Cameronian minister and martyr.

Ross, Lord William. Cavalry officer, Claverhouse's best man.

Semple, Jimmy; Servant of Hugh Mackay and boarding house keeper

Semple, Marette; Servant of Mev de Bie and wife of Jimmy.

Shields, Rev Alexander. Chaplain to the Cameronian Regiment.

Shields, Michael. Scribe to the United Societies. Brother to above.

Steel, Thomas. Chamberlain of Jedforest, Margaret Clelands's brother.

Stewart, James, Duke of York, subsequently King James VII & II

SCOTLAND c. 1690

Courtesy of Peter Gordon Smith.

PROLOGUE

THE TWELVE COVENANTERS had scoured the moors all day long, searching for William Carmichael, chief lackey of James Sharp, Archbishop of St Andrews, renegade Presbyterian minister and vicious leader of religious persecution in Fife. They had determined to take revenge on Carmichael, but he had been warned, and was nowhere in the area. Eventually the searchers rode disconsolately into Ceres village, where three of them left the party in frustration.

'We might as well pack up and go home,' said John Balfour of Kinloch gloomily. His companions murmured a general agreement.

Suddenly a youth appeared round the corner of a house and ran up to them.

'Archbishop Sharp is coming from Kennoway! The auld deil himsel! Quick! You can ambush him on the road!'

'The Lord has delivered him into our hands,' said John Balfour sanctimoniously! 'Quick, let us take him on the open moor!' The group swung their horse's heads around and headed off at a canter. Arriving at the clachan of Magus, James Russell in the lead saw a carriage heading away from them. 'That's him! That's the arch-fiend himself! We'll take him down!'

The nine covenanters set spurs to their horses and gave chase. By now the Archbishop had spotted the pursuit and cried out to his coachman to go faster. Russell, level with the carriage, could see Sharp and his daughter Isabella cowering within. One man on the box attempted to fire at the pursuers, but was dragged off and left lying in the road, whilst the driver received a blow to the head from a sword cut,

1

causing him to fall under the wheels. Grabbing the reins of the lead pair, the attackers brought the carriage to a halt.

'Come out! Come out, you murderous brute!' Balfour's voice cut like a whiplash! The Archbishop and his daughter cowered deeper inside, but were dragged out onto the road. Isabella began to plead for her father's life, but he was far more loquacious. 'Spare me! Spare me!' squealed the white faced prelate. 'I can guarantee your lives and safety if you spare me.'

'As you spared the lives you could have saved after Rullion Green?' snarled Russell, 'And many others! I call on God to witness that this is no murder, but an execution of justice.'

The Archbishop, on his knees, crawled toward David Hackston of Rathillet's horse. 'Help me! Help me, for God's sake! I'll give you money! I'll give you a great deal of money if you spare my life.' Hackston looked down at the whining prelate. 'Pitiful! I would not soil my conscience with such cowardly blood as yours. But then neither will I lay hands on an Archbishop! I will have no part in this.' Wheeling his horse around, he rode off in the direction of Ceres.

The others were less merciful and, egged on by Balfour, speedily made an end to Sharp with their swords, leaving him lying in a welter of his own blood on the lonely roadside, his daughter weeping over him.

29 May 1679, Rutherglen.

Sir Robert Hamilton led his party of sixty armed horsemen into the small town as dusk was falling.

'Douse these godless bonfires! We will have no celebrating the birthday of Charles Stuart here today! We have some burning of our own to do!' Turning to Henry Hall, 'Take a party and dig out the magistrates and and bring them to the town cross. If they won't come willingly, drag them!'

Riding into the market square, the horsemen formed a half-circle behind the cross, whilst some nervous townsfolk trickled slowly and fearfully onto the square. Henry Hall and his party arrived bringing the magistrates, some of whom were bound by their hands and being dragged by a rope around their necks.

'Here's the burgesses, Sir Robert,' he said.

'By heaven, you look a right sorry sight,' remarked Hamilton as he cast his eye along the line of trembling magistrates. 'We are here to make public our declaration of intent, and you need to hear it!' The magistrates looked ashen and one vomited at his feet. Hamilton turned away in disgust.

Rev Thomas Douglas led a prayer and gave a short address, followed by the singing of a psalm. Hamilton then read out the detested Act of Supremacy which declared the King to have supreme authority in all matters spiritual as well as temporal, and the Government Declaration condemning and outlawing the Covenants. 'We do here this day publicly burn these godless Acts at the cross, as Charles Stewart has so perfidiously and blasphemously burnt our holy Covenants through several cities in this land. We refuse to be slaves, we are free born men!' So saying, Hamilton cast the hated government edicts into the flames of the remaining bonfire, and slowly led his men out of town.

CHAPTER ONE

"MACKAY OR GRAHAM?"

July 1672. Den Bommel, Holland.

T HE FURIOUS KNOCKING ECHOED throughout the house, insistent, demanding attention.

'Marette, go and see who is making that racket,' ordered Madame de Bie, looking up with exasperation from her needlework. It was clear from the expression on the servant girl's face that this intrusion was not welcome. The knocking continued even more insistently.

Marette unbolted the door and swung it wide, to be confronted by a short, fat, red-faced man wearing a red uniform. He did not look French, like the rest of the invaders.

'Aboot time too, lassie. Is yer lady hame?' His French was uncouth and almost unintelligible. He couldn't be French. '*Is mevrouw thuis?*' worked much better.

'*Ja,mijnheer,*' squealed the frightened girl, and ran back to her mistress, followed by the short man, quite uninvited.

'You are Madame de Bie, relict of the late Chevalier de Bie, former burgomeester of this town?' he demanded.

'That is so.'

'I have to billet an officer upon ye. Will ye tak Mackay or Graham?' he demanded.

'Have you French not persecuted us enough, bringing us to this *rampjaar,* with your pillage and destruction of our quiet Guelderland?'

4

'Not French Madame, Scots,' responded the soldier. 'I am quartermaster of Douglas's Regiment, The Royals, a Scots regiment in the service of His Majesty King Louis of France.'

'Even worse!' replied Madame de Bie. 'Mercenaries!'

The little man bristled. 'We are a loyal Regiment of King Charles on loan to His Majesty of France. And like it or no, we have captured your town and are now its masters. So, will ye tak Mackay or Graham?'

'Mackay or Graham?' parodied Madame de Bie. 'Is there any difference? One will be as bad as the other!'

'They are both officers of good Scots' blood, but perhaps Graham is the better ladies' man.'

'Then I'll take Mackay,' came the immediate and haughty response.

'As you will, Madame. He'll be here the night.' And turning on his heel, the Quartermaster strode out of the house.

"Thank heaven I sent the girls to Dordrecht, away from this fearful war," she thought. However, the latest order from the French invader that all evacuees must return to their homes had robbed her of most of the comfort she had gained.

Long after dark, another knock came to the door—almost apologetic this time, though firm. When Marette opened the door she saw a tall, sandy haired officer, with his soldier servant standing respectfully behind him.

'Would this be the house of Mistress de Bie?' he asked. When the servant girl nodded, he went on: 'Be so good as to announce Capt Hugh Mackay of Scoury.' Having said this, he and his man came into the hall and waited whilst he was announced.

'Come in, come in, Captain!' said Madame de Bie from her seat by the fire. 'I wish I could say a warm welcome to my home, but I trust at least you will behave as a gentleman to a widow in your power.'

'Madame, if you would prefer I will sleep in the barn rather than discommode you. But I assure you I will respect you and your household, especially as the widow of a Chevalier in the old Green Brigade of Gustavas Adolphus. I had a forbear killed at Lutzen on the same day as that great king.'

Hearing this, her face softened. 'I am quite sure you are a gentleman, and as such I trust you will protect us from the excesses of the invaders whom you serve?'

'Madame, I am not proud of our behaviour in Holland, and I will certainly do whatever I can to protect you and your family.'

'I sent my three unmarried daughters to my sister in Dordrecht in the hope that they would avoid having to live under enemy occupation. Now the order from your French King Louis is that all evacuees must return home forthwith, with severe penalties for non-compliance. You would be of inestimable service to me if you were prepared to journey to Dordrecht and convey my children safely home to me.'

'I would need leave for such a journey, but as the Statholder has already sued for peace, and the country is under our control, I believe I might be permitted to undertake such a trip.'

With this Mackay asked to be shown his room. Marette the maid led him upstairs as Madame de Bie said, 'Oh, and there is an attic room for your man. What is his name?'

'His name is Jimmy Semple, from a devout Lanarkshire family. I bid you good night, Madame!'

♣

'Clara, my darling! How wonderful to have you safe home! Margaretha and Juliana! Welcome, my beloved children! How was your trip?' Madam de Bie fussed around her three blonde daughters, trying to hide her relief at their safe return.

'Capt Mackay was quite wonderful, Mama! We were stopped often at French check points, but we came sailing through as soon as they saw his uniform. The Royals seem to be held in high regard by the French army.'

'As they should be! Capt Graham of Claverhouse has been to call in your absence, Hugh. A very courtly officer, who gives glowing reports of your fighting against the Turks in Crete. You got a medal I hear?'

Mackay went rather red and said nothing as the luggage was carried inside.

As the days went by, Hugh grew to be an accepted member of the de Bie family. He walked to church with them on Sunday, sitting beside Clara, who somehow always contrived to be last into the family pew. Her warmth both disturbed and comforted him, and they would wander home together behind the others, with their heads very close. His military duties were few, and he seemed always to have time to join family outings.

One day Mama asked Hugh to sit down and play chess with her. The girls were out, and the house was quiet.

'Hugh, I see you and Clara getting very close. You are a guest under my roof, and I want to ask what your intentions are towards her? You cannot avoid each other, living in the same house, and it looks as though she is fond of you too.'

Hugh coloured slightly. 'I will not deny that I find Clara a most wonderful friend, and that we get along together very well, as I do with the other girls.'

'You don't fool me, Hugh! I am a mother, and I can see when one of my chicks has that special gleam in her eye!'

'Well, to speak plainly, I believe I am falling in love with Clara, and I was looking for an opportunity to ask your permission to court her. I think she is not entirely indifferent to me.'

'Indifferent!' snorted her mother. 'You men are such fools! A blind man could see she is besotted by you! John Graham remarked on it the other day, for he too seems to like Clara, but she will have nothing to do with him!'

She went on: 'But Hugh, I have a serious problem with *you!*' Mackay looked anxious. 'You are an enemy officer. You have come here as part of an invasion force. Though we like you, you are billeted on us without our leave. Your whole company is foisted upon the poor people of den Bommel, who have little enough to eat, especially since the polders were flooded to keep you French away from Amsterdam.'

'Madame, I have to say, strictly *éntre nous*, that I do not share or respect the vision of King Louis to dominate Europe and deny freedom to countries such as yours, or indeed King Charles's behaviour in my native Scotland, where sincere God-fearing people are being hounded onto the moors of the south, whilst the highlands are in a state of lawlessness. My two elder brothers were most barbarously murdered some years ago, and no effort has yet been made to bring the culprits to justice, though they are well known in Caithness county.'

Silence!

Mackay continued. 'Would it improve your opinion of me if I were to resign my commission in Douglas's and seek a post with the Stadtholder William of Orange? I have been pondering this for some time.'

Madame de Bie looked guarded. 'Is that possible? It seems very radical, and likely to get you into a lot of trouble with the French, and probably the English too.'

'I will do it gladly if you will give me permission to pay my court to Clara.'

'You love her that much?'

'I do.'

There was a stifled giggle from the door as Marette appeared with a tray of coffee. 'Oh Missus, will ye let Jimmy Semple and me be wed too?'

'It seems I must watch out below stairs as well as above,' said Madame de Bie with a smile.

June 1673.

'You want what?' spluttered Colonel Lord George Douglas.

'I want to transfer to the Dutch service,' said Mackay.

'Why on earth?' questioned Douglas.

'I have no peace in my conscience with French and British behaviour here in Europe, or at home, and I have formed an attachment in Holland.'

'Oh, it's a petticoat is it?' sneered Douglas.

'No, my lord, it's a matter of a clear conscience before God.'

'You're one of these whimpering Whigs!'

'Military discipline prevents it, else I would call you out for that remark,' said Mackay, outwardly calm but inwardly seething.

Lord George immediately realised that he had overstepped the mark. 'No, you're right man. You have an outstanding record of courage and loyalty, and the Regiment will be sad to lose you. I'm not so sure about His Majesty. But I will ask for your discharge from the French service, and since we are at least talking to the Dutch at the moment, I'll see what can be done to get you a captaincy in their Scots Brigade.'

'Thank you, my Lord. I am indeed grateful.'

♣

Hugh cornered Clara in the garden and led her to a secluded arbour where he drew her down beside him on the garden bench.

'Clara, wonderful news!' Clara turned a mild shade of pink! 'I have been accepted by Prince William of Orange!' Clara visibly paled, for she had been hoping for some other news. However, Hugh continued: 'Now I am free to ask the question that has been heavy on my heart these many months.'

Taking both her hands in his he asked gently: 'Will you be my wife?'

She threw her arms around his neck and squealed for joy! 'Hugh, I would have married you even had we had to run away together. How soon? Soon, soon! Very soon!'

'Lets go ask Mama.'

Late 1674. Den Haag.

Graham of Claverhouse and Mackay of Scoury stood silently at attention before the Stadtholder, with Adjutant-General Colyear beside him.

Prince William of Orange looked up angrily from his desk. 'What is the meaning of this, Major Graham?'

'Sire?'

'Don't play the innocent with me! You struck the Adjutant-General in a rage, because you thought he was intruiging to keep you from command of a regiment. You struck him with your cane! You well know that is a court martial offence! I could have your right arm off!'

'That Regiment is rightfully mine, Sire. Have you forgotten how I saved you in the marsh at Seneffe?'

'You have forgotten *yourself*, sir. The Regiment is in my gift, and *I* decide who will command it! Long ago I decided to award the honour to Major Mackay here. He also greatly distinguished himself at Seneffe and Grave, and I have more confidence in his loyalty to me then I have in yours. The Regiment goes to Mackay.'

'Sir. I deeply regret my argument with Colyear, but I still feel strongly that the Regiment should come to me.'

'I make you full reparation Major Graham, for I bestow on you that which is far more valuable than any regiment—I give you your right arm! Now, leave us!'

Claverhouse looked at Mackay with a face of malice. 'I'll get you for this, Scoury! First the girl, and now the Regiment! Someday, somewhere, I will square the odds! And swinging on his heel he quit the palace, and was next heard of as a captain of horse in Scotland, in the service of King Charles II.

'So we were right after all,' mused William to his Adjutant-General some months later. 'He is more loyal to himself than to me. Nevertheless he did save my life, and is certainly an outstanding soldier. Draft a letter to the Duke of York commending his military ability, especially with cavalry. I would rather have him as a friend than an enemy.'

CHAPTER TWO

"DRUMCLOG"

29 May 1679. Douglas.

'**I**T WILL GO VERY ILL FOR US NOW,' remarked William Cleland as he threw another log onto the fire. News of the Archbishop's murder had spread like wildfire, and the covenanters knew that they would be hunted down even more viciously than before.

'Aye, that it will,' replied his brother James, whilst John Haddow, fiancé of their sister Anne, merely sighed.

The three young men were in deep trouble. Though they should have been pursuing their studies at St Salvator's College in St Andrew's, they were hunted fugitives, for their names had appeared on the list of those wanted for attending secret field-preachings on the moors.

'We are forced to worship God in secret or under government appointed curates, who have little theology and even less faith. What would Knox and Wishart have said?'

'What would Wallace and Bruce have said?' hotly interjected John.

'The murder of Archbishop Sharp has given the government just the excuse it needed to persecute all presbyterians, moderate or not. They have redoubled their fury.'

'Aye,' sighed William, 'it will go very hard for us now.'

'But have you heard that the covenanting folk from Lanark to Ayr have banded together and met for worship on the moors for the last twenty Sabbath days? What is more, they carried arms, and even saw off one or two small parties of troopers.'

'We must fight!' said William. 'We are free men. We must *fight!*' So saying he headed for the door.

'And where are you off to?' asked his brother casually.

Cleland blushed. 'I just have to go up Cambusnethan way for a wee while.'

'Is that not where the Steels live?' said John in a knowing way. 'I hear young Margaret is back from Glasgow?'

William slammed the door behind him and breathed deeply as he saddled his horse. As he headed off towards Lanark over Broken Cross Muir, he calmed down and began to go over his latest poem;

> *Hollo my Fancie, whither shalt thou go?*
> *Stay, stay at home with me,*
> *Leave off thy lofty soaring,*
> *Stay thou at home with me,*
> *And on thy books be poring,*
> *For he that goes abroad layes little up in storing.*
> *Thou's welcome home my Fancie,*
> *Welcome home to me.*

'Wonder if she'll like it?' he mused as he set his face for Cambusnethan.

♣

'What in the world are ye' doin' here at this time o' nicht?' John Steel gasped. His reaction on opening the front door was not cordial!

'I hear Margaret is home from Glasgow? I wondered if I might see her for a wee while?' faltered the usually composed Cleland.

'There's mair ga'an on in this hoose the night besides lovers trysts,' responded Magaret's father in an angry whisper, 'but since you're here, you had best come ben, for you are a brave young man, and a clever one. You may be of help.' So saying he led William into the main chamber where, gathered round a blazing fire, sat a number of serious looking men.

'This here is young Will Cleland,' said Margaret's father to the group at large. 'Son of the factor to my Lord Douglas, and committed to our cause.'

William was conscious of being scrutinised by several pairs of very hard eyes.

John Steel pointed out the owners to Will. 'Robert Hamilton of Preston, the Rev Thomas Douglas, David Hackston, Henry Hall, Robert Fleming and John Balfour.' Cleland gasped! These were names he had heard in connection with the murder of the Archbishop of St Andrew's. He was in dangerous company indeed!

'The news of what we did in Rutherglen today will be all over by dawn,' said Hamilton. 'The die is cast. We have thrown down the gauntlet to the tyrant. Where do we go from here?'

'Claverhouse will be furious. His efforts will redouble to capture us. We must stand and fight now, not skulk off into the mosses when we are attacked.' There was a murmur of agreement at Hackston's remark.

'There is to be a field meeting at Loudon Hill this Sabbath.' To his surprise William found himself speaking out. 'The Hill-folk from Lanark to Ayr have been worshipping under arms for the past half year. Can we not make a stand at Loudon?'

'Aye, the lad is right,' said Hamilton, 'a stand is long overdue. How many men under arms can we count on?'

'We have fifty muskets, some pikes, and about forty men with horses. Forbye, the other men who are prepared to stand and fight will all have a pitchfork or scythe. Perhaps another fifty such.'

Silence reigned.

'And Clavers?' asked Balfour.

'Three troops of horse and dragoons, say 150 to 200 men.'

'Plus our eighty from Rutherglen. We can match him for men but not for arms.'

An angry growl went up from the gathering.

'We'll do it! By the grace of God, we'll do it!' exclaimed Hamilton. 'Balfour, do you take the horse, Hackston the right, and young Cleland,' here he gazed at William as if to read his soul, 'can we trust you with the left flank? I will be in overall command. And Thomas, will you preach the Word?'

'That I will, and right gladly Robert,' replied Rev Thomas Douglas.

'So be it then. And as our Bluidy Banner proclaims, *"No quarter for ye active enemies of ye Covenant."*'

'No quarter!' all shouted in unison, whilst underneath his breath John Steel breathed: 'Then we'll soon see which is the more bluidy, Clavers or the Covenant!'

'We must ride, for we need to be at Lanark 'ere the dawn, and Loudon by the next one.' Hamilton led the way out of the chamber and all followed... save William who hung back with a poor impression of nochalance.

'She's by the rowan tree,' whispered one of the maids who had come into the room to clear up. 'Ye ken it?'

'That I do,' replied Will, his handsome face lighting up at the prospect. Sedulously avoiding eye contact with anyone, he sidled towards another door, and was gone!

The moon was full, the night was bright, and in the shadow of the rowan tree, where Margaret and he had met and talked so often, he saw her outline.

Wrapped in a cloak her shape was hard to descry, yet her sylph like form was obvious to him. She rushed into his arms and kissed him passionately.

"Oh, Will! Will! Is it really you? I have been so afraid for you since I heard you were on the fugitives' list. And with a price on your head, too. When did you come back from St Andrews? Where are you biding? Are you hurt?'

'Wheesht, wheesht, lassie. I am well and strong. But so deeply concerned with the state of old Scotland and the vile goings on here. Where a man can be shot in cold blood for having a bible, and bairns are put to the torture to tell where their fathers are hiding. We are not free! But God has made us for freedom, and just you wait, we shall soon be free again!'

'I don't care! I want to be with you, Will. You sent me that lovely poem:

Hollo my Fancie, whither shalt thou go?
Stay, stay at home with me,
Leave off thy lofty soaring.

'That's what I want. I want you here! You can't save the world, or even Scotland singlehanded. Oh stay, stay at home with me!'

He took her hand in his and kissed the palm. *"'It is not for glory, nor riches, nor honours that we are fighting, but for freedom—for that alone, which no honest man gives up but with his life."* I learned something of our history at St Salvator's, and I believe that we are in a similar case now as Scotland was in 1320. In fact, its even worse, for it is our fellow Scots who seek to enslave us, not the English. Would you have a coward for your husband? Would you have a slave? Would you have our bairns grow up in a land where they are not free to worship God as they feel they must? You know there is no turning back now. We will own no earthly king, until we get one who will acknowledge Christ as Head of the Church!'

Margaret's tears flowed freely as he held her to his breast. 'No Will, I would have you no otherwise, though it break my heart. For our harassed mother Scotland, for our ain folk, for our bairns, and for Jesus, you must do your duty. But I will be on my knees day and night until you come home to me.'

Cleland tore himself from her grasp, and mounting with a heavy heart, turned his horse's head towards Douglas once more.

1st June 1679. Drumclog.

The worshippers gathered from early morning beneath the loom of Loudon Hill. Many had walked through the night to be able to worship on this Sabbath day according to their consciences. Many had taken cover and hid on the way from cavalry patrols which were scouring the country in their search for the men who had been at Rutherglen a few days before. Many were mired to the knees, having waded through mosses and burns on the way. But all were resolute, pious folk, who longed to be left in peace to worship God in their own way.

As had become their wont, most of the the men bore arms for self defence. A few had muskets, a few more pikes, but the majority had only pitchforks or scythes. Mounted men acted as picquets at vantage points to prevent any surprise attack, for it had been reported that Claverhouse was in the area.

Their women were there, and the children too, for this was a family affair. Some there were with a price on their heads for failing to attend the services laid down by the government, instead attending conventicles like this one. Some there who were hunted for having been found in possession of a bible, or having their children baptised by an "outed" minister driven out of his parish.

After the singing of a Psalm, an expectant hush fell on the assembled congregation as Thomas Douglas laboriously climbed up on a rock to preach.

'He was at Rutherglen you know,' whispered John Haddow to Margaret's brother Thomas Steel.

'I ken, I ken. He was at oor hoose too!'

'Naw, he wisna!'

'Wheesht!' hissed Margaret, as the assembly fell expectantly silent.

'...and we call on God to witness that we seek not the blood of any man. We seek only freedom to worship God in our own way, and to hear those ministers that we choose. We will not be cowed by those who seek to impose the royal will upon us, and to force us to use their English prayer book, when The Lord has given us freedom to call upon Him in our own words, and with the good Scots tongue in our heids.'

There was a murmur of approval from the crowd, but as it died away, a young man, whom many knew as the potboy from Scribbie Young's tavern in nearby Strathaven, elbowed his way from the rear. 'Let me through! Let me through! I hae news!' They parted to let him through, and he ran up to Robert Hamilton who was standing at the foot of the pulpit rock and handed him a letter.

'Clavers is at Strathaven,' said Hamilton, looking up from his reading. 'He has three troops of dragoons, and he has prisoners whom he is forcing to march with him, Rev John King and others.'

Just then a warning shot rang out from the picquet atop Loudon Hill. 'They are in sight,' said Hamilton.

Thomas Douglas's voice rang out clearly over the moor: 'People of the Covenant, ye have the theory, now for the practise! Self defence is always justified!' The men looked to their weapons. An angry growl went up from the congregation as the armed men moved to the front and ranked themselves under their officers, already detailed by Hamilton. Most of the women and children stayed in place, but a few of the more courageous stood behind their men in the ranks, Janet and Anne Cleland, and Margaret Steel, amongst them.

'Remember! No quarter for these enemies of our Covenant.' Hamilton's call had a mixed reaction, some calling out, 'No quarter!', but most keeping silent.

'We did not come here to seek vengeance, but to seek our rights as free men,' said William quietly to his brother James.

'Maybe no, Will, but there will be vengeance sought this day, by both sides.'

The covenanter force began to advance eastwards towards a bog which only those who lived locally knew about. As they advanced they sang a psalm in the time honoured way of covenanters facing danger. Coming to the crest of a small rise, they saw a bright green swathe a few yards wide at the bottom of the dip. To the untutored eye it seemed no barrier to either horse or foot, but the locals knew that it would not bear the weight of an armed horseman. Beneath lay a deep marsh.

As Hamilton's small force took up position, the helmets of Claverhouse's scouts appeared on the skyline, soon followed by the main body. They drew up in troop formation, with an officer on a roan horse in front.

'Yon's Bluidy Clavers!' shouted Thomas Weir. 'He burned oor farm!'

A small group of dragoons detached themselves from their troop and advanced slowly down the slope, carbines at the ready. As soon as they got within range they made ready to fire.

'Down! Down!' yelled Cleland, and his men flung themselves prostrate as the volley rang out. Some covenanters advanced to the edge of the marsh and prepared to return the volley. Soon volley after volley echoed round the windswept moor, as each side sought to draw blood, but still no-one fell. Now a full troop of dragoons advanced, and Cleland, ahead of his men, waded into the bog and brought down a soldier with a long range shot.

As the second troop advanced, his order was again 'Down!' By now Cleland's men had seen the wisdom of this, and all hit the ground save

John Morton, who could not resist having a look. He took a bullet square in the windpipe, and fell back dead into the mud. One each! Claverhouse, having reformed, now led his entire force straight at the covenanters, but to the surprise of both sides, directly into the bog. Horses struggled in the peat moss, and troopers were forced to dismount to prevent themselves sinking into the depths.

The Battle of Drumclog 1 June 1679. By Charles Edward Wagstaffe after Sir George Harvey: Courtesy of the National Gallery of Scotland.

'Come on lads, here's our chance!' shouted Cleland, as he led his men further into the bog, hacking at troopers all the way. Red coats turned brown as more and more troopers were overpowered and bogged down with their steeds. Cleland turned to wave Balfour with his horsemen round the edge of the moss to cut off any escape as the attack began to turn into a rout. William, seeing a roan horse mired to the fetlocks and recognising it as belonging to the enemy leader, struggled through the mud and grabbed the bridle. 'Graham, this is the day you meet your deserts for all the innocent blood you have shed. Come help me!' he cried, 'I have Clavers!'

But as he grabbed the bridle he lost his footing and his enemy wrenched his reins free. At that moment Thomas Finlay caught up with Cleland and plunged his pitchfork into the horse's guts, but with an enormous effort the gallant steed broke free of the morass and reached firm ground.

'It will take more than the likes of you to bring *me* down,' sneered Claverhouse as he cantered up the rise, gathering troopers as he went. He was quickly joined by his trumpeter, a lad of fourteen, and his standard bearer. But the troopers in the bog were still being worsted. Many were wrenched from their saddles, and others thrown into the mud as their horses panicked. Soon troopers and horses began to stream up the hill in the wake of their leader as they extricated themselves.

'Rally to me!' cried Claverhouse, but few were listening to their commander now. Streaming past him, those still mounted put spurs to their steeds and headed pell-mell for Strathaven, hotly pursued by the covenanter horse led by John Balfour. Cleland's foot soldiers finished off those who still resisted, taking prisoner those who threw down their arms and cried for quarter.

Claverhouse, seeing his position was hopeless, was disposed to stand and die with the remnants of his troop around him, but panic had infected all the horses and the entire party fled, Claverhouse, his trumpeter and standard bearer bringing up the rear, closely pursued by the mounted covenanters. As Claverhouse crested the rise where the prisoners of the morning had watched the battle, Rev John King was heard to shout: 'Are ye no stayin' for the efternoon sermon, Captain?' With a vicious look, Claverhouse pressed on.

Despite the exhaustion of the meleé, the superior quality of the government mounts soon began to tell, and gradually pursuit slackened. One of the last shots fired brought down the young trumpeter, but his horse continued to run alongside Claverhouse until his own steed foundered from its pitchfork wound. Claverhouse then took to his trumpeter's mount, and made good his escape with the remnants of his force.

Gradually the weary covenant horsemen began to trickle back to where Claverhouse's prisoners had been held. They were now free, but six captured dragoons, all wounded, had joined the group under guard.

Robert Hamilton arrived on his blown horse. 'What are these enemies doing alive? Did you not hear, can you not read on our Bluidy Banner: *"No Quarter for ye active enmies of ye Covenant?"'* Suddenly, without warning, he ran the nearest soldier through. As he fell to the ground a gasp of horror went up from the group. 'Now cut down these other servants of Belial!' yelled Hamilton in a rage.

'Hold! Stand fast!' At the sound of Hackston's voice everyone froze. This was the man who had refused to raise his hand against Archbishop Sharp even as his companions were hacking him to death. 'We are not here for vengeance but for freedom. Do not stain your hands with the blood of defenceless men. Mind Rev Douglas's words: "Self defence is always legal." Killing in cold blood merely disgraces our cause.'

There was a general murmur of approval and relief from the group, and a hopeful look dawned on the captured troopers' faces.

'I command here!' Hamilton's face was purple!

'By your own appointment!' retorted Hackston cooly. "Fetch up Mr Douglas and let us thank The Lord for today's deliverance.'

Later that night the tavern where Claverhouse and his officers had breakfasted rang with the sound of excited covenanter voices. The room was bulging with men exulting at their victory, not only over one of their most sworn enemies, but also the best cavalry commander in Scotland.

Robert Hamilton slumped in his seat at the table. 'What is the score?' he asked wearily.

'John Morton died in the moss,' replied Cleland, 'and we have five more badly wounded and like to die.'

'And Clavers?'

'We took down about twenty five on the moor, and six prisoners, of whom one was slain after the battle.' Cleland shot an accusing look at Hamilton, who appeared entirely unmoved.

'The order was no quarter, and I would have gladly slain the rest had these cowards not prevented me.'

'There were no covenanting cowards today!' angrily responded John Haddow. 'The only ones who ran away were Clavers and his men.'

'And in Strathaven we took down aboot a dozen as they fled through the Hole Close,' interjected Scribbie Young.

A murmur of support went around the room. Hamilton had enough sense to see that the feeling of the meeting was turning away from him. 'That's well over half a troop accounted for. We have done well today!' Most present visibly relaxed at these words of encouragement.

'So what now?' asked John Balfour, who had been in the thick of the day's fight.

'We must capitalise on our victory,' said Cleland. The government will be in turmoil, the South is ready to rise. We must band together and march against them. Now is the time to force them to listen to our case!' There was a general murmur of agreement.

'Tomorrow I march on Glasgow with all who will support me,' said Hamilton. 'Now let us get some rest. We have a hard day ahead. Mr King, you have been delivered from the enemy's hand today. Will you dismiss us with a blessing?'

CHAPTER THREE

"BOTHWELL BRIG"

21st June 1679. Bothwell.

THE ARCHBISHOP'S DEATH had led inexorably to Rutherglen, and so on to Drumclog. The covenanting victory had seen the small Drumclog force joined by many who flocked to their banner from all over the south. Most of these new arrivals held a more moderate position than did Richard Hamilton and Thomas Douglas, desiring simply freedom to worship in their own way.

The covenanting army had at one stage swelled to 6000, but after a delay of three weeks, plagued with endless to-ing and fro-ing between Glasgow, Hamilton town, and other centres, the army was now reduced to 4000, split between moderates and extremists. Any sense of unity and cohesion had long ago collapsed into endless bickering. The moderates, led by the venerable Rev John Welch, declared that they had assembled in lawful self defence, and provided they were granted freedom of worship and a free Scots Parliament, they were prepared to submit to royal authority.

Hamilton, who had shown increasing arrogance during this time, grew more intransigent by the minute, dragging in his wake those who subscribed to his rejection of royal authority, but who nevertheless mostly had serious reservations about his radical views. Rev Donald Cargill, a leading cleric and close friend of Richard Cameron, led the extreme ministers. Yet he also had strong personal links with Welch and his following, many of whom he held in high regard.

So the camp became yet more divided, not only into moderates and extremists, for the extreme party were gradually splitting further due to the intransigence of Hamilton, who went so far as to demand that the royal army should lay down its arms and surrender, and Donald Cargill with his earnest desire for any way forward which might achieve the freedom they sought whilst maintaining a clear conscience.

By Saturday 21st June, a royal army of 10 000 had assembled on the north bank of the River Clyde at Bothwell. The Duke of Monmouth, King Charles II's bastard son, was in command. Monmouth was known to be a reasonable and fair minded man, and some in the camp still felt that a peaceful solution was possible. The covenanter council of war met on the moor behind the camp.

'We are of Cameron's mind,' said Robert Hamilton.

'And what might that be?' challenged James Ure.

'He is against acceptance of any Indulgence, or of owning the king's authority.'

'He is presently in Holland and cannot speak for himself! I would ask Mr Cargill, as senior minister present opposed to the Indulgence, where he stands?'

'I am not for the Indulgence, but neither am I for bloodshed if it can be avoided. Ritchie and I have preached together, and I feel I do know his mind. We must have a day of prayer and fasting, to humble ourselves before God for our internal strife, and to seek His will.'

'We are far too late for that,' interjected William Cleland. 'Monmouth will attack on the morrow. The Galloway men who joined us on Friday are like to be the last reinforcements we will receive. If we are to fight, we had best fight soon, before our army fades away entirely.'

Immediate uproar overtook the meeting!

'Had you preached on the Indulgences as I ordered, matters would not have come to this pass,' roared Hamilton at Welch.

'When the day dawns that I accept orders on what to preach from any other than the Almighty, I will truly be damned!' retorted Welch, red in the face with anger.

'Friends, friends!' reasoned David Hackston, widely respected by all, 'We have wasted three weeks with petty bickering, when we are all come here to seek the same freedom. We have not appointed officers for divisions, we have not laid on supplies of powder or weapons, nor have we discussed tactics. All we have done is argue amongst ourselves.'

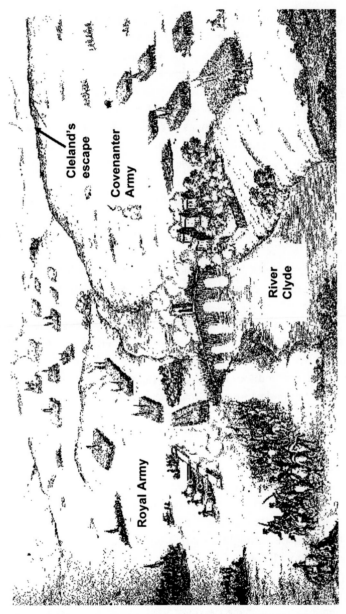

Contemporary representation of the Battle of Bothwell Brig,
22 June 1679.

'Away with you Hackston!' shouted Hamilton. 'Do I not command here?'

'By the same authority as at Drumclog! Your own!'

A mud-bespattered rider drew up and, throwing himself out of the saddle, made straight for Cleland. He whispered in his ear and Cleland blanched. 'My brother James is killed just now! The royalists caught him at the ford of Clyde.' Silence fell over the meeting. Cleland was greatly loved and respected, even by those who felt him somewhat of an upstart. He had proved himself at Drumclog though he was barely twenty. Every eye looked to him now.

Finally he spoke out. 'We have tried to frame a declaration acceptable to all assembled here at Bothwell, and we have failed, twice. We must try once more, for if we fail again, may God have mercy on us tomorrow.'

'We must appoint the best military officers at least,' said Major Joseph Learmont, standing beside James Ure.

'I have already done that, including you, Learmont! You can appoint whomever you like! I am leaving!' So saying, Hamilton abruptly stormed out of the meeting, followed reluctantly by a dozen or so, including Cleland, his brother-in-law, and Learmont.

After an uncomfortable silence, Thomas Douglas, the preacher of Drumclog, spoke out. 'I am no soldier, but even I can see our weakness. Our artillery amounts to one brass cannon. Our best officers have left us. We had indeed best draw up a final petition, and spend the night in prayer for our woeful shortcomings in the Covenant service. I move for the Revs Welch and Cargill to draw up this petition, and to call on whom they will to help. The rest of us to disperse and prepare as best we can for the morrow.'

Amidst a general murmur of agreement, the gathering broke up dispiritedly.

Early next morning, Rev John Welch brought a petition to Hamilton for his signature. Hamilton, harrassed with preparations for the battle, hardly glanced at it before he signed in his capacity as leader of the *Covenanted Army now in arms.* His only query was whether Rev Donald Cargill had played a part in its preparation, which he was assured was the case.

David Hackston and John Balfour were in command of the advance guard at the toll-gate in the centre of the bridge. 'No-one has come to check our powder and ball,' remarked James Ure to no-one in particular, as he drew his company up on the west side of the wooden bridge crossing the Clyde. The men of Glasgow and Stirling took station on his flanks. Two hundred Galloway foot, armed only with pikes, took up position on the extreme right. The solitary brass cannon was mounted to cover the bridge whilst one small troop of horse brought up the rear.

Six troops of Monmouth's horse now advanced on the bridge, sending forward six men who opened fire on the defenders. The volley was returned, and two men fell. Just then two cloaked figures approached the south side of the bridge and made as if to cross. On being challenged by Ure they revealed themselves to be the Revs John Welch and David Hume, bearing the petition to The Duke of Monmouth.

♣

'Your Grace, we bring a humble petition from the covenant men in arms here.

'We are not rebels, we seek only our God-given rights of free worship and government.'

Monmouth read the one-page document slowly. It was most unusual to receive such a brief document from a group so notorious for their verbiage. Indeed it seemed a most reasonable paper.

'Gentlemen, what you seek seems most reasonable and just. In all probability I could approve your requests, since His Majesty has given me powers to treat. However I cannot negotiate with rebels standing to arms against the king's troops. Lay down your arms and surrender and I give you my word you will be reasonably and fairly treated.'

'My Lord, I doubt they will agree to that, without some definite commitment on your part.'

Monmouth bristled. 'Do you refuse to accept the word of a prince of the blood?'

Inwardly Welch thought, 'Not only of a prince, but his father the king himself, and *his* father, and *his* father's father. They have all broken their sworn word to grant us freedom of religion.'

'Your Grace, we seek to be loyal subjects to King Charles. That we can only be if he recognizes the people's rights under his rule.'

'I'll give you thirty minutes to lay down your ams, otherwise I attack.' As he spoke, the royal artillery drew up on the rise commanding the bridge and approaches. Infantry moved in support. 'Thirty minutes, gentlemen!'

Welch and Hume started back for the bridge, passing close in front of a cavalry troop commanded by an officer on a black horse.

'Still a canting Whig I see, Mr Welch! And Hume, you have the effrontery to consider yourself a man of peace!' The words spat like venom from Claverhouse's mouth.

'Captain Graham, I will answer to God for my behaviour, not to you!'

'And I to the King,' Claverhouse riposted! 'As for God, I'll take my chances with Him!'

Hume and Welch made their way back over the bridge to the south bank of the river, and sought out Hamilton. When they delivered Monmouth's reply, Hamilton snarled: 'And hang next! What sort of fool does he take me for?'

So passed, without consideration, the last opportunity to avoid a battle which, in its aftermath, was to bring great suffering to all of Scotland.

Monmouth's artillery now began to rake the defenders of the bridge and a battalion of foot assaulted. Hackston stood at the gatehouse on the bridge, constantly exposing himself to enemy fire, and urging the defenders to continue firing. Hand to hand fighting broke out as the infantry reached the centre of the bridge, and continued unabated for two hours, after which the defenders' ammunition began to run out.

'James, go tell Hamilton that we are in dire need of more powder and ball!' Hackston shouted to Ure above the din of battle.

Ure mounted and raced up the hill to find Hamilton, but on reaching the headquarters he was nowhere to be seen. Major Learmont seemed to have taken over command.

'Major, we are almost out of ball and shot. The bridge is in danger of falling!'

'There *is* none left! Tell Hackston its hopeless.'

James Ure wrenched his bridle around to obey, but saw the enemy had already forced the bridge and were even now debouching along the south bank. Putting spurs to his steed, he headed for the enemy flank. Riding within a musket shot of the enemy line, he raced along their front, mentally assessing their strength as he rode, and then returned along the covenanter front. As he did this, he met his own troop fleeing up the hill, and rallied them around him. As he did, Learmont rode up.

'Get your men into the hollow of that wee burn there, and surprise their horse if they try to outflank us!' But the horsemen supporting the covenanter foot at the bridge suddenly broke, and streamed back through their own infantry, drawn up under William Cleland.

'Stand fast! Stand fast there!' Cleland's order went unheeded. As he and the other officers desperately tried to stem the flood, their own fleeing horsemen broke through the ranks, trampling all underfoot as they went. Panic spread to the infantry, who also broke. The right flank under Cleland had stood fast longer than the rest, for as he turned round in despair to view the battle scene, all he could see were covenanters throwing down their arms and fleeing over the hill. It was a rout!

John Graham of Claverhouse, in front of his own troop of Life Guards, rose in the stirrups. 'Now is our day of vengeance!' he called to his men. 'Remember Drumclog! No quarter! And above all, bring me Cleland, dead or alive.' His men cheered as he raised his sword hilt to his lips, and bringing it down in a swinging arc to point at the fleeing backs yelled, 'Charge!'

All along the front the sabres flashed in the sunlight. The royal cavalry swept over the crest and into the backs of the fleeing covenanters. Many there were who stood and sold their lives dearly, many there were who threw down their arms and cried for quarter, only to be cut down ruthlessly. The moor became a sea of blood as four hundred men died.

♣

'Kill them,' ordered Dalzell as he surveyed the large group of prisoners who had thrown down their arms and surrendered where they stood. The General had arrived on the scene after the battle had ended.

'What, all of them?' exclaimed Claverhouse. 'You can't slaughter 1200 men!'

'Yes I can! All of them! We will rid ourselves of this Whig scourge once and for all.'

'Not while I command here!' The Duke of Monmouth's voice cut like a whiplash. 'Is it any wonder these men rebel, when they are hunted down by the likes of you! I will not kill men in cold blood. That is only for butchers.'

"Oh, a Whig lover is it?' sneered Dalzell.

'I'll thank you to remember who I am! Now take these prisoners to Edinburgh, so that they may be legally dealt with!'

'First strip them and make them lie face down! And shoot any who move! We cannot march before dawn.'

'But many will die before that,' remonstrated a young Cornet.

General Dalzell shrugged. His order soon took effect, for a few moments later, as one wounded man lifted his head to beg for water, he was shot in the head before he could speak.

♣

Donald Cargill, panting with exhaustion, was overtaken by a trooper who felled him with a sabre slice to the head. The wound was deep enough to kill any normal man. As he fell, the trooper cried out, 'Are ye no that minister Cargill?'

'That I am.'

'Then guid luck tae ye,' said the trooper, and rode on, leaving him bleeding in the heather.

The slaughter spread far and wide, as the cold steel bit into flesh. Not only those fleeing were cut down, but even some who knew nothing of the battle walking from Hamilton town, were killed without mercy.

♣

Margaret Steel looked anxiously out of an upper widow in her father's house at Cambusnethan. What of Will and her brother Thomas? They were both well mounted and should escape pursuit. But knowing Will, perhaps he would be killed defending someone else, or be unhorsed and at the mercy of his pursuers. As she looked, she noticed her neighbour Arthur Inglis, sitting on a pile of hay in his own yard next door, reading his bible.

A troop of horse suddenly rounded the bend, and with no warning started shooting at Arthur. They missed, but riding into the yard, the leader exclaimed, 'A Whig! He has a bible!' and clove his head in two in the same breath. Margaret sceamed, and the troopers swung round as she ducked below the windowsill.

'This place is a hotbed of rebels! Search that house!'—and the troopers, dismounting, kicked the door down and ransacked the house, dragging Margaret and her father out into the open.

"You are harbouring rebels here!' It was a statement, not a question.

'We are not!' replied John Steel, as Margaret clung to her father.

'Cut him down!' and as the sabre bit deep into the flesh, John Steel fell at his daughter's feet, covering her dress with his blood.

"Let that be a lesson tae ye lassie,' said the leader, wiping the blood off his sabre on her dress. 'Mount! We have other hunting to do this day,' as they clattered out of the yard.

Margaret fainted!

♣

Night fell over the battlefield. Many would die before the dawn.

Mary Rae searched desperately for the body of her fiancé. When she found him he was still alive, though sore wounded.

'Come, let me help you tae the well, John.'

'Aye Mary, I have a great drouth, but I canna' move. I am hurt sair.'

But Mary, with the strength of love, lifted him onto her own back, carried him to the well and dressed his wounds.

♣

Donald Cargill groaned as he was turned over by gentle hands.

'Alex, its Rev Cargill!' exclaimed Gavin Semple.

'By heaven, so it is! He has often stayed with us at Earlston,' responded Alex Gordon. 'Help me lift him up.'

'He's hurt sair in the heid. We'd better bind him up first.' Taking off his shirt he tore it into long strips and bound up Cargill's head wound.

'It's very bad. I doubt he'll live.'

'Well, he'll surely no' live if we leave him here on the moor. We maun tak him to oor friends in Hamilton. My gude-cousin Effie will help us, I'm sure.' They hoisted him onto Alex's horse, and held him in the saddle as Gavin headed towards the lights of the town.

Effie Semple heard a scratching at the back window, and going fearfully to open it, she started as she saw Alex and Gavin standing there in the dark.

'Wheest, Effie, we need help.'

'There's many the day that need help, and many that's past it,' she replied tearfully. 'We have sodgers all ower the toon. But come in quietly, Mr Gordon, or rather Earlston, for I hear you faither fell today!' as she opened the back door.

Alex blanched. 'I had not heard.'

'Laud, sakes!' exclaimed Effie when she saw Cargill. 'Is he alive?'

'Barely. This is Mr Donald Cargill, friend of Richard Cameron.'

'I ken him fine. I've heard him preach. Come ben, come ben.' They carried Cargill upstairs and laid him on a bed.

'I'll tend him, but I'm alone here, for my man was out with you today, and I fear for his life. The soldiers are at every door, searching for the likes of you. Gavin, turn your horse loose, and hide your saddle in the dunghill out back.' As Gavin wrinkled his nose in disgust, 'And you put this on!' thrusting a woman's dress at Alex, 'And this wig and cap too. Sit here and rock the cradle.'

By this ruse, Donald Cargill and his rescuers escaped to fight another day.

♣

William Cleland, John Haddow and Thomas Steel had ridden for their lives when they saw all was lost, for they knew that they were all marked men since Drumclog. Drawing up on a rise they looked back. The cavalry were still distant, busy with the remains of the covenanting foot, but the leaders were already breaking through and galloping towards them.

'That's Clavers' Horse in front,' said John grimly.

'Our best hope is to get over the Clyde. They won't look for us on their side of the water.'

'You're right Will, but all the fords are guarded. You lost your own brother at one yesterday,' replied Thomas Steel.

'We'll swim the horses, and make for your family home at Cambusnethan. Surely they will hide us there?'

'They will,' replied Thomas, 'but we put them at risk.'

'They have already risked as much. We only stay the night, and be on our way before dawn. We must put much distance as possible between Clavers and us as soon as our beasts are rested.'

Once they crossed the rise and were out of view of their pursuers, they changed direction and made for a wood extending on both sides of the river. It would give them some cover for their crossing.

14 August 1679. Edinburgh Tolbooth.

The jailer unlocked the cell door, ushering in a man who was clearly a gentleman, though his cloak covered his face.

'Good day, Reverend gentlemen,' he said, uncovering to reveal the face of John Graham of Claverhouse.

'Have you come to mock us before our execution?' asked John King.

'No, I came to tell you that His Majesty has graciously signed an indemnity for those who were at Bothwell, in response to the supplication of his bastard Monmouth. It was signed at Windsor on 27 July, and is to be published here in Edinburgh today.'

'God be praised!' exclaimed John Kid.

'The indemnity will be published this morning. But I am here to tell you that your executions will still go forward.'

'What manner of evil is that! So you have come here merely to gloat?'

'You have been taken three times and escaped each time. But not this time! Your death is for your insolence to me at Drumclog. Let it be an example to all who scorn the king's officers.'

'No, Captain Graham, it is *you* who scorn the King's servants, and one day you will answer for all the innocent blood you have shed. Mr Kid here was put to the torture, even after he confessed to being at Bothwell. Is there no end to the evil cruelties in this kingdom?'

'Good day gentlemen, and may your God have mercy on your souls.'

'He already has, sir. We do not fear to die, but you should, for a higher court awaits you than the one which condemned us.'

Graham kicked at the cell door to be let out.

♣

At the market cross, the place of execution, John King and John Kid walked hand in hand. As so often with the martyrs of the Covenant, they both wore cheerful faces. This was something which continually drove the authorities to an absolute fury, but on the public scaffold what could they do?

'I have often heard of a kid being sacrificed,' said John Kid, 'but seldom a king.'

'Aye weel, John, the one we serve is both Kid and King, and we are walking in His train today.'

After they were hanged and cut down, their heads were cut off, to be stuck above the Netherbow Gate of the city where they had died.

CHAPTER FOUR

'THE EXILES'

August 1679. Rotterdam.

'**I**'**M GOING TO LAND YOU AT DELFSHAVEN,**' said Capt Hodge of the brig *Song of Queensferry.* 'Those who were at Bothwell attract less attention if they walk the last few miles into Rotterdam. Even although you are fairly safe here, it is well to remember the Stadtholder is related to the House of Stewart.'

'That's true,' Cargill responded. 'We heard Robert M'Ward, John Brown and Col Wallace were forced to move out of Rotterdam for a year despite local protests.' He turned to Robert Hamilton, David Hackston and Henry Hall who were standing beside him on the poop.

Peering into the swirling mist and rain, they could just make out the emerging Dutch shoreline. 'It's mighty flat country,' said Hamilton gloomily, 'but at least it's a refuge. I doubt I would have evaded capture much longer had we not sailed.'

'Aye, we would all have been dancing at a rope's end in the Grassmarket by now, like as not,' David Hackston replied. 'But we are alive, and surely we can find some peace here to recover and heal our wounds.' Here he glanced at Cargill, whose head was still swathed in bandages.

They leaned forward into the cold wind of the grey morning as Captain Hodge warped his ship alongside. Other than the harbourmen waiting to take the mooring ropes, there were few people on the quayside. But as the gangplank was run out, a young man, soberly clad, left the shelter of a warehouse door, and made as if to come aboard.

'Who are ye?' called the captain.

'I am sent by the Rev Mr M'Ward to meet a Mr Cargill, due from Scotland. My name is Alexander Shields.' The faces of Cargill, Hamilton and Hackston brightened. Shields paused uncertainly at the end of the gangway.

'Aye well, come aboard then. We have Mr Cargill with us.'

'I am Donald Cargill,' stepping forward with hand outstretched.

'I ken, I ken. I heard you preach at Clydesdale that day The Lord miraculously restored your voice to preach. I even remember your text: *"I will pour water on him that is thirsty."* I mind it well. I am come here to convoy you to Rotterdam, where you will be warmly welcomed as heroes from Bothwell.'

'Humph!' sniffed Hamilton, 'We might be heroes from Drumclog, but Bothwell!'

Their possessions were few, and soon the small party of refugees set out for the walk into Rotterdam.

As Shields showed the way, he could not contain his curiosity. 'Tell me how it was at Bothwell? The whole of Holland is thirsting for news, for it seems it went very ill for us? We have fugitives from Scotland arriving every day.'

Hackston burst out. 'Aye, it went ill for us indeed! We could not agree on anything! Political bickering and ecclesiastical humbug resulting in military disaster. We threw away our victory of Drumclog for a mess of pottage. Our leaders deserted us and our minsters failed us!'

Hamilton looked embarrassed, and Cargill remained silent.

'Would that we had had Ritchie there,' said Cargill quietly.

'You mean Richard Cameron? He is here, newly ordained and on his way back to Scotland even now.'

'You mean we've missed him?'

'I'm not sure. His departure was imminent. But Mr M'Ward will know.'

By now they were approaching Rotterdam, and Shields led the party straight to a coffee shop with the sign *James Bruce* swinging above the door. 'This is where all the Scots come,' he explained as he dived into the crowded place. 'There's Mr M'Ward in the corner with Andrew Russell.'

As they drew near to the table, a smile lit up Cargill's face. 'Robert M'Ward, is it you! My belovéd friend of St Andrews and Glasgow days! How wonderful to see you again!' Then, as one of the other occupants of the table wearing a broad-brimmed hat looked up, 'And Ritchie Cameron! God be praised. We were feart we would miss you.'

General hand-shaking and embracing ensued, for all were well known to the others, and had faced the same persecution for the cause of freedom.

'We usually meet here,' said M'Ward, 'so that we might not stand out. Our homes are watched by English spies. Some of us were banished from Rotterdam a few years ago. Were it not for the goodwill of the people some of us would have already been extradited back to Scotland to be tried as traitors.'

'You'll need some good strong Dutch coffee after your voyage,' said Russell, signalling to a waiter.

'This is a luxury I have not tasted for a good while,' admitted Hackston when the coffee arrived, together with a platter of *biskjuit.* Silence descended on the table while they all savoured the warmth and aroma.

'Now Donald, I am indeed glad that you and Ritchie have met before he returns to Scotland. The situation there is critical. Field preaching has fallen by the wayside, for all the field preachers who survive are either in exile or prison. Most of the more moderate ministers accepted the Indulgence after Bothwell, and the Kirk is within an ace of coming under the heel of the King once more. You know what that means?'

Cameron butted in. 'You either give up your conscience, or you give up your liberty.'

'So what would you have *me* do?' asked Cargill.

'My colleague John Brown is very ill,' replied M'Ward, 'but he and I have been struggling with the problem of the Indulgence since we were exiled here in the early sixties. We feel you can help us with our thinking. Let us go and talk with him, and then we can get you settled into a safe place to stay.'

They made their way out into the rain-soaked street, and Shields led off into a poorer area of the town, where houses huddled together more closely than on the fashionable *grachts.* Stopping at one he knocked, and the door was shortly opened by a fair haired woman of middle age.

'Marette, we are here to see Mr Brown.'

'He's not well,' Marette answered doubtfully.

'We have The Rev Donald Cargill here. I know he will want to see him.'

'But not the rest of you,' viewing Hamilton and Hackston with a jaundiced eye.

'Very well, then! Just the ministers! But may the others come inside and rest in your parlour while we visit him? They have had a long and cold journey from Scotland.'

On hearing this, Marette's face softened somewhat and she held the door wide. 'From Scotland is it? You are welcome then. Come in, there is a good fire. I'll call my husband. Jimmy! Jimmy! There's folk from Scotland here.'

A spruce little man bustled in carrying a load of firewood. Seeing Hackston, he dropped his load hastily and wrung his hand. 'Mr Hackston, sir. It's gude tae see ye again. Ye'll mind my brother was a keeper at Rathillet ten year syne?'

'Jimmy Semple, indeed I remember you. How do you come to be here?'

'I served in the Royals with Captain Hugh Mackay and married his wife's mother's maid, Marette here. Noo we run a wee bit boardin' hoose.'

'And how is Captain Mackay?' asked Hackston.

'Oh, he's Colonel now. He commands the whole Anglo-Scots Brigade.'

'Well, I can see you are well taken care of here. We will go up and talk with Mr Brown.' So saying, M'Ward led Cameron, Cargill and Shields up a narrow flight of stairs.

The Rev John Brown of Wamphray lay on the bed looking pale and shrivelled, the husk of a man. But the eyes shone brightly, and when he spoke it was evident that his mind was still very sharp. 'Ritchie, you still here? And Alex! But who is this stranger you have brought?'

'John, this is the Rev Donald Cargill, landed from Scotland this very day.'

'Man, you look sore wounded! You should be lying down, not me!'

'I took a sair ding to the head at Bothwell. But the trooper who cut me down, let me go when he recognised who I was. And God in His mercy is healing me fast.'

The four ministers then spent some time in prayer before discussing what course was to be taken on the return of Cameron and Cargill to Scotland, for Cameron was to sail on the morrow, and Cargill was already anxious to get back and carry on with the work.

'You'll have heard that Ritchie was ordained in the Scots Kirk here in Rotterdam?' said Brown.

'Indeed we have,' responded Cargill. 'It hasn't been too well received in some circles in Scotland.'

'I know, I know,' said Brown wearily. 'I have just today received a letter from The Rev John Carstares, taking extreme umbrage along with many others.'

'The point is,' said M'Ward, 'that there are virtually none left who will still preach fearlessly in the fields. Thomas Douglas is the only one still alive and at large. The others have all been hunted down, imprisoned or killed.'

'Claverhouse is after him too! He hates him as much as he did King and Kid!'

'That is why we ordained Richard here,' said Brown. 'You may have heard the prophecy that he would lose his head, and that it would be stuck up somewhere in public view? Anyone who has the courage to press forward with something like that hanging over him is the sort of man sorely needed in Scotland now.'

'And so I sail on the morrow, to raise the Covenant Standard once more,' said Richard Cameron.

'Ritchie, I will sail back with you!' exclaimed Cargill.

'Not with a head wound like that,' interjected Brown. 'You must bide here a while until it is healed and your strength is returned. You will have to face long days and nights, preaching on the moors and being hunted for it!'

'He can stay with me,' said Shields. 'I have been working on a paper setting out the justification for our stance and actions, and I would really appreciate Mr Cargill's advice.'

Marette's head appeared at the door. 'You've tired Mr Brown enough with all your havering. Be off with the lot of you!'

They rose to leave.

'I'll not be seeing you again in this life, Ritchie,' said John Brown.

'But you will in the next! How can I ever thank you for all your care and wise council?'

'By keeping the faith and ensuring that Scotland is set free from the tyranny of the divine right of kings. Only God has divine right, and He made us free to worship as we would, not as the king orders.'

♣

'He refused what?' exploded Robert Hamilton to Cargill and Shields in the parlour of Shields' lodgings.

Cargill spoke quietly. 'Robert Fleming, the minister of the Scots Kirk here has refused communion to Hackston and Balfour because they were present at the murder of Archbishop Sharp.'

'Murder! You mean execution!'

'That is a matter of opinion. He is quite within his rights to refuse communion to any whom he considers to be unrepentant.'

'You side with him! You are as bad as he!'

'I would have thought my appearance at Bothwell and my preaching would have shown that I am on no man's side. I may hold to the Covenants and stand against the Indulgences, but I will always seek reconciliation wherever possible.'

'Reconciliation! You mean surrender!'

'Do not speak to me of surrender. I stood my ground at Bothwell, unlike some!'

Hamilton was silenced, but not for long.

'You will obviously refuse to celebrate the communion tomorrow then?'

'I will do no such thing!'

Hamilton snorted, a sound which was becoming well known in Scots circles in Rotterdam. 'You are as weak as M'Ward. You denounce the Indulgence but not those who subscribe to it!'

'Indeed. We hate the sin, not the sinner.'

Hamilton stormed out!

Cargill and Shields both sighed deeply. 'We must not become embittered, but neither must we yield our stance.'

Shields nodded his assent. 'Can we get on with this declaration I have been drafting? You'll mind how the ministers of Edinburgh drafted a paper before Bothwell which might well have gained our petitions for us instead of the disaster we endured. Even Monmouth said our requests were reasonable. We must try again.'

'We shall keep trying until we succeed,' rejoined Cargill.

'I have been trying very hard not to express support for the extreme position which some, such as our recent guest, seem to delight in. Too many are breaking with their brethren over some trivial point. They do not earnestly seek freedom for the kirk and are dangerously close to seeking their own glory.'

'I am booked to sail home soon, Alex. You must press on, for I want to take your draft with me, to discuss it with Ritchie before we go public.'

On 21 November 1679, the *Song of Queensferry* sailed from Delfshaven, bound for Aberlady Bay. Aboard was Donald Cargill, accompanied by Alexander Shields, David Hackston and Henry Hall.

In Cargill's possession was the draft of a document which was to become famous as *The Queensferry Paper.*

CHAPTER FIVE

"CASTING DOWN THE GAUNTLET"

April 1680. Cambusnethan.

S INCE CARGILL HAD LANDED at Aberlady Bay in November
1679, he and his companions had moved secretly all over the south
of Scotland, visiting those still prepared to stand up for the Covenant
and resist government attempts to force them into compliance with the
Indulgences. He had met up with Richard Cameron, and they had been
joined by Thomas Douglas, so now there were three ministers prepared
to preach fearlessly in the fields. Cleland and others, who had not fled to
Holland but had been in hiding since Bothwell, were starting to form a
small band prepared to fight in defence of conventicles should they be
attacked.

Now, on the eve of the first major conventicle since Bothwell, they
had all gathered at Cambusnethan, prior to the convening of a public fast
nearby at Darmead, a traditional conventicle site. Alexander Shields on
a short visit from Holland, was also staying at the Steel's home on the
introduction of Cleland.

William Cleland looked up with a satisfied look. 'There is some
good news at last, Margaret.'

'But government troops are under orders to attack any conventicle
which they find,' said Margaret, 'and to spare no-one, man or woman.'

'Quite right my dear,' responded Will, 'but Richard Cameron has
gathered a following from all over the south-west, and this fast will be
our first public defiance of the tyrant's law since Bothwell.'

41

Alex chipped in: 'And our exiles in Holland are watching expectantly to see whether we have the courage to continue after Bothwell, or whether we will cave in to persecution.'

♣

The next day several thousand gathered on the Darmead moor to hear Cameron. Picquets had been posted to give warning of any threat of attack, and Cleland, Hackston and Hall each commanded a group of armed men who would follow their lead in the event of any threat. All was in readiness!

'Reverend Sir! The picquets are posted. There is no enemy in sight. The service may proceed,' Young Davie Semple, in charge of the picquets, reported to Cameron.

Richard Cameron's voice rang out clearly over the throng. *'"Behold, I will send my messenger, and he shall prepare the way before me; and the Lord, whom ye seek, shall suddenly come to his temple."* We are met here today, to worship God in our own way. There are those who would deny us, even destroy us, so that they may have their will with our consciences. But be not disheartened, for God is with us! We do not seek earthly power, indeed we do not seek authority over others, save to be under the authority of God and His Word. We may be hunted and harried, persecuted and pursued, but a day of reckoning is coming in Scotland! It will not be a day of human reckoning; it will be far more terrible, for it will be a day of God's reckoning! Oh, turn now from your sins...'

13 June 1680. Bo'ness.

Donald Cargill and Henry Hall were riding slowly, heading for Queensferry. Passing two men standing at the corner in clerical dress, Donald muttered, 'Keep your heid down, these look like curates.'

Taking his own advice he pulled his hat further over his brow, and kept his eyes on the road in front. Careful not to ride too slowly, the pair casually walked their horses out of Bo'ness.

'Yon's Cargill,' said the curate of Bo'ness, for it was indeed him and his colleague from Carriden who had been standing at the corner.

'By glory, so it is! We had best warn the Governor, and that quickly.'

♣

'You're sure it was Cargill?' interrogated Governor Middleton of Blackness Castle.

'Sure I am! I've seen his likeness many times. And he has a companion who looks as if he can handle a sword.'

'Guard! Guard! Mount and make ready!' Six troopers responded to the Governor's call, and were soon mounted in the forecourt.

'Do you keep an eye on two men on the Queensferry Road whom I will show you. But do not let them see you, do not get too close!'

'Sir!' The grizzled sergeant was not one to waste words.

Middleton led his troop into the shelter of a small wood overlooking the main road. 'There they are! Keep them in view. I will follow at a distance. When I call, come at the gallop.'

'Sir!'

Cargill and Hall rode into Queensferry as nonchalantly as they had ridden out of Bo'ness. Inwardly their guts were churning, for they knew that all the small ports along the Firth of Forth were watched by government spies. Riding into the yard of the Hawes Inn they dismounted, tethered their horses, and entered the tavern.

'Goodie, bring us two pots of best ale, it's a hot day for riding.' Before she had time to respond to this request, Governor Middleton, drawn sword in hand, burst through the street door.

'You are my prisoners!' he shouted! 'I arrest you in the name of King Charles!' as he took a swing at Cargill.

'He's not *my* king!' roared Hall, as he grappled powerfully with the Governor.

'Aid! Aid, in the name of the King!' shouted Middleton. Henry Hall was a strong man of undoubted courage, and the Governor was unable to free his sword hand from the vice-like grip.

'Run Donald! Flee for your life!'

As Donald made for the street door, Hall was felled by a blow from behind by a carbine wielded by Thomas George, the local Exciseman. No one else had appeared to help, and there was no sign of the sergeant and his troopers. Suddenly the tavern filled with sturdy fishwives, drawn by the commotion. Immediately sizing up the situation, they blocked the Exciseman and Governor from reaching either door, and in the confusion were able to assist Hall into the street and out of sight into a friendly home.

Meanwhile Donald Cargill had mounted the Governor's horse which had been tethered in the street, and was now nowhere to be seen. Shortly the sound of hooves was heard in the street, as the sergeant and his men appeared at the gallop. Governor Middleton, standing in the street with his drawn sword in his hand, was a picture of fury. 'Where in Hell's name have you been? I told you to stay close by!'

'We were misled by a young carle who said you needed us at the slipway to prevent Cargill escaping.'

'Well, he has escaped now sure enough, though I managed to wound him. Hall is also sore wounded and will not get far. Send a galloper to the House of Binns to appraise General Dalzell.'

'The fugitives' horses are still here in the yard,' called out one of the young troopers.

'Search the saddlebags to see if we can find any clue as to where they are hiding,' ordered the sergeant.

Two troopers began to empty the contents of each saddlebag onto the ground. 'Here, what's that paper you threw down?' demanded Middleton.

He reached down and picked up a dirty parchment roll. As he unwound it, his eyes widened in surprise.

'By heaven, we have them now! This is a formal protocol, setting out their rebellious policy in detail. We can destroy their credibility with this!'

Two days later. Kirk O'Shotts.

'This is disaster, Ritchie.'
Donald Cargill and Richard Cameron had managed to link up again in secret. There was now a price of 5000 merks on Cameron's head, and 3000 on Cargill's. Henry Hall had been captured, but had died of his wounds *en route* to Edinburgh.
Cameron sighed. 'Aye, it puts us in a very bad light, a very bad light indeed. As though we had not opposition enough.'
'The paper they seized has already been published by the government under the title of *The Fanatiks' New Covenant*. It's all over the place! Everyone is reading it! They have taken it to be our declared policy, though it was still only a draft. Henry was going to take it back to Holland for comment by M'Ward and others before we published it. He was due to sail from Queensferry the very night he was taken. So now we are not only rebels, for the draft rejects the king, but we are also accused of being power seekers, for it virtually proposes a republic! You know full well that we have never sought political power for ourselves, but who will believe this now, for warfare by prayer and fasting is a concept not understood by many? Now we are not only cut off from society, but from the kirk as well, for it advocates separation from indulged ministers to a such degree that our enemies will surely succeed in driving a wedge between the moderates and ourselves! We will henceforth be *pariahs* to the whole world!'
'Aye, we may well go down in history vilified for what we never were, war-mongers and power seekers, when all we ever wanted was to to be free to worship without interference. But our foes have now seized the initiative and are exploiting the propaganda value to the limit. We are like to be seen by all as just a bunch of murdering fanatics.'
Donald broke the tense silence. 'So we must publish our own declaration to state our case clearly and fairly, and that right quickly.'
'I have already drawn up a basis for such a declaration, and twenty-seven have signed including Thomas Douglas. I am minded to publish it on 22 June, the anniversary of Bothwell Brig. Possibly at Sanquhar? Here,' handing a parchment to Donald, 'look it over.'

'Well Ritchie, ye maun gang yer ain gate,' said Donald after reading the short paper.

'It will of course need to be refined but it must be published very soon. You may remember my sermon at Shawhead? "*Some would triumph in a great army, but know ye what it is to triumph in the work of His hands? Our persecutors may have forces and armies at their command'... Many think that if we had such an army as we had last year we would contend with them, but we need not trouble ourselves about it.*" For it is God Himself who will bring deliverance, and none other.'

'So you actually propose to declare a war against the crown?'

'I do! But a spiritual war! We may be few and poor and weak, but we have The Lord of Hosts on our side. Mark my words Donald, some day this *declaration* will shake the throne of Britain. But now we must split up. Who is with you?'

'I have Alexander Shields and Will Cleland, just we three. Otherwise we are alone.'

'You would look far to find better men, and you of all people know you are never alone. I have David Hackston and my bodyguard, so I am well escorted.'

♣

Alex and Will were keeping lookout whilst the two ministers conferred.

'Where do you think we are headed now, Will?'

'Donald tells me he wants to get up Falkirk way near the Forth. It seems he has some specific business there. But I'd like to try to call in briefly at Cumnock, to say goodbye to my sister Janet, for I fear it may be a long time before I see her again. Do you mind a bit of a detour?'

Shields' face lit up, though he strove to appear disinterested. 'No, I don't mind. Who knows when we may ever be this way again.'

'Alex, is there something between Janet and you? I'm not sure I would approve of that as her brother. There is already too much pain in these uncertain days.'

'Might the same not apply to Margaret Steel?'
'Hmpf!'

22 June 1680. Sanquhar.

In the grey morning light, the line of twenty-one horsemen led by Richard Cameron on his grey horse, plodded into the little town. Each held a drawn sword or pistol, and their faces were solemn. Riding slowly up to the market cross, one man dismounted. He held a parchment in his hand. All uncovered, and the solemn sound of a psalm floated above the rooftops. The dismounted man looked at his leader, and receiving a nod, started to read from the paper in his hand. His voice rose clear above the wind, and echoed through the market square:

"...And we disown Charles Stuart who has been tyrannising on the throne of Britain these past years," his voice rose a semi-tone, *"being under the standard of Christ, captain of Salvation, we declare war against such a tyrant and usurper..."*

The few townspeople in the square shivered in the cold wind, and drew their plaids and shawls closer around them. This could only bring trouble down on their heads, and whilst they might sympathise with the speaker and his companions, they longed to be left in peace. Too many fathers and brothers were still being hunted down by Claverhouse's dragoons after the battle at Bothwell Brig, exactly a year ago today.

'Nail it to the cross, Michael,' said the leader when the reading ended, 'and take a copy to each corner of the town and nail it up. John, Francis, Alex and young Crichton, quick now!' The men named each took a paper from for the leader's hand and trotted off, to return within a few minutes.

'Thomas, you had the Word at Drumclog, will ye give us a prayer?'

'Aye Ritchie, that I will'—and as the troop uncovered the Rev Thomas Douglas led into a heartfelt plea to God for protection and mercy. The whole troop joined in the "Amen", and wheeling their horses about, followed their leader slowly out of town. The last sight the townspeople caught of them was wending their way up on to the moors.

22 July 1680. Airdsmoss.

Cameron had spent the night at Meadowhead Farm but his followers had slept rough on the moor. When Richard joined them he found that Hackston, commanding his bodyguard, had sent out scouts to reconnoitre, but they had returned with nothing to report. The group of sixty men huddled together on the bleak moor with no cover of any sort.

'Someone's comin',' quietly called Willie Manuel. 'Looks like a shepherd.'

A bearded man in hodden grey panted his way into the group. Hackston confronted him, as he blurted out, 'Sodgers, horse and dragoons! Aboot a hunner, headin' fast frae the east. Move closer to the moss!' he urged. 'It will gie ye some cover as at Drumclog.' So the group moved to the only point of vantage, on the fringe of the marsh called Airdsmoss. There was general unspoken agreement to stand and fight.

'Come close, and let us commit ourselves to The Lord.' Richard Cameron led: *'Lord, spare the green and take the ripe.'* This he repeated three times, and then quietly spoke to his brother: *'Michael, come let us fight it out to the last; for this is the day that I have longed for, and the death that I have prayed for... and this is the day that we will get the crown.'* He raised his voice: *'Be encouraged all of you, to fight it out valiantly; for all of you that shall fall this day, I see heaven's gates cast wide open to receive them.'*

Amid priming of pistols and drawing of broadswords, the enemy leader hove into view. 'Its Bruce of Earlshall! Our father helped him out of his financial difficulties!' exclaimed Michael through clenched teeth. A hundred and twenty troopers rode at his back.

'And there's David Ramsey, a fellow student of mine at St Andrews,' added Hackston bitterly. 'This is indeed a sad day for us and for Scotland.'

About twenty dragoons dismounted and approached the covenanter's exposed flank. Hackston ordered some of his foot to head them off, and advanced himself with the horse, commencing firing on the enemy. Horsemen of both sides became quickly mired in the bog, many dismounting to avoid being sucked down with their horses. The fight rapidly developed into a general meleé, with Cameron and his followers fighting like madmen. Despite being heavily outnumbered by the troopers, the outcome hung precariously in the balance.

'Yield and receive quarter,' cried Bruce over the clash of steel.

'Never will I yield to you,' replied Cameron, and renewed his onslaught more vigorously than before.

Ramsay and Hackston confronted each other on foot. They were both excellent swordsmen and neither could better the other until Hackston was cut down from behind by three severe cuts to the head. 'If these rebels had been as well mounted and armed as us, the day would go differently,' thought Ramsey.

But Richard Cameron, deep in the thick of the fight, fell beneath the swords of the three men he was fighting at once, and as his brother fell too, the covenanter footmen began to leave the field in ones and twos, leaving their horsemen to cope alone. Many who fled, later wept bitterly that they had not stayed to die with their leader, "The Lion of the Covenant."

By five o'clock on the summer afternoon, while the sun was still high, the fight was over.

'Here, Murray, there's a guinea. Bring me Cameron's head,' called out Bruce.

'Which one is he? Ah never saw him afore.'

'There's two joints of his middle finger missing.'

The trooper examined the dead bodies roughly, kicking over those who lay face down, till he saw a hand with missing joints. 'I'll just cut aff baith hands,' he said to himself, cutting them off with his sabre, and then hacking the head off the corpse.

'Here y'are Capt'n,' holding up a sack dripping with blood. 'Yin heid and twa hands.'

'We've captured five, all wounded,' reported Ramsay, 'and nine dead. But we have lost twenty-eight killed or badly wounded. They fought well.'

'Aye, they fought well, for traitors! Bind up the prisoners and mount them. We ride for Douglas.'

'They are all sore wounded, and two cannot sit a horse.'

'Bind them up and mount them! They are all going to die anyway!'

The weary and bloodied party started over the moors, and soon the spire of St Bride's at Douglas was seen. Hooves clattered into the market place, where the troopers dismounted and refreshed themselves at the tavern. The prisoners were ignored, left tied on their mounts, in obvious distress from thirst and loss of blood.

Trooper Murray detached the dripping sack from his crupper and rolled out a head onto the cobbles.

'Here y'are, boys! Here's a fine fitba.' He and the others started kicking Richard Cameron's head about. The few townsfolk who had dared to appear looked sick, but one young woman, more courageous than the rest, carried a pitcher of water towards the badly injured Hackston.

'Here, lassie! Where d'ye think ye're gaun?' rudely asked the sergeant.

'Do you have compassion for no one?' she cried and, ignoring the troopers, gave a drink to Hackston. 'I am Janet Cleland, Will's sister,' she whispered in his ear. "Would that I could dress and bind up your wounds, but they will not countenance it.'

'For what you have done I bless you. Never fear, I am quite ready to die, for I walk close to God, whilst they do not even know Him.'

Next day. Privy Council Chamber, Edinburgh.

'My lords, there's the head and hands that lived praying and preaching, and died praying and fighting,' said Bruce, as he threw Cameron's bloodied remains onto the council table.

The Tolbooth, Edinburgh.

The cell door crashed open!

'So, old man, do you know this head and hands?'

Alan Cameron took the severed head and hands into his own hands and kissed them. *'I know them, I know them, they are my son's, my dear*

*son's. It is the Lord, good is the will of the Lord, who cannot wrong me
or mine, but has made goodness and mercy to follow us all our days.'*

The Cross of Edinburgh.

Hackston, tied to a hurdle, was being dragged backwards to his place
of execution.

On reaching the gibbet he was dragged up onto the platform and
forced to his knees. Whilst the hangman's assistants held his hands on
the block, they were severed by the hangman's axe. Hackston made no
sound while this fearful mutilation took place. The noose, already
around his neck, was now reeved through a pulley and he was hoisted to
the top of the gibbet. As he slowly strangled his body writhed in agony,
but while he was still alive they let go of the rope and his body crashed
onto the platform. The hangman knelt down with the great dirk in his
hands, sliced open the victim's breast and plunging his hand into the
cavity, pulled out the still pulsating heart.

'Behold the heart of a traitor!' The hangman held the heart up for all
to see, and then cast it onto the glowing brazier beside the gallows.
Some onlookers vomited, but most jeered! The body was dragged once
more to the block and the head was now chopped off. Thereafter the
hangman and his assistants hacked the mutilated body into four quarters,
so that it might be sent to four quarters of the kingdom to serve as a
warning not to trifle with the King's rule.

In the crowd, William Cleland, white faced, leant towards his sister
Janet.

'Most foully murdered, just like they did to William Wallace! May
God forgive me, if I do not devote the rest of my life to ridding Scotland
of such an evil tyranny!'

'God rest that brave man's soul,' choked Janet through her tears.

CHAPTER SIX

"THE KING IS EXCOMMUNICATED!"

Aug 1680. Craigmad Moor.

CARGILL, CLELAND AND SHIELDS were hiding in a bothy far out on the moors.

'It may be summer, but its gye cauld here,' exclaimed Cleland, rubbing his hands over an apology for a fire. The wood was soaking, and there was no chimney, merely a hole in the thatch of the soot blackened building. The heat given off was minimal.

'Someone coming!' called out Alexander Shields, who was keeping watch. 'Looks like one of us, alone and plainly clad. Goodness, its Walter Smith! How ever did he get here?'

As Smith drew closer he recognised Alex. 'Well, am I glad to see you! Everyone seems to be dead or in prison these days. I couldn't make the preaching yesterday, and I had a terrible job to find anyone who would trust me enough to say where you were hiding.'

By this time Donald and Will had joined the pair outside, and a general welcome took place. 'Walter! Well met indeed! There has never been a time we needed you more.'

'We thought you were safe in Holland,' said Cleland.

"How could I stay safe in Holland at a time like this, Will? *The Queensferry Paper* captured and published. Then Ritchie's *Declaration* at Sanquhar, and him and the others killed. This is no time to be hiding in Holland, this is a time that needs every true man in Scotland.'

'Aye, that's very true,' said Donald. 'Though some would call it foolhardiness rather than courage. But you are indeed welcome, for we are at a very low ebb, and the Covenant cause has all but foundered.'

Later after Cargill was asleep, the others sat and talked quietly amongst themselves. 'Donald is very cast down after Ritchie's death,' said Shields.

'Hardly surprising, since he is now the only field preacher left in the whole of Scotland,' responded Smith.

'Not quite,' remarked Cleland. 'John Blackader is still alive and free, but he is too ill to preach.'

'So what is going to happen now?'

'I think Donald is about to do something momentous. He is very withdrawn and solitary. It seems he is getting his courage up for what lies ahead. I have never seen him quite like this before.'

'He should share it with us, whatever it is, before he acts,' said Walter.

'You're right, but I don't think he is going to,' William closed the conversation.

11 Sept 1680. The Torwood.

Donald Cargill and his close friends were meeting the night before the conventicle to be held at Torwood, between Larbert and Stirling. The service promised to be very well attended, for word had gone out that something exceptional was about to happen. Exactly what no-one yet knew, for Cargill had remained solitary and silent for days. At last he spoke.

'I have chosen the Torwood as the place to make the strongest protest yet against the tyranny of the House of Stewart, for it has strong historical links with our long struggle for freedom in this land. William Wallace hid here after the Battle of Falkirk, and it was the mustering ground for Bruce's army before Bannockburn. They both called on God for help, and we shall do the same.'

'What are you planning?' asked Walter Smith with a worried look.

'Yes, will you not share your burden with us, your friends?' added Alexander Shields as Cleland grunted his assent.

'It is too great, too grievous. I must bear this burden alone,' sighed Cargill.

'We are all hunted men with a price on our heads. We are all on the fugitives' roll, and our lives have been worth nothing since Bothwell. I think we deserve an explanation.' Cleland spoke out forcefully.

'Indeed you do deserve that and much more, but if I give it not, will you then desert me?'

Cleland replied angrily, 'Donald, you know that blood is thicker than water, and we know that you have been many times within an inch of death, as have we all. No, we will stand by you whatever chances to happen.'

'Well said, Will, like a true friend. But I wonder if you will feel the same tomorrow night?'

♣

The next day dawned bleak and grey. The very heavens seemed to want to weep, as the worshippers began to gather under the cover of the Torwood, hidden from the eyes of troopers who were continually scouring the countryside in search of the solitary field preacher who still defied the king.

An immense crowd had gathered in a clearing in the depths of the forest, many having walked from Falkirk or Stirling, or even farther afield. Many seemed more curious than anything, for word had gone out far and wide, that a great event was about to occur.

And so it was!

Cargill began reading his text. '*And thou, profane wicked prince of Israel, whose day is come, when iniquities shall have no end, thus saith the Lord God; Remove the diadem, and take off the crown... exalt him that is low, and abase him that is high. I will overturn, overturn, overturn it, and it shall be no more...*'

A shudder went through the crowd and people began to shout out: 'Away with him, away with him!' The noise reached a crescendo as

Cargill, raising his voice, called out: 'Hear me friends, hear me! Do not make a judgement until you have heard what I have to say today, for it has been laid upon me by The Lord Himself. Of that I am certain.'

Gradually the shouting died away, but as Donald saw his host of last night sidle out of the crowd and disappear into the forest, he also noticed William Cleland gathering a group of swordsmen around him. Obviously he expected trouble.

As Cargill went on, it became clear that this was to be no evangelical sermon! In fact, it soon became clear that the king himself was the target today. After a short exposition on his text, he fell silent for a space and it was clear to the watchers that he was wrestling with some major inner stress. At length, taking a deep breath, he got himself under control and drawing himself to his full height, he began to speak once more.

Rev Donald Cargill's voice rang out clear and true. Even those on the very extremity of the vast concourse could hear every word, every subtle nuance.

'I being a minister of Jesus Christ, and having the authority and power from Him, do, in His name, and by His Spirit, deliver up to Satan, Charles II, king, and that on account of his wickednesses:...'

A stunned silence hung over the crowd! One could have heard a pin drop!

He had everybody's attention now!

'For his high contempt of God... for his great perjury... because he had cancelled all laws permitting a covenanted reformation, and is rather working for the introduction of popery in this land... for the innocent blood of the people of God that he has shed on fields, and scaffolds, and on the high seas...'

He went on, the crowd spellbound:

'Also, James Duke of York for idolatry...'

'James, Duke of Monmouth, for leading an army against the Lord's people...'

'John, Duke of Lauderdale, for blasphemy and apostacy...'

'John, Duke of Rothes, for perjury and adultery...'

'Sir George MacKenzie for apostacy and persecution...'

'General Thomas Dalzell of the Binns, for leading armies against God's people, and for persecuting them...'

'...this sentence is just, and there is no king nor minister on earth, who can lawfully reverse these sentences, without full repentance.'

This was the only time in his life that Donald Cargill delivered such a judgement. That same afternoon he reverted to type, and preached a sermon of compassion and forgiveness which had many of his listeners weeping. But as they walked home that night one thought occupied each mind.

The king had been excommunicated!

A few days later. Edinburgh.

'They may call me "Bluidy Mackenzie", but why-ever did that canting Whig Cargill not excommunicate "Bluidy Clavers" as well? He's killed more than I have!' Sir George Mackenzie and General Tam Dalzell were meeting with the Duke of Rothes to discuss the latest Cameronian madness.

'At least they consider me a worse persecutor than Claverhouse,' Dalzell quipped sarcastically.

'No General, you are a lot more brutal than Claverhouse. At least his cruelties have a purpose in view. You just delight in cruelty.' Dalzell bristled!

'And you would know of cruelty my Lord Rothes! I've seen you wallowing in the torture of these covenanters. Sometimes it seemed you wished you were the one turning the screw!'

'Gentlemen, gentlemen, what is the point of bickering amongst ourselves?' Mackenzie interjected. 'We are all in the same barrel in Whig eyes. At least we share this latest insult with none less than His Majesty the King, his brother, and his bastard!'

'More to the point, we have the whole adder's nest just where we want them with this excommunication. Even some of Cameron's close followers are aghast at Cargill's behaviour. We can use it against whomever we will, moderates and Cameronians alike. His Majesty will not put any limit on our treatment of any who refuse to conform even to the smallest royal decree. Cargill will hang for this!'

'Raise the reward to 5000 merks and someone will surely betray him!'

'I'm not so sure. Whatever these covenanters are, they are not cowards, and betrayal for them is a great sin. These people are not cynics like us, they would rather die than betray their friends.'

'Then let them die in great numbers!' retorted Dalzell. 'If it's a war of attrition they want, they can have one. We still have many on the fugitives' roll whom we have never ever captured, let alone punished.'

'Lauderdale is like to die soon after his stroke. Perhaps we can claim that this speeded up his death, and use that to whip up public support against them? Pity none of the rest of us are terminal!'

Rothes, who knew he was dying, remained silent. Dalyell grinned maliciously. 'Not much need. This has put the fear of God into many a heart. We must not waste this golden opportunity.'

'They already have the fear of God in their hearts,' retorted Mackenzie. 'What they don't fear is our retribution, and that's the only weapon we possess!'

Next day. Kirk O' Shotts.

Cargill and Smith had split up from Cleland and Shields right after the Torwood. 'This will mean the Grassmarket for Donald,' said William Cleland as they made their way over the soggy moor.

'Aye, it grieves me to say this,' replied Alex, 'but I fear I must go into exile again and you must come with me this time, Will. We must regroup for another venture. There is no point in you and I becoming martyrs right now. Donald and Walter will move public sympathy much more than us, despite Torwood. And Donald himself insisted we must go ahead to Holland. We need to make a new plan.'

Will was silent for a moment. 'You know full well he will not follow us. He will not leave Scotland again. He is determined to pay the full price.'

'Yes, I know. But it's going to be up to you and me in the end, Will. We have a destiny to fulfil, and our time is not yet.'

'You turning prophet as well, Alex?' asked Cleland wryly. 'But you are quite right of course, we really need a new and better plan.'

'So it's us for Holland, Will?

'It's us for Holland, Alex!'

CHAPTER SEVEN

"LETTERS FROM HOME"

October 1680. Utrecht.

T he *Rector Magnificus* **was weary.** 'Not another Scot! I can't understand why all your theologians prefer Utrecht University to Leiden?'

Alexander Shields was prompt with his reply: 'To be frank *Rector*, Utrecht is safer for us than Holland proper, or even Leiden. Some of our friends have been forced into further exile from Holland, and there have even been attempts to seize Scottish fugitives from a safe house under cover of night. Three of my friends are already registered here, and you have more Scots exiles than at any other university in the Netherlands.'

'The problem with you lot is that you never stay put, and you rarely finish your degrees! Walter Smith is a really outstanding student, but he has disappeared off somewhere, we hear back to Scotland? You people are just not serious enough about your studies!'

'We are living in very perilous times *mijnheer*. Walter Smith even now is in grave danger of his life, seeking to advance the Kingdom of God in Scotland.'

'Well, I have to admit that you are a brave and earnest bunch. I suppose we were much the same here until we threw the Spanish out of the Netherlands. We longed for freedom above all!'

'As do we! And we find the doctrine you teach here at Utrecht very congenial to our way of thinking. You hold to the teaching of Calvin, and we admire your Professor Voetius for his steadfast resistance to the Coccesian and Arminian heresies. This University takes the same stance as do our good friends the Revs Brown and M'Ward in Rotterdam. And your Professor of Divinity, Dr Leydecker, has made it clear that followers of Richard Cameron are welcome here.'

'Hmph! Some might say that we are just a hotbed of religious fanatics!'

'That's nothing new to us. We are quite used to being run down and despised. It's pretty well the fate of everybody who stands for the truth? Many of our folk have already paid with their lives.' The *Rektor* had the grace not to pursue the argument further.

'Well Mr Shields, we will accept you here as a theology student, but I trust you will be diligent in your studies and conform to our rules? And that you will live quietly amongst us, not behaving too boisterously on *kermis* days! You must arrange for yourself which lectures you will attend. They start at 8 a.m, but you are expected to attend private tuition before that. Dr Matthius Netenhuis will advise you.'

♣

The English Coffee House was packed with émigrés. Shields and Cleland had met up and been joined by Robert Hamilton, Sir Patrick Hume and Sir John Erskine of Carnock, all fugitives from Bothwell. Robert and William Blackader, sons of the only other field-preacher besides Cargill still alive, were also there. All were in an unusually cheerful frame of mind and the talking was animated!

'William, you look unwell?' Trust Hamilton to pick up something negative!

'Yes, I picked up a fever when we were on the run and living rough after Torwood. I expect Dr Blackader here will see me right.'

'Just because I achieved a distinction for my thesis on *calculi* in the bladder and kidneys, doesn't mean I'll be much use to you!' Dr William Blackader could be infuriatingly cynical. 'But I'll come and check you out anyway. Where are you staying?'

'In Leiden, at a widow's lodgings in St Anna Straat.'

'Leiden? I thought you were going to study here at Utrecht?'

'I had a mind to study both medicine and law, and they will only let me do that at Leiden. Forbye I still have a fancy to go a soldiering, and John Carnock reckons James Johnstoun's fencing school is the best in all the Low Countries.'

'Well, you are the best suited of any of us to the military life. You will surely be accepted into the Scots Brigade here, for I hear Colonel Mackay has improved the standard of the regiments beyond measure. He is a covenant man and known to be very pious.' Alex Shields was trying to be encouraging.

'My problem is that the Scots Brigade can still be ordered home by Charles Stewart if he needs troop reinforcements in Britain. And you know that would mean death for me!'

♣

'Alex, I've just had a letter from Margaret bringing me up to date with events in Scotland.' Cleland and Shields were meeting over a bottle of wine at the *Witte Hart* in Leiden.

'Just what you need to get you over the last of your fever, eh Will?'

'Yes, but the news is not good. In fact its pretty depressing. Our Cameronian cause seems to be going down the drain. Cargill's execution was almost the last straw. Someone as thoroughly decent as that, to be strung up like a common criminal!'

'Well, what did you expect after he excommunicated King Charles?'

'I suppose I hoped for mercy.'

'Hmph! They made that papist the Duke of York, King's High Commissioner for Scotland the very afternoon of his execution! Where is their mind for mercy?'

'And how is Margaret?' Shields asked in a diffident tone!

Cleland coloured slightly. 'She is well, but sad. Not just by my absence, for her brother Thomas has been forced to go to the Carolina's in company with Lord Cardross, to escape the persecution. We have Scots exiles on both sides of the globe now.'

He went on: 'She writes of Cargill's arrest and trial. How cruelly he was treated on the way to Edinburgh after capture, and how, when the

Duke of Rothes threatened him with torture at his trial he replied: "*My Lord Rothes, forbear to threaten me, for die what death I will, your eyes shall not see it.*" Rothes died on the very morning of the day that Cargill was executed in the Grassmarket!

'Moreover, she writes that the night before they both died, Rothes was in such a state of fear that everyone in the house could hear his shrieks of terror throughout the house! His Duchess, good Christian woman that she is, called in two covenanting ministers to lead him to repentance which they duly did. So you see, Cargill's ministry was a blessing even to those who hated him and hunted him down. The Duke of Hamilton, in the next room with some other peers, was heard to say: "We banish these men from us, and yet when dying, we send for them! There's something wrong somewhere!"'

He read on: 'On the scaffold, thrice the drums were beat to drown out his words to the crowd, but still many heard him as he said, "*I entreat you, be not discouraged, for this is the sweetest and most glorious day that ever mine eyes did see.*" It was just like Ritchie at Airdsmoss, for that was the day he got the crown! Walter Smith and James Boig were hanged along with him, and they were just as brave. Their deaths have made many decent people here realise afresh just what sort of brutal persecution we are up against.'

'Oh, and our old acquaintance Claverhouse is having a fine time in the south-west, arresting and killing, especially since the introduction of the *Test Act* in August! No one may now hold any office or position however humble, unless he swears fealty to the Stewarts, even in matters of conscience, so none of our friends can swear to it, and it is used as yet another excuse to remove good men from any position of authority. You see this black hackle I wear in my hat?'

'Yes, I wondered about that. What's it for?'

'You know our old Scots tradition of wearing a black feather when one has a bitter dispute on with someone? I have a dispute to settle with Claverhouse and indeed the whole House of Stewart. I will wear a black feather in my hat until justice returns to Scotland.'

'I see!' Alex was silent for a while. 'Might be a long time! But tell me about this *Test Act*, Will?'

'It's tied up with York's right of succession, and is a most confusing oath! It's designed to test one's loyalty to the Crown, whilst also professing the Protestant faith. But it makes a mockery of it, for it affirms the king as *"the only Supream Goverenour of the Realm, over all persons and in all causes as weill Ecclesiastical as Civill."* Even loyal supporters of Charles have difficulty swearing to it, it is so contradictory. The Earl of Argyle was only prepared to swear only *in so far* as it was consistent with itself, and supported the presbyterian faith. He was imprisoned in Edinburgh Castle because of this attitude, but he escaped and is now here in Holland. Ironically it was Argyle's casting vote which sent Cargill to the gallows!'

'Dear Lord! Is there no end to all this misery?' exclaimed Alex.

'Margaret says there are house meetings all across the South and in Fife, and that more and more are turning to them for solace, for it is to be found nowhere else. But they have to meet in secret. There is one which meets in her home in Cambusnethan, and another at your sister Janet's at Cumnock, as well as many others whom we ken. Forbye, there is not even one minister left alive to bring communion to this suffering remnant, yet they still stand fast for their freedom of worship.'

'Any more?'

'Well, the rest *is* rather personal, Alex.'

♣

As Cleland and Shields worked at their studies at Leiden and Utrecht, more exiles arrived every week from Scotland with fresh tales of bitter persecution. The little exile community steadily grew in numbers and influence and the Scots Church in Rotterdam flourished. Generally the Scots were liked and respected for their canny and quiet lives, but here and there a situation flared up, hardly surprising since the spectrum of exiles ranged from moderates, who had accepted the king's Indulgences, to Cameronians who rejected them out of hand. That the exiles covered such a wide range had much to do with the irrational attitude of the persecutors, who were as likely to throw someone loyal to the king into prison on a technicality as to arrest an avowed enemy of the Stewarts.

One surprising such arrival in Leiden, during the autumn of 1682, was Sir James Dalrymple of Stair who had been President of the Scottish Court of Session, but had fallen foul of the *Test Act* largely due to his association with the Earl of Argyle.

'I have come to see Sir James Dalrymple. My name is William Cleland.'

'Huv ye an appointment?' The large and very surly man who opened the door was decidedly unfriendly.

'No, but he and I are studying under Professor van Dijk who recommended me to consult with Sir James regarding my *Institutio,* since it concerns Scots Law in which he is expert. His work demonstrates the influence of Grotius and other Leiden law experts.'

'Bide there!' A pause…! Reluctantly the lackey reopened the door. 'Come ben then. He'll see ye.'

Cleland was shown into a simply furnished room where a man in his early sixties was seated by a small fire.

'Mr Cleland! Welcome! I know you by repute.'

'I fear, Sir James, my repute will not be very good in your eyes, for had I been taken after Drumclog or Bothwell, it is like you would have sentenced me to death.'

Dalrymple gave a heavy sigh. 'You are quite right of course. But now you find me with as little credit as yourself. Or rather you have more, for no-one could say you ever served two masters, and I to my shame, had a hand in cobbling together this foul *Test Act!* But we are both exiles from our homeland, and should help each other where we may. What can I do for you?'

'I have been studying law at the University here in Leiden, in the hopes of bringing a better justice to Scotland some day. I have been hunted with a price on my head, and you know only too well the harsh laws which are inflicted on my Cameronian friends.'

Dalrymple had the grace to look embarrassed.

Cleland continued: 'I have been working on the rules of evidence applied in our Scots courts, and studying your *Institutions of the Law of*

Scotland with great interest. Would you consider looking over my *Institutio Juridica de Probationibus* and giving me your views on it?'

'Indeed I would, Mr Cleland, and all the more as I hear we have a common enemy.'

Cleland looked puzzled.

'I refer of course to Colonel John Graham of Claverhouse. He is the main reason I am here in Holland. He had the infernal cheek to warn me to walk warily when I applied to His Majesty for relief in the need to take the *Test!* Young whippersnapper! And now he is taking both me and my son to court. I was forced to leave Scotland or take the oath, and I would not besmirch my conscience with that! You are the only one who has ever defeated him in the field. He bears you no good will I fear.'

'Nor I him, Sir James.'

'So let us see what we can do together to help each other. Give me some salient points from your disputation.'

'Well sir, as you are aware, the covenanters are well known for their strict regard for the truth. Practically everyone knows that they will not lie, even under duress. Yet they are tortured, not to get at the truth, but to make them lie, so that they can be falsely accused. Also their high respect for the Almighty is held in scorn. I hear even Donald Cargill's faith was impugned at his trial, when the whole world, even his enemies, admit that he was a true man of God. Such goings on are scandalous and evil, and bairns are even forced to...' Cleland was warming to his subject.

'Enough! Enough! Mr Cleland. I can see your sincerity is beyond question. I will read your paper and let you have my views. I would ask you to stay for supper, but my wife has not yet been able to join me here, and I keep a very simple establishment.' The reappearance of the large and surly servitor confirmed this.

'I will take my leave then, Sir James. Bid you good day, sir.'

'Good day sir, and be of good courage. I have a feeling one day your paper may well help to reformulate the laws of Scotland.'

♣

'Alex, will you and the others please carry me outside, for I want to see this comet before I die.' Rev Robert M'Ward's decline had been rapid since his recent fall-out with Robert Hamilton who, since his arrival, had managed to upset just about everybody in the Scots Kirk of Rotterdam with his intransigent attitude to virtually everything.

Though M'Ward was near death, Shields and three of the kirk elders were consulting him about the latest situation in Scotland, for despite his weakness, his brain was still crystal clear, and his advice was still widely respected.

Halley's Comet streamed across the sky, drawing a magnificent tail in its wake.

'Losh! That's a sight to behold,' marvelled one of the elders.

'It is that! It is that! Thank you, my dear friends. Now take me back inside where I may die in peace, unlike so many of my persecuted friends at home in Scotland.'

They carried him back into the parlour of Marette's house, where he had shared lodgings with his friend John Brown of Wamphray since they had both been exiled. Once he was comfortably settled on the couch, the elders departed, and he was left alone with Shields.

'Tell me Alex, what news of Scotland?'

'I've just received a letter from my brother Michael who is in hiding around Lanarkshire. There are some hopeful doings afoot. Let me read it to you.'

'Wonderful!' murmured M'Ward.

Alex extracted a letter from his coat pocket, and sat down beside his friend.

'This letter seems to have had some high adventures to judge from its state.' The paper had obviously been soaked at some stage and was covered with black smudges on the outside. 'I think our messenger, Earlston, had a hard job to get it here safely. He sailed on a collier, and at one stage had to hide in the hold when they were boarded and searched by an English frigate.'

'That's like as not.'

'Well, here goes,' said Alex. 'It's dated at Muirkirk, Lanarkshire,16th March, 1682. Michael is now scribe to a new organisation called the United Societies, and he seems pretty well informed.'

'Go on.'

> *"Dear Brother,*
>
> *The persecution continues very hot under Claverhouse, Grierson of Lagg, and the like. But we do not lose heart! All the home fellowship groups in the South-West have now been linked into Societies, and the Societies in each County are then linked into a District Society, which sends Commissioners to a General Meeting. You will see that we are organised like a presbyterian church with congregations, presbyteries and a general assembly, although we are not quite so formal. About 80 Societies, comprising 7000 men and their families have come together for mutual support and encouragement. That means we have about one-fifth of the people of the south-west in our Societies, virtually all who still refuse to bow the knee to Charles Stewart.*
>
> *We do not permit anyone who takes any government oath or pays the Cess, (a tax used to finance the troops who persecute us), to share in our Communion, or indeed anyone who appears in a government court willingly. Many of our folk are dragged into court on trivial charges, such as not attending the service of the appointed curate, and quite a few are tortured during investigation. It is not only men who are dealt thus harshly. Isobel Alison and Marion Harvie glorified God in the Grassmarket recently, and little children are bullied and ill treated to make them reveal the hiding places of fathers and brothers. Yet we stand fast under all this, though it is hard to prevent our people reacting in anger to such brutality. So while we now require each man to be armed, we absolutely forbid any revenge taking, or the use of weapons other than for self defence or rescue.*
>
> *Of course our enemies give us no credit for this, and continually accuse us of needless violence and murder, but we believe that these "killing times" must pass, and we Scots will once again be free to worship according to our consciences. Clavers is made Sheriff-Depute and has virtually unfettered*

power from Galloway to the Pentlands, so government troops are free to abuse as they wish, making the Highland Host of 1678 seem tame by comparison.

At our first General Meeting on 15 December 1681, there was a strong feeling that we must go public with a new declaration of purpose. We have no ministers left alive to guide us just now, but one young man named James Renwick has proved very helpful in formulating what has become known as the Lanark Declaration. Renwick was present at Donald Cargill's execution, and was so greatly moved that he resolved to join our cause. I think he will be of great service to us in the future.

Fifty of us rode into Lanark on 12 January 1682, and made our Declaration there. We also burnt the Test Act. In retaliation the council hangman burnt the Solemn League and Covenant, together with the Rutherglen, Sanquhar and Lanark Declarations at the cross of Edinburgh where King, Hackston and so many other honest men suffered. Forbye they fined Lanark town 6000 merks for allowing it to be read there.

At our second meeting at Muirkirk, only yesterday, it was determined to send Sir Alexander Gordon of Earlston to Holland as emissary to Europe for the United Societes. You will recall he saved Donald Cargill after Bothwell? He has left us to travel via London, and I have given him this letter which I pray may reach you safely—someday!

May The Lord be with you.
Your loving brother,

Michael."

♣

It was September already. Sir James Dalrymple's lodging wore an unusually festive air. The street door stood open, and people of various ages and stations were streaming in and out. Lawyers, students, soldiers and clergy were all recognisable, but the one unifying factor was that they were all Scots.

William Cleland elbowed his way through the crowd to greet his host. 'Will! Welcome indeed!' Relations between Cleland and Dalrymple had warmed considerably with the passage of time. 'My wife has finally been able to join me, so that is a good excuse for a party. As if we needed one! I've just had two hogsheads of good Scots ale shipped over from Leith, for I know how you students long for some home-brew in this foreign land.'

Dalrymple took Will by the elbow. 'There is someone here I want you to meet.'

He led Will up to a tall man who carried himself with a military bearing. 'Colonel Mackay, may I introduce you to one of the budding lawyers in Leiden, Mr Willam Cleland?'

Mackay took Cleland in with a deeply appraising look.

'Mr Cleland, I am very glad to meet you at last. I have heard much of you since that day at Drumclog. I trust you prosper here?'

'Sir, I press on with my legal and medical studies, but in my heart I know I am cut out to be a soldier. Once I complete my *Disputatio* I am minded to approach you to see if I might serve in the Scots Brigade?'

'I hear you are a sensible resolute man, but what experience of soldiering do you have?'

'Not much. In fact, other than Drumclog and Bothwell, none at all.'

'And we can hardly call Bothwell a success, although I hear you carried yourself with great coolness and determination. You and I have a common ill-wisher in Graham of Claverhouse, I think?'

'I have heard so, Colonel.'

'Well, at least you defeated him the field, which I cannot claim.' ("Better in the field than the bedroom!" thought Mackay as he excused himself.)

Cleland cast his eye around the room and saw Alexander Shields in deep conversation with two men, one of whom he recognised as Robert Hamilton, whom he had not seen since Bothwell. Shields looked round and beckoned him over. Cleland went rather unwillingly, for he had no desire to get involved with Hamilton.

'Will! So good to see you again!' There was no mistaking the warmth of Alex's greeting. 'You know Sir Robert Hamilton of course.' The two men glowered at each other and said nothing. 'But have you met Sir Alexander Gordon of Earlston? He was at Bothwell too, and rescued Donald Cargill.'

That sounded better to Cleland, and he gave Earlston his hand. 'Sir Alexander! What are you doing here in Leiden? Banished in exile like the rest of us?'

'No, Mr Cleland. I am here as emissary for the newly formed United Societies. Perhaps Mr Shields has told you about them?'

'Yes, I am glad to hear that some people still stand firm against government pressures to conform. But here in Holland, we have heard of some Covenant followers killing innocent people, and abusing those who oppose their view.'

'You are quite right, not all the abuse has been on the one side by any means. Not surprising really, considering how everyone's rights have been trampled underfoot. But I do assure you that now, even in cases of extreme provocation, the United Societies will not countenance violent behaviour.'

'And what of Sharp's killers?' asked Cleland with some acerbidity.

Earlston looked embarassed, but Hamilton burst in angrily. 'You mean executioners! You yourself saw Hackston barbarously murdered in Edinburgh, and John Balfour of Burley still hides in the moors of the South-West.'

An awkward silence ensued.

Earlston continued: 'We are painfully aware that some violent incidents, often by those not of our number, have portrayed us in a very bad light. We are now striving to ensure that we behave as Christians should, whatever the provocation. The only occasion now when United Societies members may use their weapons is for self defence, or to rescue our captured brethren. Unfortunately there are some who pretend to be with us but in fact are ne'er-do-wells who cause us much harm by their irrational actions. The authorities lose no opportunity to lump us together, so the followers of Richard Cameron are miscalled even by those whom they would befriend.'

'But you have had no ministers since Cargill's death. Who leads the Societies?' Alexander Shields sounded concerned. 'How do you ensure your doctrine is right?'

Hamilton butted in: 'That's the whole point. The Solemn League and Covenant set forth the need for freedom of doctrine, worship and church government as long ago as 1642. All these are matters that Charles Stewart claims must be decided by him alone, his by divine right!' Hamilton snorted.

'We are planning to send four young men over here for theological training.' Earlson sounded enthusiastic! 'One of them in particular is an outstanding young man, James Renwick. He and the others are due to arrive before the end of the year.'

'Y'know,' said Will, turning to the others, 'it would seem two things link us all; being Scots and a dislike of Claverhouse.'

'Have some more of this good Scots ale, Mr Cleland. Just arrived from Leith.'

Will glanced at the rest of the group who were rather ostentatiously drinking water! 'Thanks—I will. But I'd give a lot more for a really good dram!'

♣

James Renwick knocked nervously on the door of the imposing house in the best part of Groeningen. It was opened by a pleasant looking serving woman of middle age, wearing the traditional white Dutch kappie and clogs.

'*Mijnheer?*'

'*Ik zoek Professor à Mark, alstublieft.* I am looking for Professor à Marck, if you please.'

'*Hij is nu thuis, Kom binnen alstublieft.* He is at home. Please come in!'

Renwick stepped into a cool tiled hall, hung about with pictures, some of which he recognised as from the schools of van Rijn and Vermeer, along with earlier paintings from the Dutch renaissance period.

A tall grey figure, serious of visage, entered. 'You'll be young Renwick, no doubt?'

'I am indeed, sir. But newly arrived from Scotland.'

'Hamilton,' said the grey man brusquely. He did not extend his hand.

'Sir Robert!' Renwick made a small bow.

'No! None o' that here. Just plain Robert Hamilton. You may have heard that I now represent the United Societies on the continent, and that Earlston has been recalled? But you are welcome, for we looked for you lang syne. Your compatriots have been here for a month.'

As if on signal, two young men burst unceremoniously into the hall. 'James! At last! We heard you were captured. Welcome indeed!' William Boyd and John Flint, whom the Societies had sent for ordination training ahead of Renwick, were relieved. Joyfully they conducted him into a comfortable parlour, where a distinguished, grey haired man stood in front of the fire, warming himself.

'Mijnheer Ren-wick,' he emphasised the 'w', *'Kom binnen, kom binnen.* Its very cold outside.'

Hamilton spoke: 'This is Professor John à Marck, Professor of Divinity and Church History here at Groenigen University. He has been good enough to permit the three of you to stay in his house during your studies. You will be safe here.'

'Thank you Professor. I trust we do not inconvenience you?'

'I am honoured to have you under my roof. My good friend Rev William à Brakel from Leeuwarden has a very high opinion of the courageous stance of your Scots Societies and their insistence that they will not be dictated to by anyone in matters of conscience. It's a very Dutch attitude!

♣

Robert Hamilton actually looked pleased for once! 'Rev à Brakel and I have solicited the Classes (presbytery) of Groningen on your behalf, to ask if they will ordain you. Professor à Marck has spoken out very favouraby on your behalf. It seems that you have excelled at your studies, as well as being most expeditious.'

James Renwick allowed himself a grin!

The three young ordinands filed nervously into the chamber where the Classes of Groeningen were assembled. Both Boyd and Flint knew they were fortunate to be present, as their testimonies had not been ready when called for, whereas Renwick's had. But the Classes had decided to examine all three candidates together.

The President spoke: 'We are well aware of the persecution which the church in your native Scotland is experiencing. We also realise that many Scots clergy have accepted the King's Indulgence, and have returned to their pulpits under condition that they do what they are told by the crown, even as to what to preach.

'Here in the Netherlands we know only too well what religious persecution can be. Perhaps we have even suffered more than you, for we had to endure the Inquisition, until we finally threw the Spanish out and gained our independence. We well realise that you cannot obtain instruction in reformed theology in your own universities, and that although some of you have completed degrees at Edinburgh or St Andrews, you could not accept laureation, since you were obliged to refuse to swear to that evil *Test Act* which conflicts so violently with our Christian consciences.'

'So far, so good,' thought James.

'Therefore, after solemn and serious consideration, we have decided that, providing we find you sufficiently committed and capable to perform the work of ministry within the reformed church, that we will ordain you, even though all the kings of the earth should object to it! For are we not a part of the holy catholic church, and therefore free under the Almighty to direct our affairs without let of hindrance?

'Mr Boyd and Mr Flint, since we do not yet have your testimonies to hand we must delay you until that is rectified. You are therefore excused. Mr Renwick, you will please remain. Your friends,' glancing at Hamilton and à Brakel, 'should wait in the church next door, in case we have need to call them for testimony.'

Then followed a four-hour grilling of young Renwick by the entire assembled Classes. The whole process was almost derailed at one point when James was informed that he must subscribe to the catechism of the Dutch church.

'Sir, I greatly regret that I cannot conform to that!'

'Cannot? Or will not?'

'I cannot! My call is to serve the persecuted people of Scotland, and I have already subscribed to the National Covenant. Although we may be separated, driven out to the moors, hunted down and killed, we are still a part of the true Church of Scotland. I must subscribe to the Confession and Catechism of the Church of Scotland, else have I no right to minister there. Times are hard enough, but I will not be a schismatic in my own land!'

'Very well said, Mr Renwick,' interjected a member of the Classes, 'but this is without precedent.'

'Reverend gentlemen, when the martyr Richard Cameron was ordained at Rotterdam, he took the Scots Confession.'

'True,' replied the president, 'but he was ordained by Scots ministers, and in the Scots Kirk here.'

'But for the same ministry as I am called to! Wherever in Scotland the true testimony of God is needed. My parish is the whole of Scotland.'

'Let us consult.' The Classes drew into a huddle. After a few minutes they resumed their seats and the President spoke again: 'As I said, we are free under God to direct the affairs of His church as we believe He would wish. We believe it is indeed God's will that you should minister to those in Scotland who have been deprived of the Ordinances of the Church by a tyrannical king, and we will therefore accept the Scots' Confession in your case. We will now proceed to ordain you.' The other members signified their assent with a loud "Amen."

'Now you may call in your friends, and we will lay hands upon you.'

Hamilton, Boyd and Flint entered, followed by à Brakel, à Marck, Alexander Shields and William Cleland. As they gathered round James to lay hands on him and pray, they noticed that his face, which had a beatific expression, shone.

He wept!

♣

Early the next day a message arrived for à Brakel, to the effect that the Scots ministers in Rotterdam had serious problems with Renwick's ordination, and that it must be stopped. 'Too late!' said à Brackel. 'What's done is done!'

'I think perhaps the hand of God was in this?' murmured William Cleland.

'One can hardly expect this sort of thing to go smoothly, for James's ordination was bound to upset many in Scotland,' replied Shields. 'But Ritchie's prediction that the throne of Britain will be shaken is starting to come true.'

CHAPTER EIGHT

"HOMEWARD BOUND"

June 1683. Rotterdam.

'**I MUST GET OVER TO SCOTLAND!** June already, and still hanging about here! Earlston captured at Newcastle, and now imprisoned in the Tolbooth on suspicion of implication in the Rye House Plot; Claverhouse made Privy Councillor, Dalzell Commander-in-Chief and taking a hand himself in torture! How much worse can it get?' James Renwick was very distressed.

'Robert, you are the Societies' representative here. Can you not get me a passage home?' James was agitated enough to do what few people would venture to do—nag Robert Hamilton.

'There is a ship lying at Brill bound for Burntisland in the Forth. I think we might get you a passage on her.' Hamilton was not used to be treated in such a cavalier manner but young Renwick and he had struck up a surprisingly close friendship with a good deal of regard on both sides. Hamilton did not grate against Renwick's gentle nature, as he did with most.

♣

'Ah canna' sail with this wind, sur.' Captain Munro was not happy. 'Can ye no' pray me one up, you that's an ordained meenister?'

'Perhaps I am not intended to sail with you. I have been much pestered by some of the other passengers who are continually in their cups and seeking to give offence by trying to force me to drink to the health of King Charles. I had thought that here in Holland I would be free of such pressures.'

'Weel laddie, ye are noo on a Scots ship, and we fall under Scots law, so to drink the king's health is no crime. Ye seem ower pernickity with your company.'

Renwick turned away from the Captain in disgust and spied a familiar figure walking down the quay through the driving rain. Despite being hunched up and rendered almost unrecognisable by a large broad-brimmed hat, the gait was unmistakably that of Alexander Shields.

'What Jamie, still here I see?' he called out.

'Aye still here in this windswept, wet world. Where else would one get so much rain with a westerly gale?'

'Perhaps in Scotland, Jamie! I have found a ship which should take you there. You will be a lot safer than on this ship, for the other is Dutch. Get your stuff together and get yourself ashore! We need to get over to Texel where they also await a more favourable wind, but there is more chance of getting one there than here.'

'I'll be glad to. Bide there. I'm coming.'

Once Renwick had lugged his bag ashore, Alex had a surprise for him.

'I'm sailing with you too. I can't stay here any longer when things are at such a pass at home. And I have booked your passage under the name of James Bruce. Not much of a pseudonym I know, everyone will think you are in the coffee business! But your own name is already too well known by the authorities both here and over there.'

Later. Texel Harbour.

A very small barque was moored alongside and remained so for for some days even after Alex and James had boarded their new ship. Captain van Deventer seemed happy enough to have them as passengers, and let slip in conversation that his Scots wife had a cousin on the fugitives' roll. But he was less forthcoming as to his landing place. When pressed, he revealed that it was his intent to go south-about, through the English Channel, and so gain the west coast of Scotland rather than land his passengers on the east coast, which was heavily patrolled by the military. This gave them some concern, for these waters were patrolled by English frigates which stopped and searched any suspicious vessel. When they finally put to sea, a full gale was still blowing and the little ship made heavy weather into the eastern reaches of the English Channel.

'I'm going to have to run for shelter in Rye, Mr Renwick. We are fortunate not to have been driven on to the French shore with this gale, for we won't ride it out in this *klein schip.* '

'But surely Rye is a very dangerous place for the likes of us? The plot to assassinate the king there was only discovered recently and is the reason why the Duke of Monmouth, Sir John Cochrane and others have fled to Holland. Surely they will be on the lookout for Whig sympathisers?'

'Don't worry Mr Renwick, we are too small to attract attention, and anyway, things have quietened down in the last few months.' It seemed to James and Alex that the captain was a mite too glib for their comfort.

Sure enough, once the ship was made fast alongside, an exciseman escorted by two soldiers came aboard and was closeted with the captain for an hour. During this time the two friends were much alarmed, but the visitors went ashore with protestations of satisfaction. The two friends were concerned that the captain might have informed on them for the price on their heads.

But the next day dawned fair with a good sailing wind, and after beating out into the open channel, they ran before the easterly breeze, making good time. When the barque was hailed by a guard boat at the harbour entrance, to their concern Captain van Deventer called out that he had some passengers aboard, but that he knew nothing of their political attitude. They felt sure they would now be boarded and searched, but were merely waved on and wished good sailing! Later they discovered that the captain was carrying contraband, the proceeds of which he shared with the exciseman, so they were saved by his duplicity. In any event, they were well pleased to be quit of the English mainland.

After an uneventful voyage they put in at Dublin, and were set ashore to await a ship for Scotland. After some searching they finally found one, and after a heated argument with its captain who wanted to put them ashore at a recognised port, they were finally landed by small boat on the Ayrshire coast between Skelmorlie and Largs. From here they could easily get up on to the moors and disappear.

On the moor above Beith they paused. 'Well my friend, this is where we part. I am for Edinburgh, and you go to seek your brother Michael somewhere in Lanarkshire. But since he is scribe to the United Societies, our paths will surely cross again soon.' Renwick held out his hand.

As Alex grasped it, he replied, 'Before long James, I feel sure.' Little did either of them know that before they met again, Shields would have been captured, tried, and consigned to the Bass Rock.

22 Nov 1683. Cambusnethan.

'We must thank you Mr Renwick, for bringing us this news about Will.' James had found shelter with the Steel family before his first public appearance since his return.

'It is I who must thank you for your shelter, Miss Steel. I know your family has suffered much.'

'And I thank you for bringing us the news that my brother is still alive.' Janet Cleland had heard little of William since he had escaped to Holland, nearly three years before.

The next day a large crowd had gathered on Darmead Moor to hear the new minister of the United Societies preach his first sermon. His voice rang out, loud and clear: *"Come my people, enter thou into thy chambers, and shut thy doors about thee: hide thyself as it were for a little moment until the indignation be overpast."'*

A sigh ran through the crowd, and some began to weep. 'He is using Donald Cargill's last text, when he preached at Dunsyre the week before he was taken,' one whispered to another.

'Aye, we hae' a godly leader again. We can stand firm once more.'

'And the bairns can be baptised.'

'And we maun hae communion again!'

Many breathed a silent prayer of thanks.

10 June 1684. Paisley.

'Do you, John Graham, take this woman, Jean Cochrane to be your lawfully wedded wife; to have and to hold from this day forward; for better, for worse; for richer, for poorer; in sickness and in health; to love and to cherish; until God shall separate you by death?'

'I do!'

'Do you, Jean Cochrane...'

The nave of the partially ruined Paisley Abbey was crowded with an elite gathering. The congregation were not quite at ease with each other, since Claverhouse, persecutor of covenanters, was marrying Jean Cochrane from a notable covenanting family. Her uncle, Sir John Cochrane, was wanted in connection with the Rye House Plot of the previous year. Nevertheless there were many who hoped that this marriage might provide some healing for their troubled land.

As Claverhouse and his bride left the abbey, the guard-of-honour, formed by troopers of Graham's own regiment in brand new scarlet tunics, formed an arch of sabres beneath which the bridal couple passed. Trumpeters blew a fanfare, and mounted kettle drummers flourished a tattoo.

With every outward appearance of joy the bridal couple led the guests, headed by Lord William Ross the best man, and Jean's sisters the bridesmaids, across the green sward to the Place of Paisley, Jean's childhood home, close by the ruined Abbey.

As the wine began to flow the guests noticeably relaxed. Supporters of Crown and Covenant alike began to converse with each other, and the party promised to be both happy and noisy. When all was at its height, with cheerful music encouraging the younger ones to dance, Claverhouse led his young bride on to the floor. They had scarcely started when a uniformed officer, dishevelled and muddy, forced his way through the revellers and drew Lord Ross aside.

'My Lord, I must speak!'

'Devil take it, Elphinstone! Can you not see we are at a wedding, and that of your Colonel to boot!'

'I know, my Lord, I know. And I am indeed sorry to intrude, but I have an urgent dispatch for Colonel Graham from General Dalzell. I need you to call him aside.'

'What can be urgent enough to call out a man on his wedding day between the service and the marriage bed?'

'A party of armed covenanters are heading this way, into Renfrewshire!'

'I'll call him!' William Ross wove his way through the dancers, and caught Claverhouse by the sleeve.

'What's that, you say? I can't hear you, William!'

'Urgent message from General Dalzell, sir. Trouble!'

'They might have let my wedding day pass at least!' He took the message and read it carefully. 'It seems that about eighty armed rebels from a conventicle at Black Loch were pursued by our troops, but they lost them around Hamilton. It is feared they are heading this way, toward Paisley. We must head them off!'

'Elphinstone, you can still ride?'

'I can indeed sir!'

'You'll find Colonel Buchan south-east of Ayr. Give him my compliments and ask him to meet me at Newmilns as soon as possible. With all his force. Now ride!'

'Sir!'

'William, take your troop and what dragoons you can muster, and scout towards Muirkirk. I will take twenty Horse Guards from here and search towards Lesmahagow. Rendezvous at Strathaven tomorrow night!'

'But this is your wedding night! You must stay!'

Claverhouse looked angrily at his young friend. 'William, do not presume to tell me my duty! Now go!'

As Ross swung on his heel to leave, John Graham looked around for his bride of a few hours. She sat half-recumbent at at table, surrounded by the women of her family. Lady Katherine Kennedy, Jean's mother, was in a spitting rage. 'Just what you would expect from these godless Grahams! Any opportunity to hunt down a few harmless worshippers!' But Jean's grandmother, the Countess of Dundonald, was all concern and fussed around the bride like an old hen.

John Graham took his wife by the hand and led her gently out of earshot.

'My love, I have to go. You do know that, do you not? I have to follow the path of duty, even today. Especially today. *"I could not love thee half so much, loved I not honour more."* '

'Oh John, don't quote poetry at me at a time like this!' Jean was on the verge of tears. She was not quite sure which prevailed in her, anger or sorrow. 'Of course you must go. But mine will be a very lonely bed tonight! Why can you men not live at peace with one another?' She threw herself into his arms, and it was with the greatest difficulty that he detached himself from her embrace... but eventually he did!

The last his bride saw of her groom on her wedding day was his back, at which rode half a troop of Life Guards.

Having fruitlessly scoured the moors in search of fugitives for a day and night, Claverhouse, Buchan and Ross met up at Strathaven next day as planned. 'This place holds evil memories for me,' John Graham said gloomily, looking morosely round Scribbie Young's Tavern. Everyone was exhausted with long hours in the saddle, searching through bogs and mosses to no avail.

'Time to return to Paisley I think sir?' Lord William Ross was the soul of tact, for he had been with his leader long enough to know how he thought.

'Yes, you are right William! Colonel Buchan, you should head south, back towards Ayr. William, take a break and meet me at Paisley on Friday.' So saying, Claverhouse executed a perfect caracole and rode off into the gathering darkness.

♣

Lady Jean Graham tossed and turned on her vast bed. Suddenly through the night came the sound of hooves in a hurry, and she knew that it was her lover returned. Clad only in her shift, she ran down the broad staircase and out into the night air. John Graham, muddy and weary, slid off his horse and let it go.

'I always said I would take you only in your shift, my dear.' And lifting her into his arms, he climbed the stairs to their chamber. As he kicked the door shut with his boot, the crash echoed through the great house.

CHAPTER NINE

"TO THE BASS ROCK"

11 Jan 1685. London.

ALEXANDER SHIELDS WAS PREACHING in the Embroiderer's Hall in Gutter Lane. Since he and James Renwick had parted on the moors more than a year had passed. Alex had spent some time as chaplain of a ship running to and fro from the Low Countries, specialising in ferrying exiles and fugitives, for the captain was a man of sincere presbyterian principles. They had experienced many narrow escapes, which they attributed to the grace of God.

But the reformed faith was also growing in places other than Scotland. Towards the end of 1684, Shields was invited to London, to serve as amanuensis to Dr John Owen, a non-conforming minister of high repute who ran his church in the Embroiderer's Hall in Cheapside. Alex was licensed to preach by a group of dissenting Scots ministers in London, and proved a popular preacher.

Shortly after his return to Scotland, James Renwick had published his *Apologetical Declaration,* in which the Cameronians for the first time had threatened reprisals on their persecutors. The government promptly drew up the *Oath of Abjuration* in reply, denouncing the *Declaration* and requiring all suspects to take the *Oath* and swear fealty to the crown. This new oath began to replace the *Test Oath* as a means of bringing dissenters to heel, and anyone suspected of the slightest disloyalty was made to swear to it on his knees before witnesses, or to be condemned to peremptory execution.

Alexander was preaching to a congregation of about sixty people in an upper room at the Hall. That morning he had had a strong premonition of impending trouble, and so he set two men to keep watch for any military activity in the area.

"Naphtali is a hind let loose." My friends, I speak to you today on the subject of liberty. While all men long to be unchained, to be liberated from their dungeons and not to be enslaved; there is a liberty beyond mere bodily freedom. I speak of spiritual liberty, for *"If Christ hath set you free, you shall be free indeed!"* So do not let any man, however exalted he may be in church or state, deprive you of that freedom! It is yours by right!'

At that instant the door burst open and the City Marshal, drawn sword in hand, strode in with two soldiers at his heels. 'In the King's name, I command you to surrender!'

'What king would you be meaning?' answered Shields quickly. 'By what authority do you disturb the peaceful worship of Christ? You dishonour your king sir, by making him an opponent to the worship of God.'

This infuriated the Marshal, who thrust himself into the midst of the congregation, laying about him with the flat of his sword. 'I have better things to do than stand here arguing with the likes of a Whig like you. You're all under arrest, the lot of you!'

'There's only three of them and sixty of us!' Alex cried. 'Come help me run them down the stairs!' He started to work his way through the press to get at the Marshall, but hands grabbed him and stopped his progress.

'There will be more soldiers downstairs. We must not antagonise them!'

'They are already antagonised, and that by a simple appeal to their decency and respect for God.'

But the nervous prevailed, and the whole congregation were taken to Guildhall, to appear before the mayor. On the way several broke away from the party and were seen no more. One of these was Alexander, who escaped down a side street. But reaching the end, he turned the wrong way, and found himself facing the rabble which had gathered before the Guildhall in order to see the sport being made of the nonconformists. They grabbed Alexander and forced him to the ground, kicking and scratching him unmercifully.

'Knife him in the guts! Bloody Whig! Rioting in our peaceful town! Kill 'im! Bet 'e's a foreigner; Irish or Scot as like as not! We'll fix 'im!'

Fortunately there was a strong guard at the gate, and four soldiers dragged him from the hands of the mob and into the courtyard. 'Orl right mate,' said the corporal of the guard. 'On yer feet! Ye have to see the mayor, he'll fix you worse than this rabble, I'll be bound!'

Shields found himself reunited with his group of worshippers and brought before the mayor. 'What was your business in the place where you were detained?'

'We were at the worship of God, your honour.'

'What is your trade then?'

'I have no trade.'

'Then you are a gentleman?'

'Not as you would have it, sir. God provides for my needs.'

'So you are a vagabond then? We know how to deal with the likes of you here.'

'No sir, I am no vagabond. Just that I have no steady employment at present.'

The mayor's eyes lit up. 'He is a Jesuit then! Search him!'

Even under the duress of the situation, Alexander could not prevent himself feeling the irony that he was being mistaken for a Roman Catholic priest. But just then, the court orderly found his bible in his coat pocket and handed it across to the mayor, who examined it carefully. 'Why does this bible lack the Book of Common Prayer at the front? You are a great rogue, and I am minded to commit you to Bridewell Prison, where you may get a good whipping.'

Shields was thoroughly alarmed at the prospect of being sent to the notoriously worst jail in the city, but the mayor continued. 'I set bail at thirty pounds. Take him away!'

Next day Alex was back in court. 'Alexander Shields, you are hereby charged that, along with others, *you did with force and arms, riotously, unlawfully and tumultuously, assemble and meet together to disturb the peace of the kingdom, under colour and pretext of the exercise of religion, and after another manner than that according to the liturgy*

and use of the Church of England... this in open contempt of our
sovereign lord the king, his laws, crown and dignity.

'Prisoner at the bar, how do you plead?'

'Not guilty!'

'And from what country do you come?' demanded the Recorder, Sir
Tomas Jenner.

'I am a Scotsman born and bred,' answered Alex.

Jenner burst out: 'These pestilential Scots flee the laws of their own
land, where they can be tortured at will, for they have laws to extract a
man's thoughts and then hang him for them. But they come down here
to England, where they expect to profit from our mild and reasonable
laws, even though they are all foul rebels and murderers! Will you take
the Oath of Allegiance?'

But the Lord Mayor, a more reasonable man, interjected. 'Will you
engage never to go to this type of religious meeting again?'

'Sir, I cannot do that and keep my conscience clear before God.'

'What more do you need?' screamed Jenner. 'Tell me, were you at
Bothwell? Your name is on the fugitives' roll.' Shields remained silent.

Further questions followed without any pause for answer:

- 'Was it rebellion?'
- 'Do you own the murderous Apologetical Declaration?'
- 'Was the killing of Archbishop Sharp murder?'

'None of these questions refer to my indictment. I will answer
nothing extraneous to that with which I am charged.'

'Then you are committed to Newgate Prison pending further
evidence,' ruled the Lord Mayor. The court stood as he withdrew.

♣

On 2 February 1685, King Charles II died.

The cell in Newgate Prison where Shields and the other religious
prisoners were held, was cold, dark, and nasty, separated by only a grille
from the chamber where thieves, robbers and highwaymen were kept.

The turnkey clanged the door open. 'Aw right, a' you that's Scotchmen, you're a' on the move. Get your stuff ready, you leave tomorrow.'

'Why, what has happened? How can you send us out while there are charges still pending here?' The rumour that they were to be repatriated for trial had gone through the prison, and Shields was anxious to avoid such a move if possible.

'You've heard the king died last month?' Indeed they had! The prison had echoed with the news for days! 'We are letting you off, so that your own country can take care of you.'

'You mean torture and kill us!' said Shields.

'Well, that's no' my problem,' retorted the jailer.

♣

Next morning several prison officers entered the cell loaded with manacles, and handcuffed the Scots two by two. The senior officer announced, 'You are all charged with high treason, and will therefore be transported to Edinburgh to stand trial before a Scottish court!'

Thereupon the eight Scots prisoners were marched through the streets toward the Thames, accompanied by the jeers of the crowd. To add to their shame, they were brought out at the same time as some criminals due to be hanged at Tyburn Hill. The manacled prisoners answered nothing to the mocking shouts of the crowd, but one woman onlooker, bolder than the rest, cried out: 'This is for being at a protestant meeting. Take heed to yourselves good people, and see what evil times we live in.'

The prisoners were taken by boat downstream to board the *Kitchen Yacht* at Greenwich. 'Up ye come then, laddie.' The soldier who hoisted Alexander up the gangway spoke with an unmistakable Scots accent.

'You're a Scot then?'

'Aye, we are frae Dumbarton's Regiment, and its glad we will be to see the hills o' hame again. And its sorry we are to be taking our countrymen there in chains.'

'Not as sorry as we are,' replied Alex.

After a very stormy passage of three days, during which time conditions for the prisoners, chained in the lower deck and fouled with their own vomit, were execrable, the *Kitchen Yacht* came alongside at the port of Leith. Thankfully the prisoners made their way down the gangplank and on to Scottish soil. A small crowd had assembled to see them arrive.

An elderly woman, supported by a young man, burst from the crowd and threw herself weeping upon Alex. 'Alex! Alex! My dear boy! What a sight you are!'

'Mother! And brother Michael! How came you here?'

A party of Grenadier Guards waited on the quay to escort the prisoners into Edinburgh. 'Naw then, no fraternising with traitors!' said the sergeant in command. 'Separate them,' he ordered two of his men. 'And the rest of you form a screen to keep them apart from the crowd. Stand back! Stand back!' He clearly feared a rescue attempt. Alex's mother and brother were roughly manhandled back into the crowd, but not before his mother had given him a loving hug which brought tears to his eyes.

At eight o'clock that night the prisoners arrived at the Edinburgh Tolbooth, weary to the bone, having marched from Leith in their chains. They were forced into a cell so crowded they could not sit down.

'Not much of a homecoming,' grimaced Alex, to no-one in particular.

♣

Next morning Shields was brought before the Privy Council. Sir George Mackenzie, excommunicated by Donald Cargill, was the Lord Advocate. Alexander realised he would get little mercy.

'Are you Alexander Shields from the Merse, and were you taken at a conventicle in London?' asked the President.

'Yes, I was taken at a meeting for the worship of God, which I prize above my liberty.'

'Well, that may be so, but being a Scotsman, you have been sent down to us to be tried.'

'My lord, if it is a crime to be a Scotsman, that seems very dishonourable to our native land.'

'Do you own the authority of King James?' asked Mackenzie.

'I am surprised that you ask such a question! And I plead to a great indisposition of body and mind, having been brought from Newgate prison, through a gale, marched to Edinburgh, and spending last night on my feet.'

'If you do not own the king, then all the indispositions in the world cannot save you from hanging.Take him down!'

Ten days later, the surviving prisoners who had travelled with him took the Abjuration Oath before the High Court. One had died before reaching Edinburgh.

♣

Alex was again before the High Court. 'You were born in Haughhead?'

'I was.'

'Then you are familiar with Captain Hall of Haughead in the Merse?'

Alexander realised that they were trying to trap him into a connection with Henry Hall, who had been with Cargill when the Queensferry Paper was seized. But he knew that particular Hall was from another Haughhead, in Roxburghshire.

'I know no-one of that name in the Merse.'

Sir George Mackenzie came on the attack: 'Were you at Bothwell?'

'You must prove that if it is my crime.'

'Not much proof needed! Your name is on the fugitives' roll. Do you subscribe to the treasonable document emmitted by these foul renegades called Cameronians, declaring war on the king?'

'I decline to answer.'

'But you *must* answer, sir!'

'I see it is a misery to be a Scotsman. I've been in many countries and never heard of such an imposition on anyone.'

'It is a misery to deal with rascals like you! Will you take the *Abjuration Oath*? If so, you may have your liberty. You must answer by Wednesday. If your answer is "no", you will hang on Friday.'

'But that oath denies me my inalienable right to freedom of thought, which is subject to no tribunal under heaven.'

'If it were left to everyone to disown authority whenever he pleases, such freedom would destroy human society,' riposted Mackenzie.

On Wednesday he was before the High Court yet again. He had still not seen the *Apologetical Declaration*, only the government proclamation condemning it. On this he had written his sentiments in the margin. *I disown all treasonable declarations and the horrid principle of assassination, but I humbly believe that this proclamation is not enough to extort a confession from me that the declaration is treasonable in itself.* But before he was called before the court, one of his old lecturers from University days, Sir William Paterson, now Clerk to the Privy Council, sent for him, and in the rush he forgot to take his notes with him.

'Mr Shields, I am heartily sorry to see you come to this pass. You were not of this opinion about government when you were my scholar. You are still young, with your life ahead of you. Do not throw yourself away on some hopeless cause.'

'Sir William, I do not believe that any man, even the king, has the right to dictate another's conscience, especially his manner of worship. I also do not consider mere lineal descent is enough to make a man a king. He must act like a king and govern his subjects in a kingly way. The *Declaration of Arbroath* speaks as strongly for us today as it did for all Scots in 1320. *"If the prince shall leave the principles he hath so nobly pursued... we will immediately endeavour to expel him as an enemy... and make another king."* We have been suffering under Stewart tyranny since James VI went south to take over the English throne in 1603. Even before that anyone who held to the reformed faith was persecuted. I consider it necessary for my salvation not to go against the measure of light which the Lord has given me.'

'You sound like a Quaker, to make conscience your rule.'

'Would that I had the courage of a Quaker, Sir William.'

'And now you talk like an Arminian, with your freedom of thought.'

'Sir William, I am an orthodox Calvinist, but I can recall no writing that denies me freedom of conscience as a result.'

'Well at least you have remembered some of what I taught you!'

From this interview, Alexander was led directly before the High Court. The Clerk of the Justiciary did not waste words. 'If you do not disown this Cameronian *Declaration*, you will die.'

'Am I not even to be allowed sight of what I am disowning? Is this Scottish justice? Sir Thomas Jenner spoke truth at my trial in London— about the cruel and unjust laws in Scotland!'

'Very well! The *Declaration* will be read to you.'

The Clerk read slowly and ponderously...

'Our intent is to *"testify to the world, that we purpose not to injure or offend any whomsoever, but to pursue the ends of their covenants in standing to the defence of the work of reformation and of our own lives. ...We utterly detest and abhor that hellish principle of killing all who differ in judgement or persuasion from us, it having no bottom upon the word of God"'* The paper went on to threaten certain of the Cameronian persecutors; not only their military enemies and politicians, but spies and informants, malicious bishops and curates were required *'to take warning of the hazard ye incur,'* and whilst self-preservation was described as a *'sinless necessity',* it was clear that persecution had reached a point where the more extreme elements might well break out spontaneously into individual action, and this therefore, was expressly forbidden by the document.

'You have heard it read. What do you think of it now?'

Alexander Shields pondered for a moment. 'It seems to me to have been issued by a party suffering great distress as a result of oppression and rigorous persecution under the law. They seek to frighten their persecutors by threatening to fall back upon defensive methods which they have not yet used, but which now seem the only means they have left to defend themselves. I do not believe the government Proclamation reflects it correctly. They say they abhor assassination and arbitrary attacks upon individuals; they speak of the defence of their religion, lives and liberties. I cannot disown all these; I cannot disown the Covenant and the work of Reformation; I will never disown these principles.'

At this the court erupted, many crying out 'He is a dead man!' but the Lord Advocate broke in, and vociferously stated that there was no intention to force Shields to disown these principles. 'Will you renounce the *Declaration* in so far as it declares war, and asserts it lawful to kill those employed in the king's service? You may have one day more to consider your answer.'

This caused him great distress, for at this point Alex was beginning to wonder how far he could go to save his neck while still remaining true to what he believed in. When he was taken back to the Tolbooth some ministers who had accepted the Indulgence came to see him and urged him to take the oath, saying that he could do it with a clear conscience before God. 'You should know that Argyle himself took the oath only "in so far," so you are in good company.'

'As I recall, Argyle sent Cargill to the gallows and was himself later sentenced to death,' responded Alex wryly. The next day when called before the Court, he capitulated partially. This was to haunt him for the rest of his life.

'Will you swear?' asked Mackenzie.

'I will swear only to this:

"I do abhor renounce and disown in the presence of God that pretended declaration, in so far as it declares war against the king, and asserts that it is lawful to kill all employed by him in Church, State, Army or Country."

'Thus far will I swear, and no farther. And may God have mercy on my weakness.'

'Said like a gentleman,' said one of the bench.

'If I have not said it like a Christian too, then it is all wrong.' Alexander was already beginning to feel pangs of conscience, in the knowledge that he had not had the courage to stand as fast as Cameron and Cargill. But at least he could now go free!

Sir George Mackenzie addressed him: 'This Court is now finished with you.' Alex breathed a sigh of relief. 'But I have instructions that the Privy Council intend to bring fresh charges against you. I therefore recommit you to be held in the Tolbooth, pending the pleasure of the Privy Council.'

Alex very nearly broke down. He had been abused and examined repeatedly since his arrest in January. It was now 26 March 1685, and his resistance was at an end.

♣

On 29 April, Shields was arraigned before the Privy Council. The King's High Commissioner Lord Queensberry and the Lord Chancellor, the Earl of Perth were present, and there was a suave looking member of Council whom Alex knew with certainty to be Major-General John Graham of Claverhouse. Bluidy Clavers himself. His heart sank!

'Alexander Shields,' Perth the Chancellor opened. 'We have here a letter purporting to be from a certain Mr Target, addressed to a Mr Forbes in Holland. Any anwer to be directed to you at the home of a certain Mr Robert Young. You should know that Mr Young is already a prisoner in the dungeons of Dunottar, and has been examined under torture. We suspect that Forbes is no other than that notorious primacide, John Balfour of Burley. You keep dubious company indeed, Mr Shields. What is more, in your letter you express regret for taking the prescribed oath. What have you to say?'

'The Court before which I took the oath was satisfied, my Lord. What is done cannot be undone.'

'Do not make sport with me, young man! I have it on good authority that you bitterly regret taking the oath.'

'My lord, what is the reason for this re-examination? Am I to be forced to take the oath again?'

'Indeed you are, and if you do not do so, and retract all your reservations, you will surely go to the gallows. And who, pray, is this Mr Forbes?'

'I decline to answer.'

'I remind you that I have the power to put you to the torture. General Dalzell recently brought back some thumbkins from Europe, which he says are highly effective.'

Alex went pale. 'Since you already suspect his identity, I can only confirm it.' This was said with a great deal of reluctance.

Queensberry asked, 'Why would you be friends with a murderer?'

'He is not a murderer, but an executioner.'

Perth broke in: 'Do you not know to whom you are speaking, young man? This is His Majesty's High Chancellor for Scotland that speaks to you. Address him as "Your Grace".'

'Í am not particularly bothered who I am before. Was it not one of our own kings who said that every man was as good a man as the monarch, though maybe not so rich?'

The Commissioner had his dog with him in court. It had been trained to terrorise the prisoners at the bar, and had been straining at its chain throughout this exchange. At Shields' last comment the enraged Perth let slip the chain, and the dog bounded across the courtroom and leapt on to his chest, knocking him to the ground, biting and barking furiously until it was restrained and taken outside.

'The prisoner is to be confined to the Court of the Guard until further notice. Take him down!'

Shields was pleasantly surprised with his treatment by the soldiers of the guard, who expressed great sympathy for his predicament. One even allowed him a lady visitor.

The cell door opened and a shrouded figure came in. Alex was delighted, but much concerned, to recognise Janet Cleland, her features shielded by a plaid. 'Janet! What are you doing here? Surely this is too dangerous for you?'

'Alex, we must act quickly! The sentry let me in without the knowledge of his officer. You must escape! We hear that you are to be allowed out for air daily to the Nor' Loch, with only two escorts. You must make a run for it!'

'Dearest Janet, I am far too spent to run any distance. I would need a horse to get away.'

'That is just what we plan. On 4th May there will be a group of friends at the lochside with a horse. They will mount you and prevent the soldiers shooting or chasing you. We have effected many such rescues of our people. Oh Alex!' With this Janet clung to him, and with a sob buried her face in his coat. 'I have as good as lost my brother Will. I cannot bear to lose you too!'

As Alexander held her to his breast, the sentry entered in haste. 'Quick! Quick! Oot o' here missus! Oor officer is comin'!' So saying he grabbed Janet by the elbow and dragged her out of the cell without giving Alex any chance to say goodbye.

♣

The morning set for the escape dawned wet and blustery. 'Just the sort of day to get clear away into the Pentlands,' thought Alex. But he was doomed to disappointment.

'Get your stuff t'gether. Wé're movin' ye tae the Tolbooth. General Dalzell's orders.'

'But am I not to have my exercise?'

'No' the day. Let's go.' And with that, Alexander was taken under close guard, back to the Tolbooth.

The next morning he was before the court yet again. For the umpteenth time the question came: 'Were you at Bothwell?'

'I hardly think I am tall enough to be of much use to any army, king's or covenant.' At this quip everyone laughed, save the three bishops present who asked to confer with Shields apart. Accordingly he was brought privately before the Archbishops of St Andrews and Glasgow, and the Bishop of Dunkeld. After a lengthy harangue, Glasgow spoke out: 'We have regard for your youth and trust that you will not throw your life away out of sheer obstinacy, but we can ensure your life only if you will agree to conform to three requirements. First; that you will go to hear the appointed incumbent, whether curate or minister, in whatsoever parish you may live. Second; that you refrain from preaching yourself, and Third; that you promise never again to support the lawfulness of any resistance against the king.'

'I could not live with myself if I were to subscribe to these.'

'Then you may die by yourself without them,' said St Andrews, and the three bishops departed in a huff.

Shields collapsed in a dead faint on the floor!

He was to languish in the Tolbooth for a further three months before being sentenced to the Bass Rock *"to be kept and detained there until further orders."*

♣

The Bass, a bleak inhospitable rock rising out of the Firth of Forth, lay two miles offshore from Tantallon Castle. It had been used as a prison since 1671 as part of government policy to break the spirit of the most uncompromising covenanters. It was garrisoned by soldiers, and the only natural inhabitants were the gannets. Landing was dangerous and sometimes impossible, for at times the waves broke right over the prison wall, some thirty feet above the sea.

As Shields boarded the small boat which was to row him out to the Rock, the main hope he had was that he might meet again with some old friends like Rev John Blackader, father of William and John, and Major Joseph Learmont, who had commanded at Bothwell after Hamilton ran away. There were a total of thirty-seven prisoners, of whom three were clergymen. Surely he would know someone?

The sea was running high, but as the boat neared the slipway the steersman showed no sign of nerves. 'Steady boys,' he growled. 'Backwater port. Way 'nuff!' Putting the tiller hard over, he brought the boat neatly alongside the slip, but the waves rode it up and down to an alarming degree.

'Out!' he snapped at Alexander, who with his hands manacled in front was unable to help himself. As he jumped for the slipway, the boat fell away, and he fell into the water between the boat and the slip. He would have gone to the bottom, with little chance of survival, had not two of the soldiers grabbed the chain between his hands, and hauled him soaking to safety.

Alexander Shields was a prisoner of the Bass!

CHAPTER TEN

AN ABORTIVE EXPEDITION

April, 1685. Rotterdam

W HILE SHIELDS WAS DEFENDING HIMSELF before the courts, momentous things were happening elsewhere. With the death of King Charles II in February 1685, his brother James, Duke of York, a declared Roman Catholic, had ascended the throne as James VII of Scotland and II of England. At last others besides the covenanters were becoming alarmed at the possibility of catholicism being enforced in both kingdoms, and nowhere was this more evident than among the Scots exile community in the Netherlands.

On 17 April 1685, a meeting was held in Rotterdam, the purpose of which was to plan an expedition to Scotland to overthrow James. A simultaneous expedition was planned for England. Those present at the meeting were: Archibald Campbell, 9th Earl of Argyle, who had been sentenced to death but escaped on 20 Dec 1681; Charles Campbell, his son; Sir John Cochrane of Ochiltree; John Cochrane of Waterside, his son; Sir Patrick Hume of Polwarth; George Hume of Bassinden; George Pringle of Torwoodlee; William Denholm of Westshiels; George Wishart; William Cleland, victor of Drumclog; Advocate James Stuart of Goodtrees; and Gilbert Elliot of Craigend.

At this meeting it was resolved to mount an expedition to Scotland *"to declare and undertake a war against the Duke of York, and to restore the true religion and the native rights of the three kingdoms."* The expedition was under the command of Argyle, with Sir John Cochrane as second-in-command. It was decided that the Revs William

Veitch and George Barclay, together with Captain William Cleland and Pringle of Torwoodlee, would be sent on ahead to raise support.

The expedition against England was to be under the leadership of the Duke of Monmouth, the victor of Bothwell Brig. His position had changed dramatically in that he now found himself on the same side as the covenanters he had defeated. As an illegitimate son of Charles II, he had a tenuous claim to the throne, but like so many others in this period of confused British politics, he was now an exile in Holland.

The Scots ministers in Amsterdam supported the venture, but Sir Robert Hamilton, representing the United Societies, remained non-committal, requiring confirmation from Rev James Renwick before making any recommendation.

♣

The dark loom of the Northumberland coast lay close as the two Williams, Cleland and Veitch, landed at low tide on the sands of Druridge Bay. 'Head due west,' advised Captain James Law, who had ferried them ashore in a small boat. 'After you cross the Devil's Causeway head north-west for the Cheviots. You'll see them easy. Mr Veitch, you have directions to Lord Gray's at Wark? And Will, you know how to reach your friend Thomas Steel, the Chamberlain of Jedforest?

'That I do, and right well, Captain.'

'If pursued, you both have precise directions to the hideout above Carter Bar? Thomas Steel hid out there in 1683, with the troops searching so close he could hear their every word. Even their dogs didn't find him.' With a silent handshake the two set off across the coastal plain, and by first light were hiding in Thrunton Wood.

'We should stick together until we cross the border into Scotland,' said Cleland. 'Yonder is Cheviot Peak. If we cross south-west of it, we will both have an easy downhill to our destinations.'

'Looks pretty uphill to me!' said Veitch. 'I've got used to flat Holland. How high do we have to climb?'

'Only about two-and-a-half thousand feet,' replied Cleland. 'In the old days we would not even have noticed it.'

'These are not the old days, Will. The only thing that feels old here is me!'

'Well, we'll lie up in this wood today, and set off in the gloaming. You should be in Wark by dawn, and me in Jedforest.'

♣

As Cleland left the shelter of the forest to cover the last few yards to the Chamberlain of Jedforest's residence, he spied a blue clad figure on the terrace. The figure held her hand up to shield her eyes from the rising sun and then began running towards him. 'It can't be,' he thought, 'but it might be? By glory, it is!

'Margaret! Margaret! Is that you?'

Any doubt was dispelled as Margaret threw herself into his arms. 'Will, oh Will! At last, at last, you are back! You are home with me!' After some time elapsed she drew his arm under her own with both hands and smiling, led him into the house.

'How did you know I was coming?' he asked.

'I didn't. I am here visiting my dear brother and his wife. It was pure chance.'

'I don't believe in chance. It was heaven sent.'

♣

'Great matters are afoot, Thomas.' Cleland and his future brother-in-law were later closeted in the study.

I'm sure they are, Will. Here, let me top up your glass before we go on. You look like you need it.' It was very late, for the two men had had some difficulty getting William away from his fianceé, but finally the ladies had retired, and the two friends were able to get down to business.

'So what's afoot?' asked Tom.

'Invasion! Argyle to Scotland, and Monmouth to England! Simultaneously! In May.'

'You mean this month! That's not much warning!'

'Even as we speak they will have sailed from Amsterdam. Argyle is heading north to his own lands where he hopes to raise a strong force. Monmouth's expedition heads for southern England.'

'And what force do they have? Just a few emigrés I suppose, and then expect everyone to rally to their banners? Just like that?'

'Just like that!'

'Does the Earl not know that Atholl is already waiting for him in Argyle with a strong force, and that the clans in general are opposed to *MacCailean Môr*? Already the minor Campbell chiefs are in prison in Edinburgh.'

'But his second-in-command is Sir John Cochrane, and I and others have been sent to the borders and west country to muster support.'

'Cochrane of Ochiltree! Cochrane is Lady Clavers' uncle! My wife helped hide him in '83 at the time when I built the hideout on Carter Bar.'

Cleland bristled. 'He's good covenanting stock, and you know it! Forbye his son is also committed to the venture, so the family is committed up to it's neck!'

'And what does Argyle hope to achieve? Put Monmouth on the throne? Or even himself?'

Cleland looked somewhat embarrassed. 'It's not quite clear, Tom. We plan to restore the protestant religion and the "native rights" of the three nations.'

'You mean you have not even decided on a king? And whatever does "native rights" mean? Ireland included too! It seems you have a really half-baked scheme here.'

'But will the west not rise? Clavers and others are going quite wild, murdering and maiming, even executing women!'

'True, we call these the "killing times," but Renwick leads his Cameronians well, and we still have our free worship on the moors. We may long for a righteous government whether by king or council, and there are many who long to see James and his papist ideas thrown out, but we must know for whom we are fighting.'

'But King Jesus...'

'Don't be sanctimonious with me, Will! You of all people! You are not some ranting Whig, but a level-headed leader of men. We have never sought the rule for ourselves, even though there are some with republican leanings amongst the Cameronians. You know we do not seek power for ourselves. We stand for freedom.'

'So you will not join us?'

'The borders have not been as brutally treated as the south-west. I suggest you rather try there. Although Lord Cardross and I were forced to flee to the Carolinas, I have been allowed to return and live openly, thanks to the good influence of the Marquess of Douglas. One day we will have a new king, of that I feel sure, but the time is not yet. Now we had best try to get some sleep. There's the sun already above the Cheviots. Time for bed.'

♣

William was heading over the moors for Douglas. His main purpose was to consult with the Marquess, but he would fain have taken Margaret as far as her home in Cambusnethan. However there was no question of them travelling together, for Cleland was a hunted man with a price on his head, and under no illusions that if taken he would suffer immediate execution. His way lay over the high moors, with a constant eye open for army patrols. Bypassing Biggar, he came down the shoulder of Tinto and soon raised the spire of St Bride's Church at Douglas. He entered the town carefully, pulling down his hat and wrapping his plaid close around him, making sure his *Andrea Ferrara* was not obvious. He knew every nook and cranny, and soon was at the back door of his brother-in-law John Haddow. When he scratched gently on the door, none other than his sister Anne opened.

'Will!' Startled, Anne pulled him inside quickly and closed the door behind him. 'What in the name of goodness...' she began, but he silenced her with a finger to his lips.

'It's all right. I am not being followed,' he assured her. 'What are you doing here in Douglas?'

'After Bothwell we decided it was better to open up the old house, and for me and Janet to live apart. And John was allowed to return from the Carolinas where he had been exiled with Cardross and others. But the situation here is very dangerous, for Lord Ross's troop is in the market place even now, and Clavers himself is expected! You must get out!'

'I've only just got in!'

'And it's me that's right glad to see you alive and well, for I thought you were still over the water, or maybe dead or in prison!'

'I have been back only for a few days. I saw Margaret at her brother's in Jedforest, and now I am come to see My Lord of Douglas.'

'My John and all the baillies have been summoned to the market place. There's big trouble afoot. Rumour has it that Renwick has been seen in the area, and they are scouring the moors for him. You must get out!'

'And Janet?'

'She is safe at Cumnock. She went there after Richard Cameron was killed, that day she gave Hackston a drink. She has been on the suspect list ever since, but they seem to have let her be, seeing she is only a woman.' Anne tossed her head, as much as if to say: "Only a woman! What do they know!"

'But she is well?'

'Oh aye, well enough. Save that she has taken up wi' some minister body that lies in the Tolbooth of Edinburgh. I fear she will be badly hurt. Now go, and God be wi' ye!'

'What's the best way out of town?'

'You'll mind that secret passage under this house? Take it and you will come out by Castle Dangerous. His Lordship is at home but be careful!' So saying she gave her brother a tearful hug, and pushed him down the stair to the cellar, giving him a candle and tinderbox as she did so. William remembered the passage from boyhood days when he used to sneak out at night to fish in the Douglas Water. He lit the candle, and pulling up a trapdoor concealed under a thick layer of sawdust, descended a ladder into the dark. Bent low, he followed the passage until he saw a faint grey light ahead. The passage he knew emerged amongst some rocks outside the village from whence he could easily reach Castle Dangerous under cover of night.

Cleland waited in the dark until the lights of the castle began to go out one by one. Finally the only ones still burning were on the first floor, where the family slept. Standing below, he threw small stones at the partially closed shutters of one particular window and soon a head appeared. 'Who's there?' a querulous voice demanded.

'Jamie! It's me, William.'

A suppressed cry of joy sounded from above. The young Earl of Angus and Cleland had been firm friends since Angus was a child. 'Wait there! I'll come down and unbolt the door.' In less than a minute he had done so, and Cleland stood once more within the Douglas castle, where he had spent much of his boyhood. 'Will, my father will be so very pleased to see you! Me too, for since my parents separated things have been very hard at home.' Young James led the way up the staircase, and pausing outside his father's bedroom door, knocked gently.

'Who's that?' demanded a gruff voice.

'It's me, father. I have someone here you will be glad to see.' The door swung open and the grey head of the Marquess of Douglas stuck itself out.

'By heaven, William, is that you? By all that's wonderful!'

'Indeed it's me my Lord, and it's right glad I am to see you again.'

'I know why you are here! We have had correspondence from Holland. You are in grave danger here. You must get away, out to the moors!'

'I must speak with you first, sir. I have a commission from My Lord of Argyle and Sir John Cochrane.'

'Come in! Come in! Jamie, go organise food and drink to be brought up. And be careful. Speak only to those servants you know we can trust.' Turning with a wry look to Cleland, the Marquess remarked, 'We even have Clavers' spies in our own house now.' Angus gave his father a baleful look and disappeared downstairs.

'Argyle has already sailed, and met with little support even in his own country,' Douglas began.

Will looked surprised. 'We are not entirely without any intelligence here in Lanarkshire, Mr Cleland. We hear that he is near Dumbarton and perhaps about to cross the Clyde. The highlands have proved a great disappointment for the Earl.'

'But will the lowlands not be more supportive? Most of the persecution has been here in the south. Surely there are many who will rise against a papist king?'

'William, you must go to other places and talk to the lairds. Few of the nobility will support your cause, they are too much afraid of losing their lands and titles. But the bonnet-lairds are all covenant men and may be able to raise the countryside. Your big problem is to find mounts for your force. Virtually all Clavers' men are mounted, even the militia. Without horses you will be outmanouvered, for you cannot possibly hope to defeat the government forces in a pitched battle, save for one possibility.'

Cleland looked worried. 'And what might that be, my Lord?'

'You must convince the Cameronians of the United Societies to fight for you. They can muster several thousand armed men, and are the only semi-disciplined body in the south-west, even though they are continually accused of being unprincipled guerrillas. They even disciplined those responsible for the death of two Life Guards, Kennoway and Stewart. No-one else, other than the regular army, has even a semblance of discipline. You led them to victory at Drumclog and they have not forgotten you.'

'I know James Renwick from his days in Groenigen. I go from here to seek him, but I guess that may prove difficult. I hear he lies very close?'

'You'll probably find that your sister Janet knows better than anyone where he is hiding. Amazing woman, your sister Janet,' said Douglas wonderingly. 'I can't believe she is not married yet. I suspect she must have a lover who has been exiled, or in prison.'

Will remained very quiet.

♣

It was a short day for Will from Douglas to Cumnock, and he rejoiced to be on the open moors in daylight, for he was on his own turf and his way led over the high tops of Cairn Table and Wardlaw Hill, so he was not forced to travel in the dark. Coveys of grouse whirred up suddenly before him, and the cry of the whaup echoed over the sundrenched moors. It was a good day to be alive, and even better to be striding over his native heath. Below to his right lay the village of Muirkirk, near where Richard Cameron and his brother had been slain, but Will was in a light mood and whistled as he trudged through the heather. Reaching the outskirts of Cumnock at dusk, he waited for dark before venturing near his sister's home. Standing in the lane outside, he gave the old family signal, an owl hoot. 'To-wit-to-woo, to-wit-to-woo! To-wo-hooooo!' Immediately the response came, and a side door opened. A slight form slipped silently out into the lane and ran to Will.

Brother and sister embraced with the fierceness that continual fear for a loved one's safety engenders. 'Thanks be to God, Will, you really are alive!'

'Alive and well, my dearest sister, and still seeking the fulfilment of my vow the day Hackston was executed.' They clung together in silence for a while, overcome with memories and sadness. 'But here I am, still strong for the cause. I hear you are chief messenger for the Cameronians these days?'

'Come inside Will, we have much to talk of, and events are overtaking us every day. You must be famished?'

'I wouldn't say no to some of your famous venison pie, for I long for simple Scots fare like oatcakes and tattie scones. They are sorely lacking in Holland, and since I got over here I have been mostly visiting the gentry, where such common fare is looked down upon.' Soon he was seated at the table with a huge ashet before him, loaded with food. 'I have actually eaten in the past week, you know, Janet.'

'Aye, but not my food,' answered his sister as she sat down beside him and looked at him lovingly.

'So what's your news?' they both asked simultaneously and then laughed.

'I'm here to raise support for Argyle and Cochrane, who hope to prevent York retaining the throne and turning Scotland into a papist nation.'

'And how are you faring, Will?'

He looked somewhat shamefaced. 'Not too well, really. The nobility are afraid to risk losing their lands and titles, the lairds are willing, but so harassed by Clavers and his ilk, that mustering for any kind of training has been well nigh impossible, and the common people are so oppressed that just staying alive takes all their strength. There is nothing left over for rebellion.'

'The people do not seek a war. The humble shepherds and ploughmen long to be left in peace, and not be harried into some appointed curate's services, but to be left to worship in their own way even if it's in secret. But there are some ne'er-do-wells hell-bent on violence,' she admitted, 'and your only real hope is the United Societies led by Renwick. Yet he absolutely refuses to countenance any use of force, other than for self-defence or rescue.'

'That's not what I hear!'

'One hears a great deal these days—much of it vicious lies. Every violent act, whether criminal or religious, is blamed on the Cameronians, but in fact they are the only group which disciplines their own offenders. But "blame one, blame all" is the government cry these days, and so no differentiation is made between an old man reading his bible and an armed highwaymen robbing innocent travellers. All are grist to the government's mill of brutality and revenge.'

Brother and sister talked deep into the night, Janet telling of finding supplies for hunted fugitives and journeys as messenger for the Covenant cause. She had become a mistress of disguise and had ventured as far as Edinburgh bearing important letters. Her courage and resourcefulness had become a byword in Cameronian circles.

'And what's this I hear of a certain minister body?' asked Will.

Janet looked at him sharply. 'Where did you hear that?'

'From my Lord of Douglas, no less.'

'Well, it's all your fault!' she said accusingly.

Will looked as bemused as any man will when accused of something he knows absolutely nothing about.

'You met Alex Shields in Utrecht and Leiden,' she said accusingly.

'Well, what of it?'

'What of it? What of it! You told him all about me, and he came here when he was searching for his brother Michael after he landed near Largs in '83.'

'And?'

'We fell in love, you great fool! And now he's under trial in Edinburgh, and I'll never see him again!' Janet broke down in a fit of weeping.

'But you are already promised to James Scot of Lanark!'

'I am indeed already promised to James Scot of Lanark,' and Janet sunk her lovely head even lower, and wept even more bitterly!

Will remained silent. He seemed to be silenced quite a lot these days!

♣

Later that night he sat up writing a report for Cochrane, now rumoured to be south of the Clyde. He hoped Janet might find a reliable courier prepared to carry it, but his real fear was that she might insist on taking it herself.

> *"Sir John,*
>
> *I believe that if you knew the risks I have taken, and the efforts we have made, you would be satisfied with our progress. I have met and talked with many people, nobles, lairds and peasants alike. Clavers and his troops have been very active against us, and this has delayed us somewhat. But I do believe with God's help, that many undecided people will come out on our side, providing Mr Ker* (Argyle's pseudonym) *makes it clear that he is committed to the work of reformation. He should speak fair to all whom he meets, and not be too arbitrary. Neither should he be upset by what they may write. Letters are being intercepted.*

Hold as strongly as you can where you are, and keep the enemy as busy as may be. In eight days I hope to kindle a beacon on Loudon Hill which will be a sign that we are ready to muster. Send me whatever intelligence you have to Moffat-well as soon as possible. I will have a woman there with a knot of red ribbons on her right arm daily. Pass your information to her. She is trustworthy. We are short of horses, but well supplied for arms.

The more you can vex the enemy, the better for our cause. Things begin to look hopeful here in Lanarkshire.

Your obedient servant,
W C"

1st June, 1685. Carsphairn Forest.

Cleland took off his soaking hat and cloak and shook them vigorously as he entered the lonely bothy. 'Scotland does not get any less wet, for sure! What would I not give for a glimpse of the sun!' He had already forgotten his carefree day on the moors above Cumnock.

'You mean like in Holland?' quipped James Renwick.

'Goodness James, you are really hard to find! Why do you hide always in such outlandish places?' Cleland had been walking through the pouring rain for two days, avoiding all roads, to reach Renwick's hideout in Carsphairn Forest.

'I chose Carsphairn because the curate here is a loyal government man, and they think the people hereabouts are of a like mind. But they fool themselves. Some of our members killed his predecessor, but it was clear self-defence! Even so, we expelled them from our Societies, for we will not countenance vengeance. Nevertheless I am the most wanted man in all of Scotland. Death to me would be as a bed to the weary.'

'That may be true, but there will soon be others higher on the wanted list.'

'How so?' Renwick had recently had a number of escapes which could only be described as miraculous. 'Clavers' men harry us by day and night. They seek me from Edinburgh to Galloway. They actually executed two women by drowning this month, and since the Sanquhar Protestation, anyone refusing to disown it, is to be immediately killed before two witnesses, *whether they have arms or not!* We lost some men after we rescued prisoners from Kirkudbright last December, and Clavers actually had MacMichael's dead body dug up and hanged on a gibbet! Small wonder I wander alone in wild and lonely places. The moors are my friends, far from the evil of men.'

'James, I need badly to talk with you before the next United Societies' Meeting. There are great matters afoot.'

'Greater than the Lord's work?'

'This *is* the Lord's work!'

'How so? Our next meeting is planned for 12 June. Tell all! Withhold nothing!'

'Argyle has landed in Scotland to re-establish the old religion. Monmouth is doing the same in England. We badly need the Cameronian Societies to come in with us, for you have many men who can bear arms.'

Renwick, normally a quiet individual, burst out angrily, 'Are you serious?'

'Deadly!'

'Will, you are a man of war, and I am a man of peace. Certainly we both long to see old Scotland restored to her former freedom and honour. But you could not have chosen worse for your leaders.'

'How so, James?'

Renwick sounded exasperated! 'Argyle had the casting vote that sent that saintly Donald Cargill to the gallows. The leopard may change his spots, but can a Campbell? He may have his following among Clan Diarmaid, but here in the lowlands his name is greatly despised. And if you succeed, who is to be king? Monmouth?'

Again Cleland looked embarrassed. He had realised during his first interview with Thomas Steel that the expedition had not been properly thought through. Every disaffected man was not anxiously waiting to take up arms against the king without so much as a proper plan in place, and it seemed that Argyle's hope that the highlands would flock to his banner had not been realised. Monmouth's expedition must have sailed by now, but no news, or even rumour, had filtered through of goings on in England. This was ominous.

'No James! Monmouth does not seek the crown!'

'Then who does? For if the Duke of York, (I will not call him King James), is overthrown, who is to fill the vacuum? Or are we looking at another Commonwealth? The last one was not good for Scotland. Monmouth is excommunicate by Cargill, and the Societies will not follow an antichrist. He may have behaved well at Bothwell, but he is still the illegitimate spawn of Charles Stewart. And as for Cochrane, did you not know that it was he who betrayed Richard Cameron's whereabouts the day he was killed! You have really excelled yourselves this time! Politicians have absolutely no finesse at all!'

'My goodness, for a man of God you talk very straight!'

'Have not Cameronian ministers always done so? Are we not the only ones who continue to speak out under the repression which our homeland suffers? We are not known for cowards, whatever else anyone may think of us!'

'So will you not bring it to the Meeting?'

'I surely will. But I hold out little hope for a positive answer. I think Will, maybe we should pray a wee bit together?'

In the event, the General Meeting planned for 12 June 1685 never took place due to increased military activity in hunting down fugitives. By the time the next meeting took place at The Knypes on 24th July, both Argyle and Monmouth were dead. The beacon never flared on Loudon Hill, the woman with the scarlet ribbons never received any intelligence, and the Cameronians never took the field.

20th June, 1685. Carter Bar.

In the meantime William Veitch had had a very frustrating time. Arriving at the hamlet of Wark just south of Coldstream, he discovered that Lord Gray's estate actually lay at Chipchase Castle, near another Wark close by Newcastle and several days journey south. However, once having got there, he had a much more enthusiastic reception than Cleland in Scotland. In fact, as he was passed on from house to house, there was such a response to Monmouth's arrival, that word about it soon got out, and he was forced to take shelter in the Steel hideout.

This shelter lay amongst rocks high on Ark's Ridge above Carter Bar, with an immense view down to Jedburgh and Hawick. It was an excellent lookout post for early warning of approach from any direction save south, and was so well camouflaged that the heather had regrown right over it, hiding it completely. Only those in the secret were likely to find the concealed entrance which one had to crawl through, hidden between two uninteresting rocks. Thomas Steel had hidden here in 1683 at the height of the Rye House reprisals. Twice a week Sanders Stevenson, one of his foresters, brought food and such news as there was to Veitch. It was now mid-June, and the tension of waiting was unbearable. 'There are evil rumours from Ayrshire way,' said Sanders gloomily.

'I must have more than rumours. Can you not fetch Mr Steel here so we can talk? We need to make a plan.' Before dawn Veitch heard a rustling at the entrance. Cocking the pistol which he had loaded and primed before trying to snatch some sleep, he waited anxiously.

'William, don't shoot! It's me! Thomas!' Veitch silently exhaled the breath which he had been holding.

'God be praised!'

'You won't say that when you hear my news! Argyle is taken near Paisley, and Cochrane and his remnant were broken at Muirdykes,' gasped out Steel.

'Then all is lost!'

'Aye, looks like it! But we need confirmation. There is so much rumour flying around, and so much movement of horse, foot and dragoons, that all is total confusion.'

'What of Will Cleland?'

'He was at Douglas the last I heard. I managed to procure two blank travel permits from someone we know in Edinburgh. It's weak enough cover, but it is sheer suicide to move without one at present. I'm going to try to get one to Will. It might help him until he can escape back to Holland. He'll need a false identity of course, but he already goes under the pseudonym of William Cunningham. The other pass is for you.'

CHAPTER ELEVEN

"THE MAJOR'S TALE"

A T LENGTH THE ILL-FATED ARGYLE EXPEDITION had set sail from Amsterdam in three ships. Ill fortune struck immediately, as William Spence and Dr William Blackader were captured in Orkney, where they landed on 14th May to seek intelligence and support. Bad fortune continued to dog the expedition throughout the highlands, and finally Cochrane reached the lowlands on 16 June, by crossing the River Clyde three miles above Dumbarton with about 150 men, all that was left of the expedition. Argyle himself was captured on the same day.

Mid-July 1685. Annandale.

Major James Henderson and William Cleland had met up in Galloway a month later, after many vicissitudes.

'I suppose you heard that Monmouth was defeated at Sedgemoor and taken captive on 8th July,' said Cleland? 'Chances are by now he is dead. Argyle is already executed. Our adventure is finished.'

'Did you not get any support here in the south-west?' questioned James.

'Many were for the cause, but the whole situation depended on the Cameronians coming out. Had they been prepared to fight, we would have had a viable fighting force of dedicated men. But while they were for a change of government, or even of crown, they were not for Argyle or Cochrane. Some few under Daniel Ker of Kersland might have rallied, but without James Renwick's blessing our case was hopeless.'

'So where is Kersland now?' Cleland noticed James wince as he took his coat off.

'He is hiding on the next door farm, along with fifteen followers. But James, what ails you man? You are in some pain.'

Henderson looked sheepish. 'I took a bullet in my shoulder at Muirdykes, and it's troubling me somewhat.'

'Laud sake, James, you mean to say you have been walking around with a bullet in you for a week and never told anyone?'

'It doesn't help to complain. But since you have some skill in medicine Will, perhaps you might help me now?' Whereupon Cleland's medical training in Leyden was promptly put to good use; water was boiled up, and he began to probe with the forceps from his travelling medical kit.

'Here, drink this!' Cleland poured a generous measure from a large flask he fished out of his coat pocket. 'Ferintosh! Never travel without it,' he said. 'One of the good things from the highlands. Made in Culloden, the sort of place one never hears about, but you never know when you might need a good dram!'

'You'll have heard of the debacle we experienced in the highlands, I expect?'

'Hmm! Yes! Hold on, I've got it!' Cleland triumphantly held up a musket ball in his tweezers. 'Now you can talk more easily.' The conversation went on late into the night as they caught up with each other's news.

Taking an enormous swig straight from the flask, Henderson began his tale: 'On 16 June we were at an ale house at Kilpatrick on the north bank of the Clyde, unaccustomed to company such as ours. Sir John Cochrane of Ochiltree and Sir Patrick Hume of Polwarth were in a great quandary, for there was no sign of the Earl.

'"Where's Argyle?"' demanded Polwarth.

'"Gone! Maybe to Glasgow, maybe back to Argyle, I don't know. For all I know he has been taken. The whole thing is a disaster!"

'"How many men have we left with us?"

'"About 500, all hungry and weary to the bone. The highlands have brought us nothing save sorrow and suffering, and Argyle has led us very badly. We need to get south to our own lands."

'"You mean over the Clyde?"

'"Over the Clyde, to the lowlands. We might stand some chance amongst our own people and on our own turf, but we have none here. I have just received this despatch from Will Cleland. Here!" Throwing it on the table, Cochrane rose and left the inn.

'The remaining expeditioners were in various stages of relaxation, some sleeping on the hard ground, others making thin porridge over small fires. There was a general stirring of interest as the two leaders emerged. "Gather round boys! Gather round." Slowly the weary men raised themselves and gathered around the inn steps with surly and discouraged expressions.

'"The Earl of Argyle has left us! You are no longer beholden to him. Our expedition has failed, and we must move quickly, for we are all hunted men. Sir Patrick and I are for crossing the Clyde and making for our own country. You are all free to go your own way, or come with us, as you wish."

'"So, who is with us?" asked Polwarth. About 150 indicated their intent to follow the leaders. The rest began to fade away, and the roads leading out of Kilpatrick were soon clogged with weary figures anxious to escape.

'"Very well, let's move!" ordered Cochrane, leading the way down to the river. Two boats were drawn up on the bank, and twelve men got into each. "We'll send them right back for you," he said to those left standing on the bank. The river was about 200 yards wide at this point but, the tide being out, an expanse of sand and mud extending in front of each bank. I was in the front boat.' James Henderson continued, 'I cried out, "There's a troop of horse on the brae, and four or five hiding behind that old boat lying there!" Those in our boat made ready to fire their muskets.

'"Hold your fire!" ordered Sir John. "Wait until the main body is in range. You won't harm those behind the boat." They paddled on.

'"Now boys, they're in range! Present! Fire!" A volley rang out, killing one horse and wounding three others. The men hiding behind the boat ran back to their troop, mounted, and the whole lot beat a hasty retreat.

'"Well, if that's a sample of what we are up against, we should have an easy day," remarked Cochrane as he disembarked, sending the boats back for the others.'

'"These were only militia," responded Hume. "It will be a very different story when we come up with Clavehouse's regulars."

'"We'll abide that when we face them," retorted Cochrane.

'"Yon big house up there belongs to a king's man," I said. "I know this country well. He will be out with his troop as like as not. He keeps a good larder and cellar, so we can refresh ourselves before we proceed." Accordingly the remainder of our force helped themselves liberally to the food and drink available, before preparing to march. The stable was full of horses, so we decided to mount as many as we could, and head south in an attempt to join up with Monmouth in England. No word of his progress had reached us, but we felt he was surely faring better than us in the north.'

'As we left, we saw the troop we had put to flight joined by a further two troops, so we marched up the hill and took up a defensive position in a steading protected by a stout thorn hedge. "These cowards will not attack us in this strength,' said Cochrane. 'Come, let's force them to fight in the open." He divided us into three companies of fifty under himself, Polwarth and me. We advanced in line, and all three troops beat a hasty retreat, not stopping until they were out of sight.

'"It seems we are to have more success here than in Argyle's country," said Polwarth.

'"Cowards!"'

Henderson continued: 'The next day, 18th June, we marched south, but as evening fell we saw two troops of horse approaching us in good order. As we climbed up the small hill at Muirdykes, they drew into formation before us. "Now we have a different story," I thought to myself, for I recognised the troop leaders as Lord William Ross, one of Claverhouse's lieutenants, the other being another Capt William Clelland, a cousin of yours I think, Will? I thought, "Is there no end to this madness of intercine warfare, families fighting each other?"

'They discharged a volley at us and looked ready to charge, but Sir John called out, "Steady lads. With God's grace I will lead you safely off this field."

'They fired another volley, badly wounding Thomas Archer our young minister, but we took to our halberts and found again, as at Drumclog, that the enemy would not close with us if we took cold steel to them.

'Lord Ross then came forward under a flag of truce, and Sir John went to meet him. "You have behaved as brave men should. What is the point of throwing your lives away on a cause which is already lost? We will grant you quarter, if you only lay down your arms."

'"We despise your quarter!" answered Cochrane. "We are here in the cause of the protestant religion and freedom. You are fighting for popery and royal domination. You should be ashamed of yourselves as Scotsmen." While this discussion was going on, the rest of us, now only about 75 strong, had taken up position in an old stone-walled sheepfold. As the flag of truce withdrew, Sir John rejoined us and divided us into two flanks. "Load and make ready boys," he ordered. "When they attack, wait for my signal before you fire. Then right flank, give them a volley! Left flank, await my second signal. Then we take them on with cold steel and stop them getting over the wall. Everybody ready?"

'"Ready sir!" came the answering chorus.

'One enemy troop rode right up against our right flank, which gave them a hot reception, but thinking our muskets were now empty, they pressed home the attack, only to be hit by a second volley from our left flank at very close range. Several saddles, including Captain Clelland's, were emptied. His troop wheeled off in disorder, whereupon George Brysson leapt over the dyke-wall and wrenching the captain's scarlet coat from his recumbent form, stuck it on top of his halbert, and waved it derisively at the enemy, who milled about in disorder before settling again into ranks.

'"Stand by boys! They've taken casualties! This time they will come harder at us. Take courage, and stand fast, for our cause is good! Here they come again!"

'This time the attack was led by Lord Ross, but again was beaten off with such determination that, had he not worn a breastplate, he would surely have been killed. Several more saddles were emptied, and once again the troop retreated in disorder. We ourselves had one killed and two wounded. It was a bitterly cold day and Brysson went to look for his coat, which he found covering the wounded Tom Archer, who was nearly dead from cold and loss of blood. We carried him in and Sir John, telling us to look out sharply, led us in prayer, for we covenanters are quite used to watching and praying simultaneously.

'As it began to grow dark, Ross's men surrounded us, but well out of range. "They are afraid to attack again," said Cochrane, "for though we may be outnumbered, they will call up reinforcements before dawn. Let us acquit ourselves like men, and leave this field with honour. Load your pieces! If we can avoid them in the dark, good! If not, let us fight our way through."

'It was a cloudy night, so when it was quite dark we moved out silently in skirmishing order. But we made no contact with the enemy, and it eventually became clear that they had left the field and retreated to Kilmarnock. After about a mile Sir John reckoned we should be safe. "We have lost many good friends since we crossed the Clyde two days ago. Are you prepared to give your word that you will not part from us without my permission? Otherwise we may all be lost."

'So we agreed to stick together, and Sir John led off again into the night. We marched hard all night, and you can imagine our dismay when daylight began to dawn, and we saw that we had walked in a circle, and were back near our battle site of yesterday. I went to a nearby house to seek shelter in their barn, where we lay low all day. Our leader was overcome with shame at leading us thus, but in fact it proved to be providential, for throughout that day we watched dragoons scouring the countryside, but none came near us. That night we marched again, but this time we had a guide, and so arrived safely at a friendly farm before dawn. At last we felt that we were in more friendly country for most of the local populace were for the Covenant. In the evening a messenger arrived, bearing the news that the Earl of Argyle had been taken prisoner.

'Sir John called us together. "Argyle is taken, and there is still no news of Monmouth. I must now free you of your oath, and charge you to save yourselves as best you can. You have all fought well!"

'We parted in great sorrow. George Brysson, myself and two others headed south for Annandale, resolving to travel by night and lie up by day. After many weary days travel we knocked at the door of a lonely farmhouse. When the good widow who lived there heard our tale, she told us that she had some of Renwick's Cameronians hiding in her own house, and so could not take us in. But she sent us to her neighbour, who kindly hid us in his barn. That night one of the Cameronians came by asking where the four new arrivals were hiding, and he brought him to us. Imagine my joy,' said James, 'when I recognised our visitor at the lonely farm where we were hiding near Dalry as none other than yourself, Will.'

'So where do we go from here James?' asked Cleland.

'We must make our way back to Holland, if we can. The Cameronians here will guide and shelter us, I feel sure.'

♣

Cleland and Henderson spent many wet and weary days hiding out on the moors, occasionally taking shelter in a "safe" house for a time. Finally, reaching the outskirts of Cumnock at dusk, they waited for dark before venturing near Will's sister's home. Standing in the lane outside, once more he gave the old family signal. Again the response came, and a side door opened which Will and James slipped silently through.

'So you're still alive and still in Scotland?'

'You sound very angry, Janet.'

I'm not angry, you great fool! I fear for your life every day! Going underground in Annandale, and no word of any sort for weeks!'

'We have been harried by troops all the way, sister! We have had to travel by night, and usually lie low in a moss or peat hag for the day. It's a very damp business.'

'So where are you bound for now? Back to Holland, or skulking here?'

'Janet! Can you not be more welcoming! We have been at the risk of our lives daily for months now.'

'You think you are the only ones risking your lives? King Louis of France has revoked the Edict of Nantes, so all the French Huguenots are fleeing to wherever they may, Holland, the New World. There is rumour some have even gone to Africa!'

'God help them all! Their persecutors will now be out in the open, just like ours. These are woeful times for protestants all over Europe.'

'There's worse,' burst out Janet. 'Alex had been sentenced to the Bass! I'll never see him again!' She burst into tears, and as her brother tried to comfort her, James Henderson stood by looking very embarrassed.

'How do you know all this?' asked Will.

'I had a letter from 'Phemie Learmont, up Lanark way. Her father is on the Bass too, and like to die there, for he's over eighty!' She burst into a new fit of sobbing, as if her heart would break.

Later, after supper, when James Henderson had retired to the first dry bed he had enjoyed for months, brother and sister talked together far into the night. Janet had calmed down somewhat, though she still broke into fits of silent weeping.

'We are headed back to Holland, James and I. We have not given up yet, and I have great hope of William of Orange taking up our cause. There are some very influential Scots at his court, Carstares and others. They carry much weight with William.'

'You can't leave yet!' said Janet angrily.

'Whyever not?'

'Because of Margaret!'

Will felt a cold hand close over his heart. 'What of Margaret? She is not ill? She is not imprisoned? She is not dead—is she? What of her?' Now it was his turn to feel sick!

'You cannot leave until you have married her! Since that day at Drumclog she has waited and pined, and if you don't marry her, I truly believe she will fade away altogether.'

'But I am a hunted man, already condemned to death and with a price on my head. No hearth! No home! Nothing! I cannot ask Margaret to marry a man in my position!'

Janet sighed! 'Can there be anything more stupid than a man? Home, safety, security! What is that to a woman in love? What she wants is you in her bed, even if you have to take to the moors the next day!'

♣

The Marquess of Douglas and the Earl of Angus stood beside each other, father and son warming their behinds at a roaring fire in their Douglas home of Castle Dangerous. Captain Cleland and Major Henderson sat relaxed in wing chairs, each with a large glass of port in hand.

'Well William, turned out like we thought, eh?'

''Fraid so my Lord. Total disaster.'

'And Renwick let you down?'

'I don't think that's quite fair, sir. Argyle and Cochrane were both anathema to the Cameronians! And Cargill excommunicated Monmouth! We did not choose our leaders well, and though the Cameronians were for our cause, the most they could get to was a position of benevolent neutrality.'

'So they let Argyle and the others pay with their lives?'

'No more than the price many Cameronians have already paid, and I am sure will pay again!'

'So William, are you really one with them now?'

'I really am one with them, my Lord.'

'So am I,' interjected the young Earl of Angus, 'Body and soul!'

23 Feb 1686. Cambusnethan

'Do you, William Cleland, take this woman, Margaret Steel, to be your lawfully wedded wife; to have and to hold from this day forward; for better for worse; for richer for poorer; in sickness and in health; to love and to cherish; until God shall separate you by death?'

'I do!'

'Do you, Margaret Steel…'

The Cambusnethan Church was packed, although it was nearly midnight. The place was bright with candles, for it had been a long time since there had been such a joyful celebration here. Margaret looked stunning in a simple white dress and wearing her mother's lace veil as she entered the church on the arm of her brother Thomas Steel. Behind her, Janet, 'Phemie and Alison, wearing dresses of covenant blue, completed the tableau.

'Is there a ring?' Rev William Vilant looked nervous, as well he might! If it got out that he had married William Cleland, he himself might end up on the Bass. Not only that, but the church was full of hunted men, who had flocked to their friend's wedding in defiance of their pursuers. Piquets had been posted at all the entrances to the town, just as if it had been a conventicle. It would take a brave band of troops to attack this gathering!

James Henderson looked embarrassed as he searched through his pockets for the ring. With a sigh of relief he fished it out of a waistcoat pocket, and Will placed it on his bride's hand. 'With this ring I thee wed...'

♣

"Oh stay, stay at home with me!" Margaret held Will close as he prepared to take his leave a few days later. 'We have had so little time together, and now you are off to the continent again!'

'My dearest, you know I swore an oath when David Hackston was executed that I would live my life to set old Scotland free from tyranny. I have to go!'

'How I wish you would *"Leave off thy lofty soaring, and stay at home with me!"*

'You write it, but why do you not do it! When will I see you again? Will I *ever* see you again? You are so cruel to leave me here alone, while you go off adventuring.'

'Margaret! You know you can't come with me. James and I will be hard enough put to it to get back to Holland on our own, and if we are caught it will be death for sure!'

'I would rather die with you, than live without you!'

'I know, dearest. But I believe we shall both live to see our children grow up in a free land.'

'Children! Children! How are we ever to have any children if we are always apart?'

'You may be carrying one even now.'

And so he left her sorrowing.

CHAPTER TWELVE

"SUMMONED BY KING JAMES"

30th June 1685. Den Bommel.

THE NARROW STREET RESOUNDED to the hammering on the door. Although Hugh Mackay, commanding the Anglo-Scots Brigade of the Dutch Army, and his family lived at Den Haag, he and Clara often sneaked off for a few quiet days at her old home in Den Bommel. The thundering continued, now accompanied by a loud voice shouting, 'Colonel Mackay! Express and most urgent dispatch from His Majesty King James!'

Clara groaned and rolled over to dig her husband in the ribs. 'Hugh! Wake up! We'll have the whole town awake in a minute. What can King James want with you?'

'Nothing good, I'll be bound,' said Mackay as he rolled out of bed and went to the window. 'Who's that making such a racket in the middle of the night? Identify yourself sir, or I'll have the guard on you!' He looked down on to a mud-bespattered figure in the uniform of his old regiment The Royals. Behind him drooped a horse in the last stages of exhaustion.

'Dougie, is that you? Wait, I am coming right down.' Hugh Mackay threw on a dressing gown, ran barefoot down the stairs and opened the door. Major Dougie Elphinstone virtually fell into the hall. 'Man, you are fair exhausted. What brings you here?' as he helped the messenger into the parlour and sat him down in an easy chair before the dying embers of the fire.

'Here, drink this!' as he thrust a large goblet of claret into Dougie's hand.

After a few gulps, the visitor visibly pulled himself together, rummaged in his coat pocket and held out a parchment to Mackay. 'Personal from the King!'

Hugh quickly broke the seal and read the contents. As he did so, he visibly paled.

'Do you know what's in here?' he demanded.

'Well enough! Your Brigade is recalled! Monmouth has invaded England and Argyle Scotland. His Majesty has few troops of the calibre of your brigade, and as is his right, he requires your urgent help to quell this insurrection.'

Mackay looked very dubious. 'H'mm,' he equivocated.

'The expedition was mounted from here in Holland, and well you know it! If you do not respond immediately, and with all the force at your command, your previous loyalty to the British crown will count for nothing!'

'I will have to clear this with the Stadtholder.'

'Already done, sir. Another courier left London at the same time as me.'

'Well, I can see I have no choice. Dougie—you will carry a reply?'

'If I can have a fresh horse, I am ready to ride.'

'You always had the most amazing stamina. Refresh yourself, sleep if you will. But bear word back to the King that his Brigade is on the way.'

'I have your word on that?'

'You have my word!'

8 July 1685. Greenwich.

Mackay stepped ashore from the fast packet which he and his command group had taken from Amsterdam. The six regiments of the Anglo-Scots Brigade were to follow as soon as possible, but with Monmouth already in the field, King James had summoned his commanders with all possible expedition.

The familiar figure of Major Dougie Elphinstone stepped forward to greet him. He was much smarter than the last time Mackay had seen him spurring down the street at Den Bommel.

'Welcome General! His Majesty is glad to have you here.'

Mackay looked at him quizzically.

'No mistake sir, His Majesty has been pleased to gazette you Major-General,' said Dougie. 'My felicitations.'

'Thank you Dougie. I had not expected this.'

'The king is very pleased with the speed with which you sailed, and by bringing your command group with you, you have demonstrated the commitment of all your regiments.'

'I have indeed!'

'You may not have heard yet, but Monmouth was defeated at Sedgemoor two days ago, 6th July. By one of your old comrades-in-arms, John Churchill.'

'Indeed! Then His Majesty will not need our Brigade!'

'Not at all! Not at all! He wants you here in case things flare up again. He has few troops of the calibre and steadiness of yours, and awaits your urgent attendance in London.'

'Very well.' Turning to his colonels and their adjutants, he ordered them to mount. 'Lead on Dougie! We're at your heels.'

♣

Mackay had not met James since he became king, and was quite unprepared for his gracious reception. 'Thank you for coming, General. We have great need for loyal troops such as your Brigade. It's hard to know whom to trust these days.'

Hugh felt most uncomfortable. Surely James knew that his personal sympathies lay with the protestant cause in England, which is why he served the Stadtholder, not Louis XIV of France. He muttered something unintelligible in reply.

'And We wish to honour you also in your native Scotland. We are aware that you have not been to your ancestral estates in Scoury for many years, and so We propose to appoint you to our Privy Council in Scotland.'

Hugh felt even more uncomfortable!

August 1685. Scotland.

Mackay was relieved that Claverhouse was not present when he was sworn in as a Privy Councillor in Edinburgh, having gone to his country seat at Dudhope only a week earlier. Hugh's loyalties were severely strained by the honour James had set upon him, for his sympathies lay much with the persecuted in both kingdoms. Nevertheless he held his commission from James, not William the Stadtholder, and even though there had been some strains in the command structure of the Anglo-Scots Brigade, they had responded immediately to the summons to come over and help deal with Monmouth and Argyle. He was nevertheless relieved that the rebellion had been put down before his Brigade arrived, so he did not have to take the field with divided loyalties.

He had hoped to travel north to Scoury after his swearing in, for he had not been to his ancestral home since he left in 1672. But he was summoned urgently back to London to attend the king's review of his Brigade at Hounslow Heath. En route he spent a night with the Chamberlain of Jedburgh Forest, whose father he had known in his youth. To his surprise, when he entered the drawing room, Mackay found a face which he had known in Holland. 'I believe you are familiar with Mr William Cleland,' said Thomas Steel, his host.

'Yes indeed, he and I have had some serious talks over the water. But do you not take a grave risk introducing him here to me, a Privy Councillor?'

'General, we know you to be a man of honour and therefore bound by the laws of hospitality, so we trust to your discretion. It was not William who was so anxious to meet you, but this young lady here.' Mackay looked at the young woman standing beside Cleland. The features were so similar that they were clearly closely related, startling blue eyes, firm chin and fair hair. 'General, may I present Miss Janet Cleland.'

Mackay looked closely. This girl possessed a vibrancy which was most uncommon. Whilst her brother was of a serious disposition combined with an incredibly strong will, Janet clearly lived life to the utmost, with a vivacity and sparkle which it was impossible to ignore. Nevertheless, right now she looked very nervous.

'I have a big favour to ask, General.'

'If it is my power...'

'Oh, it's in your power right enough. The question is, does it conflict with your conscience?'

'Well why not ask me, and let me decide?'

Janet took a gulp. Everyone else in the room was hanging on the conversation with keen interest, for it concerned them all.

'You are well aware that certain of the people of Scotland are being hunted and persecuted because of their faith? Women have been tied to stakes and drowned in the sea, old men have been summarily executed merely for reading the Bible, the bodies of godly men have been dug up and hung on gallows. I could go on...'

'I am well aware of the evils which are being perpetrated here under the guise of good governance. I have met many of your countrymen in the Netherlands, where they have been forced to flee to escape persecution here. Most of them are sincere and good people.'

Thomas Steel butted in. 'We also know your reputation as a godly soldier. Bishop Burnett, who is related to Robert Hamilton the Cameronian emissary in Europe, describes you as the most pious soldier he has ever known.'

'That's probably due mostly to the influence of my wife and her mother.'

'That's as may be. But your reputation precedes you.' Cleland had the advantage of a number of discussions with Mackay in Holland.

Janet broke in: 'Please can we stop going round and round with polite compliments, and address our main concern?'

'Quite right, Miss Cleland,' responded Mackay. 'Let's get to the point!'

'The point is...,' William began.

'The point is,' burst in Janet, 'that the most godly men in all of Scotland, the field preachers of the Covenant, are all in prison now and like to die there. James Renwick is the only one still active in the whole kingdom, and his days are likely numbered too.'

'That is true,' responded Mackay, 'but what has that to do with me?'

'They've all been sent there by the Privy Council,' said Thomas. 'Mostly by your fellow councillor, Claverhouse. I believe you know him quite well?'

'I know him very well, but your intelligence is seriously at fault if you think he and I are friends. We may serve the same king, but our opinions differ quite violently.' The general spoke with feeling!

'Our petition is that the ministers imprisoned on the Bass Rock and at Blackness Castle be released, or at least moved to some place where conditions are more humane. We have already petitioned for Rev John Blackader to be moved, for he is old and ill, and will surely die soon if he is left there.' Janet coloured as she spoke. 'But the Privy Council will have none of it!'

'We would ask you to plead this case with Claverhouse. He is close to the king, and we believe that, if he could be won over, our request might be acceded to.'

'Do I detect some personal concern, Miss Cleland?'

Janet bit her lip and blushed scarlet!

Major General Hugh Mackay continued his journey south next morning, deep in thought.

September 1685. Hounslow Heath.

'Your Majesty, your Anglo-Scots Brigade is drawn up in review order. There are two hundred and forty-one officers, and three thousand and seven men on parade. Sire!' Mackay, Brigade Commander, brought his sword to the recover with a flourish.

King James acknowledged the salute with a slight bow, and began to ride slowly along the front rank of Mackay's own regiment, which headed the parade. Close behind the King rode his aides-de-camp, led by Brigadier John Graham of Claverhouse.

'Your Majesty, may I present Lieutenant-Colonel James Mackay, my brother and commander of Mackay's Regiment.' Again James bowed, but made no comment. The inspection continued until the King had reviewed all six regiments on parade. As the party drew up at the front of the parade to receive a final Royal Salute, James leant over in the saddle and spoke to Mackay. 'Your Brigade is the best We have at Our command. We are glad to have them here, and We commend you for your diligence in their training, and the expedition with which you answered Our summons.' Turning to Claverhouse he said, 'Do you not agree, Brigadier?'

Claverhouse went red in the face and made an unintelligible reply.

Later in the marquee which had been set up to entertain the royal party, Claverhouse cornered Mackay. 'Scoury, I suppose now that you are a Privy Councillor and outrank me, you think you can replace me in the King's good books?'

'I do not seek to upstage you, Brigadier Graham. I am about to sail for Holland and you will probably never see me again. But I do have one favour to ask of you.'

'You ask a favour of me? Huh! That's pretty rich!'

'Nevertherless I will ask it, and trust to your honour that you will consider it seriously.' He knew that Claverhouse would not be able to ignore a challenge to his honour.

'You and I are both men of conscience. We may have different views, but we both hold to these views with total conviction.'

John Graham nodded. He was obviously taking Mackay's words seriously.

'There are some men of sincere conscience in Sotland who are languishing in prison and like to die. The Privy Council, you and I, put them there, and the Privy Council has the power to save their lives.'

'You speak of these rebellious spawn the Cameronians?'

'I speak of their ministers who seek to lead them to Christ.'

'To hell, you mean! Even their icon Calvin denounced rebellion!'

'You cannot deny that you have hounded them and brutalised them, and they have not responded with like violence.'

'What of Kennoway and Stewart, and the Curate of Cairsphairn?'

'Yes, it's amazing how these three deaths are called up time and again, despite those responsible having been expelled from the

Societies. On the other hand, scores of covenanters have been executed, and hundreds imprisoned and tortured, many by your orders!'

Claverhouse remained silent for a moment. 'Then what would you have me do, Scoury?'

'I would have you propose to the Council that those ministers in prison should be released on condition of good behaviour, or at least moved to a more humane place. To be sentenced to The Bass is a death sentence, and well you know it!'

'I will consider the matter. I make no promise, but I will consider it.'

'And I thank *you*, sir. I know you for a hard man, but I believe you to be fair.'

♣

Claverhouse stood on the quay at Greenwich and watched as Mackay and the leaders of his Brigade boarded the sloop to return to Holland. 'Wonder if we will ever meet again,' he thought.

Little did he realise that next time he met Mackay, the outcome would be his own death!

CHAPTER THIRTEEN

"ESCAPE FROM THE BASS"

August 1685. The Bass Rock.

A LEXANDER SHIELDS WAS MARCHED UP through the prison area, not far above the waterline, to the Governor's house. He found himself in a large cold room, with a grim looking man in uniform seated behind a table. Otherwise the room was bare. Alex dripped on the floor and shivered. It was a cold day and there was no way he would warm up after his ducking at the landing place, unless he could remove and dry his clothes.

'Mr Alexander Shields!' It was an accusation rather than a question. 'You are quite famous, sir.'

'And who might you be?' asked Alexander angrily, only to receive a blow to the kidneys from the butt of his escort's musket. He gasped in pain!

'I'll ask the questions here, I am the Governor! I hold the power of life and death over all on this Rock.'

'You hold no power over me, other that that which God allows.' Another agonising blow to the kidneys, which laid Alex out on the floor.

'It would seem your God allows me quite a lot of power at the moment,' said the Governor in a dangerously controlled voice. 'You breathe, eat, drink and sleep at my discretion. I am so pleased to have another of you canting ministers in my tender care. I have two others, one of whom I expect to die very soon.'

'And what is that to you, sir?'

'To be candid, very little indeeed! I think the Rock and the world will be well rid of all your type, Mr Shields. Put him with Blackader— maybe the smoke will choke him to death. Take him away!'

The soldier grabbed hold of the chain between his still manacled hands, and unceremoniously dragged him from the room. Once outside he produced a key and removed the manacles. 'It's me that's gye sorry tae treat ye this way,' he said. 'The Governor will hae us brutalise the prisoners tae break them, and when we are wi' him we maun pretend.'

'You pretend pretty well!' remarked Shields, rubbing his aching kidneys.

'Follow me, if ye will, sir,' and the soldier led Shields back down to the prison level where there was an open courtyard, into the wall of which were set a number of heavy doors and barred windows. The sea spray burst over the top of the wall periodically, and the courtyard was awash with bitterly cold water. The escort led the way to a doorway set back in the wall and up a few steps. Unlocking and throwing open the door with a resounding crash, he cried out, 'Here's another Reverend gentleman tae bear ye company Mr Blackader.' Rancid black smoke billowed out of the open door. 'Aw right! In wi' ye!' and giving Shields a good shove, the door clanged shut behind him. Alex half fell down the shallow flight of steps and ended up on the floor. He retched in the thick black smoke that filled the place. When he recovered sufficiently to get up on one knee, he was able to see better, for the smoke thinned as one got higher. He was able to descry at the end of the room, on a wooden shelf about waist height, an old man, coughing violently.

'Reverend John Blackader?'

'Aye, that's me. I've been here since April '81, and I fear I'll not be much longer.' He broke off into a fresh fit of coughing.

'We must get you moved to a better place.' Alex was deeply concerned. 'I know your sons in Holland.'

'There is no better place. This is the best and driest cell there is.' At that a burst of spray crashed through the barred opening that looked over to Tantallon Castle. 'Whiles I stick my head out to breathe some fresh air,' said the old minister.

As the months went by Alex grew more resigned to his condition. John Blackader died in January 1686, to the great sorrow of all the prisoners, for he had been their spiritual father, encouraging and strengthening them, even as his own strength ebbed away. Even the Governor showed some slight remorse as his body was rowed away for burial on the mainland. The only ministers now left on the Rock were John Dickson, minister of Rutherglen when the *Declaration* was made there in 1679, and John McGilligan of Fodderty.

The Bass Rock, Courtesy of David Morrison

The prisoners were allowed to walk on the Rock in pairs at the whim of the Governor, for John McGilligan's influential friend Lord MacLeod had remonstrated on his behalf when he visited the Bass. Alex welcomed these breaks, even though the weather was often foul! The wind was so fierce that one day a servant girl was blown off the top and dashed to her death in the breakers below. After Blackader's death, Alex had been moved to another cell which he shared with John Dickson, so the two ministers usually were let out to walk together.

'What would I not give for some fresh meat,' said John, as they sat in the small herb garden on the summit of the Rock. 'Do you think they might sell us one of these scrawny sheep?'

'I doubt it, for they are destined for the Governor's table. But I hear the guards will get one a gannet for a few pence?' said Alex, 'Or an egg for a ha'penny?'

'Quite right, my good friend, but have you ever tasted gannet?'

'It's got to be better than the awful salt beef we get fed. I reckon we get the reject barrels from the navy!' Pulling a cherry from one of the stunted trees ringing the garden, 'Here John, fresh fruit!'

'Save your cynicism for someone else. I've been here for six years, and I don't find it funny! I've not even had one visitor.'

'Look at that wee chapel! How nice it would be to have a service up here instead of down in the prison block.'

'They'd never let us all out together for it, and anyway its full of ammunition! Pretty godless use for a nice wee kirk!'

'Talking of visitors, Major Learmont is due to for a visit by his wife and daughters next week. He has asked if I might meet with them also. I'm not really sure why, for I had not seen him since Bothwell until I arrived here, and I don't know the family very well. But it will be wonderful to see and speak with women again.'

Dickson pulled a wry face. 'Lucky you! Lucky him! He's only been here since '83!'

'Yes but he was in hiding for sixteen years before that. He must be the oldest prisoner. Near eighty!'

♣

As the boat with Mrs Learmont and her three daughters approached the landing place, there were faces at every barred window overlooking the slipway. Fortunately it was a calm day and the ladies landed safely, assisted by an unusually unctuous Governor. 'Your husband awaits you anxiously, ma'am.'

'Pray, take us to him directly!' Mrs Learmont was not about to be overly gracious to her husband's jailer.

When she and her daughters were ushered into the interview room in the Governor's house where Major Learmont waited, she gave a cry and rushed to embrace the grey figure huddled in a chair.

'Joseph! Joseph! What have they done to you!' Turning fiercely to the Governor she said, 'I see the rumours are true, and that you do hound these elderly saints to their deaths!' For once the Governor was at a loss for words.

'Wheesht, wheesht, Jeannie. You will not help me by such speech. Let us not waste this precious time together. And my beloved daughters! How wonderful you were allowed to come over!' They came forward to embrace their father.

'But who....?' The question died on the old man's lips, as his wife let out a warning hiss.

'He hasn't seen Janet, our eldest,' in an explanatory aside to the Governor, 'for many years. She has been overseas in Holland.'

Whatever condition his body might be in, Joseph's mind was still razor sharp, and he realised that something was afoot. 'Janet, my dear, how wonderful to see you. I expected only your sisters,' as the other two girls came to hug their father.

'Might we have some privacy?' asked Mrs Learmont haughtily.

'Someone must be present whenever a prisoner receives visitors, ma'am. Colonel Graham's orders.'

'But we need hardly detain you yourself, Governor. Is there not some subordinate who might do the job as well?' The Governor hesitated, torn between demonstrating that he indeed had subordinates, and a desire to hear what went on for himself. Eventually he went to the door and called out.

'Corporal! Ask Lieutenant Brown to step this way!' Brown was generally liked by the prisoners, because he was treated badly by the Governor who resented his family connections. He arrived at the same time as Alex, which was just as well, for Alex could not control a start as he realised that this was not Janet Learmont, but Janet Cleland!

'Look Jeannie. Here is our old friend Mr Alexander Shields come to say hello.'

'Dear Alex, how are you faring?' Mother was observing the proprieties, as she shook his hand, ignoring his pale and wasted looks.

'You remember our daughters, I am sure? 'Phemie, Alison and Janet.' Each of the girls bobbed a curtsy at her name, but the width of the room remained between Alex and them. 'Mr Brown... might it not be possible for us to be private as a family for a short time?'

'It's more than my commission's worth, ma'am. But I will go and sit out of earshot in the far corner of the room. That's the best I can do.' Charles Brown felt sorry for old Learmont who, in his opinion, should have been pardoned long ago and allowed to go home to die. Besides, they can hardly be plotting to escape from the Rock. No one has ever managed that!

The family huddled round their elderly father whilst Alex and Janet stood slightly to one side. 'We're hoping to get you off this Rock,' whispered Janet.

'Not possible!'

'Not to escape from the Rock, but to have you transferred to Edinburgh Tolbooth, and to escape from there.'

Alex felt the beginnings of hope stirring deep inside him. 'They will never countenance moving ministers, of all people. We are the most dangerous to them, and the most hated.'

'Mackay's last act before he returned to Holland was to request Clavers to move the ministers on the Bass to better quarters ashore.'

'And when did Clavers ever listen to Mackay?'

'He was pretty curt at the time, but we hear from our contacts in the Privy Council that he has since brought the matter up. Who knows what may be achieved through prayer, dear Alex.' She reached out to grasp his hand, but as she did so, the Governor burst into the room, and seeing Brown in the corner and the family huddled together, shouted, 'That's it! Interview over! Do you take me for a fool? Madam, take your leave, and take your ill mannered brood with you!' With which he virtually dragged Mrs Learmont out of the room, followed by her weeping daughters.

'Go! Go, Janet! And God be with you, my dearest.'

'And with you my love.'

8 Oct 1686. Edinburgh Tolbooth.

The Lords of His Majesty's Privy Council do hereby grant, order, and warrant to Colonel Graham of Claverhouse, Commander-in-Chief now upon this place, to cause bring in prisoners to the Tolbooth of Edinburgh by a sufficient guard, the ministers that are at present prisoners either in the garrison of the Isle of Bass or Blackness...

Waus, keeper of the Tolbooth, was always glad to see old acquaintances delivered back to his care. 'Sign there Mr Waus,' said Lieutenant Brown, 'and they're all yours.' Hastily pocketing the delivery note, Charles Brown beat a hasty retreat down the High Street and disappeared into Steils' Tavern which the city train bands frequented, not re-emerging until the *wee sma 'oors,* and looking decidedly the worse for wear.

'I suppose ye'll want the superior accommodation?' asked Waus mockingly. 'I've nae room in the Iron Hoose, so ye'll just have tae tak whits left.' He escorted Dickson and Shields to a small stuffy room close under the eaves, which barely had space for the two bunks it contained. 'Ye'll be comfy here, I'll be bound,' slamming and locking the door behind them.

'Well, at least it's dry,' said Alex with a grimace.

♣

'Are you no the lucky yin, Mr Shields. There's a leddy tae see ye. A Miss Learmont. Says ye were on the Bass wi' her daddy.' The turnkey leered at the female figure standing on the landing. 'Ah cannae let him oot, ye ken missie. Ye'll jist hae tae step inside. Chap on the door when ye're finished.'

Alex and Janet could hardly contain themselves while the heavy door was being unlocked, and no sooner was it closed behind her, than they fell into each other's arms. John Dickson, embarrassed, tried to be as inconspicuous as he could.

'Janet, how did you get in?'

'The keeper knew that Major Learmont's family had visited him on the Bass, and that you were present, so I think he felt that made it acceptable for him to do the same. But listen carefully Alex, for we have a plan.'

Alex looked anxiously through the barred grille in the door, but the landing outside was quite empty.

Janet went on: 'We have planned your escape for 22 October.' Turning to John Dickson, 'John, we need your help. I am sorry we cannot liberate you both.'

'You know that I will be glad to help. I've been in prison so long now that I wouldn't know where to go.'

'Bless you, John. Now Alex, stop looking like a lovesick cow and listen.' Shields gave every appearance of attention. 'I will come to visit on that day wearing two dresses, and with a spare bonnet hidden in my reticule. The guards get slack around midday, looking for their food to be brought, and usually a pint or two of porter with it. Some of them even slip out to see their lassies in the High Street. So I will arrive just before midday and be locked in with you. You put on the other dress and bonnet. You must prepare a dummy to wear your clothes. You have straw in the mattresses for that? We have bribed Udney the deputy-keeper, to let two out where only one came in. It's dangerous, for we may be betrayed, but it's as good a chance as we are likely to get.'

'But...'

'You'll pass easily, for you are shorter than me.' Alex could not deny it! 'If your friend Sir Alexander Gordon fooled Clavers' men in a woman's dress after Bothwell, you can do it too! John, when we are let out, you must be in evidence. If they ask why Alex is lying on the bed, tell them he has prison fever. That should keep them out of the cell!'

♣

On the appointed day the plan went perfectly, and soon after noon Alex found himself at liberty, walking down the High Street with his beautiful Janet by his side. Passing the sentries at the Netherbow Port, where Richard Cameron's shrivelled head still adorned a spike, they were soon on the road to Colinton. Once there they could take to the moors and Janet's local knowledge should keep them hidden from enemy patrols, as they made for the safety of Lanark and the covenanting country beyond.

♣

Janet and Alex had safely reached Lanark, and were in hiding in the Learmont's house. The secret vault where Major Learmont had hidden for sixteen years before being captured and sent to the Bass, still provided an escape route in the event of a surprise visit from the authorities.

'They searched our house in Edinburgh,' said Mrs Learmont, 'and arrested our two serving women, Isobel Boyd and Janet Anderson. Someone in the Tolbooth may have overheard you addressed as Janet, my dear, and jumped to a wrong conclusion. Fortunately both women knew nothing of the escape plan, so you should be safe enough.'

'Yes, but what about you!' burst out Janet. 'You saw Alexander on the Bass, all three of you, and I passed for a Miss Learmont in the Tolbooth.'

'We will put out trust in the Lord, and be quite safe,' said Mrs Learmont. 'If we return quietly to our Edinburgh house, there is nothing they can pin on us, for we had no hand in the escape. So your secret is safe with us. Not but that we would gladly have gone to jail for your sake, for it doesn't look as if my Joseph will survive the Bass.'

'We leave tonight,' said Alex, 'by the secret passage. And we will not tell you wither we are bound, so that you can truthfully deny all knowledge of our whereabouts.'

Three days later. Cumnock.

'I have to join James Renwick and the Cameronians in Galloway,' said Alex.

'My duty as a minister lies there.'

Janet and he were sitting disconsolately beside the Lugar Water.

'I know. I know,' Janet sighed. 'Will there ever be a time when we can just bide quietly at home? William is back in Holland, leaving Margaret heavy with child, and how many other good women are widowed or alone because of these accursed times!'

'Janet, my dear, I have something I must say to you.' Janet went white at his tone. She knew there was bad news on the way. Taking her hand which lay limply on her lap he went on with downcast eyes. 'You know I love you?' She gulped! 'You know that I have never loved any other woman, and my heart is yours forever?' Janet choked her tears back.

'But.' (Why did there have to be a *but*? Always a *but*.) 'You know very well that I have committed my life to God's service, and that when I join Renwick, my life will be worth nothing.'

'It's worth nothing now! On the fugitives' roll, price on your head, escaped prisoner! To whom is your life worth anything except to me?' Her tears flowed unchecked now, as she looked at her lover through the mist. 'You are telling me that you cannot love me anymore. You are telling me that you cannot marry me! You are forcing me to marry James Scot.'

'James Scot?'

'Yes! James Scot!' she screamed at him. 'I have been promised to him since before you and I met. By my dead father! I had just got the courage up to tell him that I would not marry him, despite the family implications of land and seizin', and now you tell me you can't marry me!' She threw the beaker of water in her hand full in his face and made as if to rise, wrenching her other hand from his grasp.

'Janet! Janet! Do not let us part like this.'

'Dear Lord, will these killing times never end? For a loving God you ask too much of your servants!' But she allowed Alex to gather her into his arms one last time, as her sobbing gradually subsided.

So they parted there, on the banks of the Lugar Water.

CHAPTER FOURTEEN

"WITH THE HILLMEN"

5 Dec 1686. Galloway.

'**JAMES, THANK GOODNESS** that I have found you at last!'
Rev James Renwick was seated by the fire in his Wood of
Earlston hideout, where Sir Alexander Gordon had sheltered from his
pursuers after evading them at Hamilton. Lady Earlston was directing
her staff in the preparation of food for a conventicle to be held nearby
on the morrow.

'Alexander Shields!' James Renwick looked pleased. 'We heard that
you had escaped, but you seemed to disappear completely afterwards.
No doubt you went to ground as so many of us have? I am truly glad to
see you, for I am sorely in need of help hereabouts. There is only me to
minister to the whole of the Societies.'

Shields turned to his hostess. 'Lady Earlston, what news of your
husband?'

'Still in jail, Mr Shields! From the Tolbooth to the Castle, to
Blackness Castle, to the Bass, and back to the Tolbooth. The sentence of
death after Bothwell still hangs over him, and they play with him as a
cat does a mouse, examining him under torture and bringing out the
"boot" to threaten him with. But the Governor of the Bass seems to have
taken pity on him and has permitted me to visit my husband. So we have
been blessed even in the midst of our tribulation, for Thomas was born
to us last year, and as you see, I am carrying again.'

'And what news of your nephew Sir Robert Hamilton in Holland?'

'That great fool! Since he ousted my husband as representative of the Societies in Europe, he has alienated so many from our cause! He seems to offend a great many people!'

'I have always found Robert Hamilton a true friend to me,' interjected Renwick with a warning look. 'But let's move on. As I said, Alex, I could do with some help, but I cannot ask you to play any active role unless it is approved by the General Meeting. Too many of our people have gone off at a tangent and put us in a bad light. As though things were not bad enough already!'

'May we have some private converse, James? I haven't seen you since that day we parted on the moors above Largs. It's been three years and I have some serious unburdening to do.'

The two clergymen climbed the earthen steps leading up from the dugout, into the wood which dripped with dankness. After they had spent some time in prayer together, they both felt encouraged.

'James, I have to confess my failure under interrogation to live up to the standards of Cameron and Cargill.'

'Whatever do you mean, Alex? We had our observers in the courtroom all through your trial, except when you were before the Privy Council. You behaved magnificently!'

'Then you must know that I capitulated on the *Abjuration Oath*, for I swore to it in part.'

'In part? Which part?'

'They tried continually to get me to condemn your *Sanquhar Protestation* and to subscribe to their grossly biased understanding of it. I was not even allowed to see your document, or indeed even their Oath. So finally in the hope of saving myself from the gallows, I agreed to this statement:

> '*I do abhor renounce and disown in the presence of God that pretended declaration, in so far as it declares war against the king, and asserts that it is lawful to kill all employed by him in Church, State, Army or Country.*"

'Thus far I went and no farther! And may God and you have mercy on my weakness.'

'You may have erred Alex, or perhaps been weak, but you have confessed it, and from your tone I feel sure you are repentant. You did no more than Argyle himself in 1681, for he took the *Test*, "in so far!" You handled it better than a lot of our brethren who have been similarly interrogated.

'I hope I may prove more true than Argyle at least, for he sent Donald Cargill to the gallows.'

'That he did, Alex. And I think he regretted it every day until his death!'

Shields visibly relaxed. He had longed to unburden himself to Renwick for a long time. 'James, I am really longing to see my brother Michael. Do you know whereabouts he is?'

'You will see him at the next General Meeting. Right now he is somewhere in Ayrshire.'

♣

Wanlockhead, the site of the next General Meeting of the United Societies, lay high in the Lowther Hills, north-east of Sanquhar. Alexander Shields stood outside the farmhouse all day, anxiously watching for a distant sign of his brother on the road from Leadhills. Suddenly he felt two strong arms grab him from behind and, as he strove to release himself, heard his brother's voice in his ear.

'A fine picquet you would make! Clavers would be upon us ere you sounded the warning!'

'Michael! Where did you appear from? I have been keeping a sharp lookout.'

'Not sharp enough, brother. I am a hillman now, and travel far and fast by ways not known to others.'

'So I perceive. But well met, brother. Now give me a proper hug!' with which Michael promptly complied.

'I had so hoped you would visit me on the Bass. Your letters were a comfort, but nothing to your presence. I have not clapped eyes on you since the day I landed at Leith from the *Kitchen Yacht*, when the soldiers prevented you and mother talking with me.'

'Alex, I am just as hunted as you are now. Had I visited the Bass it is like I would never have left! As secretary to the Cameronian Societies, I know everyone and everything. I dare not fall into their hands. So I have become the compleat hillman, experienced in woodcraft and moordwelling. Always on the move, always in secret.'

'Well, since you seem to know it all, I would be glad if you brought me up to date. News on the Bass has been mighty scarce, and since I escaped I have been so much in secret that I have hardly heard a word.'

'Tell me first, how came you here? How did you escape? Who helped you?'

'I cannot tell you that, Michael. I have promised never to reveal who helped me escape, for it concerns someone very dear to my heart.'

'Ah well! I hear you escaped in woman's clothes, so I will not seek to impugn any lady's honour.'

'You'd better not, brother!' Alex bristled like a bulldog.

'Peace! Peace! I'm just glad to have you back, Alexander.'

The brothers talked deep into the night, for Alex wanted to be as informed as possible before the meeting the following day. Michael recounted how, despite James Renwick's faithful service to the Cameronian families scattered all over the south and Fife, there were some who sought to bring him down, not only from outside the Societies, but also by a few self-important troublemakers from within.

Michael went on: 'There have been so many scurrilous accusations against him, but he merely says that it is the price for following Christ, who was Himself despised and rejected of men. The servant is not greater than his Master, so he just keeps plugging away, ministering humbly and assimilating the pain.'

'What sort of accusations?'

'Oh really ridiculous things, such as that he excommunicated all the ministers in Scotland! As if Donald Cargill's excommunication was not enough to last us all for several lifetimes! And that he has no effective ministry, although he baptised three hundred children in his first year here!'

'There's more?'

'There's more! That he is a drunkard and a glutton, whereas he barely even eats enough to stay alive. He has often said when pressed to eat, that he never stood up from the table, but that he could have eaten the same again.

'He has even been accused of being in cahoots with the military who hunt him down, on account of the number of his narrow escapes which can only be described as miraculous.'

'But…' Michael was warming to his subject, 'much more dangerous! We are being attacked at the very heart of the reason for our existence, for we are accused of setting up our own government and courts. Since *The Solemn League and Covenant* in 1643 we have had but one aim; to be free to run our own worship, doctrine, church government and discipline, without any man, even the king, imposing his will in those areas. We are ruled in matters of conscience by God, and God alone, and we will hold to that even at the cost of our lives. But we do not seek temporal power or the crown! They call us a state within a state, but that is calumny. Had they not stolen away our freedom of conscience, we would still have been loyal subjects of King James.'

The General Meeting convened on 22 December 1686.

'I wish to inform the Meeting that Mr Alexander Shields arrived at my place of refuge at Earlston Wood on 5 December,' James Renwick opened. 'Many of you will know of his suffering for the Covenant, since he was tried in Edinburgh and immured on the Bass. We have had correspondence anent him from our dear departed colleague, the Rev John Blackader. I too corresponded with him on the Bass, concerning the new *Vindication* of our position that I have been working on.'

William Boyd, who had received his license to preach from the Classes of Groenigen before Renwick's ordination there, stood to speak. 'I knew Mr Shields in Holland and had a high regard for his position in the faith. But I have heard that during his trial, he retracted from the *Sanquhar Protestation,* and that he even accepted the authority of that man James Stewart who calls himself king. Before we proceed further, I must ask Mr Shields to clarify his position.'

'Mr Shields has unburdened himself to me in that respect,' replied Renwick. 'But rather let him speak for himself.'

Alex rose to address the Meeting. 'I find myself bound to admit with great sorrow that I did indeed deny part of the testimony which is acknowledged by these Societies, for I did partially own the authority of the so-called James VII, and I did take the *Oath of Abjuration* in an effort to save myself from certain execution.'

A heavy sigh rose from the meeting. Alex went on: 'I do not seek to excuse or justify my actions. I did not show the resolution which one should expect of one who walks in the footsteps of Cameron and Cargill. But I do most humbly repent of my weakness, and certify that I do stand for all that is contained in Mr Renwick's *Vindication.*'

The meeting simultaneously exhaled in obvious relief!

James Renwick rose again. 'I have discussed the position at length with Mr Shields, and find that he not only agrees with our principles in every detail, but that he also has suggested a number of improvements which will strengthen our public declaration. I have been together with Mr Shields for some time now, and found him not only repentant for his moment of weakness, but also a most effective minister in prayer and counsel. Which of us who can say that we would not have had a moment of weakness under such trial? I have no shadow of doubt as to his sincerity.'

There was a sound of general agreement from the assembled company. James continued: 'You know how stretched we are for ministers with our people spread all over the south and in Fife. I would ask the Meeting to Licence Mr Shields as a Preacher of The Word, with a view to his ordination as soon as possible.'

After some discussion this was agreed to, and Alex became a licensed preacher to the United Societies. Thus began a close association between two outstanding, but quite different young men. Renwick the pastor *par excellence*, for whom no hardship or danger was too much to endure in order to bring help and comfort to the suffering Society people, and Shields, the brilliant theologian and logician, who nevertheless also had the ability to sway his hearers for Christ, but in a less emotional way than Renwick.

It was a perilous time for them both. In a letter to Robert Hamilton, still in Holland, Michael Shields described the current climate of persecution:

'The hand of persecution lies hard on our people. The prisons are filling up daily, with many under threat of death. Some have been summarily executed in the fields, and courts up and down the country are taking a roll of our names, whilst offering freedom to those who go to Mass, Quakers, and all who attend services under government appointed curates or Indulged ministers, but interdicting under pain of death, those who gather on the moors, or anyone who dare give us so much as a drink of water. We are the only ones left in the whole kingdom who continue to hold out for our freedom of worship.'

The next General Meeting was being held at Frierminion, a lonely clachan between Sanquhar, where Richard Cameron had thrown down the gauntlet to the House of Stewart, and Muirkirk close to where he had been killed. The significance was not lost upon those attending. Neither was the fact that they stood at the junction of three great covenanting counties of Ayr, Lanark and Dumfries.

For three days the commissioners discussed and wrestled with the *Informatory Vindication* just completed by Renwick and Shields. This was intended to be the definitive Cameronian statement of faith and action. It sought to explain their point of view about virtually everything they disagreed about with the crown and the established church. It was well understood that the government would inevitably condemn it regardless of content, but it was designed as a statement both to the church universal, and the public at large.

Michael Shields read out the resolution: 'It is resolved that this *Informatory Vindication* be printed and published forthwith, that Mr Alexander Shields be commissioned to attend to this. Further that an amount of £120 Scots be set aside to defray the expenses involved.'

After the meeting, the brothers Shields and James Renwick were deep in consultation. 'It's all very well to commission me to get this document printed and published,' complained Alex, 'but it runs to about five hundred pages in print. I can hardly just walk into John Bryce's print shop in the Saltmarket of Glasgow and ask him to publish it! There is no doubt that it will be vilified as a treasonable paper in the same way that every document of ours since *Rutherglen* has been. This will cost both printer and publisher their heads in Britain. I'll have to go to Holland!'

May 1687. Utrecht.

'Well, here we are back on our old stamping ground,' remarked Alex to his brother. 'I wonder if Professor à Marck might take us in?'

Alexander's old professor was glad not only to give the brothers shelter, but to advise them about printers.

'Professor, you know I have been working on my own *Hind let loose* while in prison on the Bass Rock and after my escape? My brother and I have come to Holland specifically to arrange for the publication of James Renwick's *Informatory Vindication*, which will be of interest to the likes of you, as the definitive Cameronian statement of faith and policy. But my *Hind* is nearly complete, and I am keen to get both published while we are here. Have you any suggestions where we might start looking for a publisher?'

'There are quite a few willing to produce contentious works, particularly if they have a reformed theological bent. But you must remember that the English king still has some influence here as the Stadtholder's wife is his daughter. I suggest you go and talk to Dirk van Ackesdijk or Ernetsus Voskyl. The latter may be particularly helpful, as he only started his business as recently as 1685, and he holds strong protestant views. But they are all keen for business, for our economy is somewhat depressed at present!'

'Right Professor, thank you. At least you have given us something to work on.'

'But probably better still, what about Mr John Haddow right here in Utrecht? He has offered to print the United Societies martyrology, *The Cloud of Witnesses*, at his own expense.'

'Is he not William Cleland's brother-in-law from Douglas? He arrived here with Lord Cardross when they escaped from the Carolinas, after the colony was wiped out by disease and the Spanish.'

'I believe he is! I must also say that these documents will be of considerable interest for the church here in the Netherlands. Certainly

Rev William Carstares who advises Prince William, has a keen interest in whatever comes out of Scotland.'

'We are also bit short of cash to pay for the printing!'

The Professor looked embarrassed! 'I'm afraid I can't help you there! Not my department!'

♣

Michael Shields scratched his head and looked worried. He always hated having to write to ask for money, even though the purpose might be good.

> *To Monsieur Rosin, at the House of Jan Claesan Duyn in New Street, Emden*
>
> *Monsieur,*
>   *Since you are well known to a close friend of ours, Sir Robert Hamilton of Preston, and he informs us that as a Huguenot you have suffered greatly for the cause of Christ, I make bold to approach you to request a loan of funds, so that we may publish my brother's magnum opus,* A Hind let loose, *which is a major treatise on the need for religious freedom, especially in our native land of Scotland.*
>   *I rejoice to tell you that Mr James Renwick's* Informatory Vindication *has already been published here in Utrecht, and copies will soon be available in Scotland and England.   I enclose a copy for your perusal and information.*
>   *If you are willing to advance a sum of 300 Guilders upon sufficient security from my brother and myself, we will be able to proceed with publication, thereby, as we believe, advancing the cause of Christ and protestant freedom in Europe.*
>
>   *I have the honour to be sir,*
>   *Your most obedient servant,*
>   *Michael Shields.*   *Utrecht. 29 July, 1687.*

October 1687. Rotterdam

James Bruce's coffee shop was, as usual, crowded with Scots émigres. The Shields brothers had managed to secure a corner table away from the main flow of customers. They were seated with a military looking man, whom we recognise easily as Captain William Cleland.

'We are headed for home Will,' opened Alex. 'Our mission here is complete. The *Vindication* is published, my *Hind* is already on the press, and Carstares says that he thinks the Stadtholder will be interested in it, as it gives the latest position from a group to whom he looks for positive support. But now it is time for us to return to support James Renwick and the Cameronian Societies. Will you not come with us?'

'My time is not ripe yet, Alex. Soon, but not yet! Next time we will win an overwhelming victory. Next time we are going to change the face of Scottish history. Next time Richard Cameron's prophecy about the throne of Britain will come to pass, when the House of Stewart is overthrown.'

'Do you know something we don't?' asked Michael.

'I know that the leaders and thinkers in both England and Scotland are starting to realise that King James is surreptitiously preparing the way to restore catholicism in both kingdoms, and to destroy the influence of all non-papists. I also know that recently James, alarmed by preparations for war here in Holland, has summoned the Anglo-Scots Brigade again as he did in 1685. But this time the Stadholder refused permission for the rank and file to leave, and of the two hundred officers of the brigade, only sixty were willing to go. General Mackay is now openly for the Covenant cause and will be one of the leaders of the invasion when, not if, it happens. I am a soldier at heart, and I know my duty is to support this expedition however I best can. Probably once again going ahead as a scout, to prepare the way.'

There was stunned silence from Alex and Michael.

'How do you know all this?' whispered Michael.

'Because of my work in 1685. Although Argyle's expedition failed, my secret work has been recognised by "Cardinal" Carstares who has the ear of Prince William himself, as well as others such as the Earl of Leven. And Claverhouse is now a Major-General, second-in-command in Scotland. I don't wish to seem arrogant, but it has been said that I am the one person he fears. That is probably not true, for I doubt if he fears anyone, but it is being said!'

'So you are going to be an *agent provocateur* once more?' asked Alex.

'Not quite. Although I may have some use as a reconnaissance spy in advance of any invasion, this time I believe I will also have a command role to play.'

Alex looked dubious. 'How are you going to achieve that, William? You did not even have sufficient influence to be accepted for service by the Brandenbergers after you got back here in '86, even though most of your companions were. All the Regimental Colonels will be noblemen. I don't disparage your ability to lead men, or your military capabilities, but you are going to need a lot more influence to command anything!'

'Alex, what would you say to a regiment of Cameronians?'

This time the Shields brothers were truly stunned into silence. Both let out a suppressed whistle, and thought deeply.

'William, are you mad?' at length commented Michael.

'You both know that had the Cameronians taken the field in '85, despite Argyle and Cochrane, we might well have won Scotland.'

'And this time we will?'

'This time we will! I believe that a regiment of Cameronians will make a significant difference, not only to an invasion from Holland, but to the future religious freedom in Scotland. Our main problem is snobbery. We Cameronians are humble folk, and few nobles espouse our views. At best we have a few baronets. But we are men who hold an earnest conviction that we are free before God. Our patience has been sorely tried by the brutal persecution since Bothwell, yet Renwick has been able to hold his people in check. What other group in Scotland has such discipline and fighting ability?'

'Clavers' Horse!'

'Well, he *is* the enemy!'

'So what do you propose?'

'The Marquess of Douglas has been a good friend to my family, and his son, the Earl of Angus, will soon be old enough to accept a

Colonelcy, even if he cannot actually take command yet. In that case, the Lieutenant-Colonel will command.'

'And that will be you?'

'I hope so. Jamie Douglas and I have been very close since he was old enough to fish. And I practically grew up in the Marquess's house. Sir Patrick Hume of Polwarth was on the Argyle expedition and has a lot of influence with Prince William. Forbye I am known to General Mackay, as are you Alex, and am assured of at least a captaincy in the invasion force.'

'How does Mackay know of me?' asked Alex.

'Because it was my sister Janet who interceded for you to be moved from the Bass, so that there was a chance of your escape. Surely you knew that, Alex?'

Alex took a long time to answer. 'No-o-o! I didn't know.'

'What's wrong, Alex? You've gone as white as a sheet!'

'You are aware that Janet and I have broken up?'

'I certainly was not, my friend! I have had no word from her since my marriage, which was prior to your escape! Post from Scotland is being intercepted more than previously. I am deeply sorry to hear it, for I had hoped you and I might be even closer than before.'

With a wry smile Alex responded, 'I still hope we can be close friends, Will.'

'Closer than you think. I want you for my chaplain in the regiment. Would you accept that post?'

'I would be very keen to fill such a post Will, but as you know I am a man of peace, and I seek reconciliation wherever possible.'

'I know you are for peace, Alex, but some of your writings seem to contradict that. Part of your *Hind* even seems to support tyrannicide.'

'Perhaps it is somewhat dissimulatory to say that my head and my heart are not always in agreement? What I wrote, though it contains a great deal of personal stuff, was actually presenting the formal Cameronian position. You will recall as far back as 1682, it was resolved that no-one should act independently in any matter involving policy? I do not for one second support murder, but in very exceptional circumstances, I do support execution. That is why I have at times

defended the Archbishop's death, call it what you will. Of course our
enemies castigate us all as violent and unprincipled anarchists!'

'That is why I wrote *Hind,* to try to restore some balance to the
public mind. But you must remember that my writing expressly covers
the church in a seriously broken state. The United Societies have in fact
been a model of forbearance, with only three violent deaths being laid at
our door, four if you count Hamilton's behaviour at Drumclog. In every
case they were clearly for self-defence or rescue, and the suspected
persons have been ejected from, or refused entry into, our Societies.
Compare this with scores of our people executed, both formally and in
the fields, hundreds imprisoned, tortured, or sold as slaves to the
Carolinas, ears cut off, faces branded, women drowned, services of
worship attacked! Surely posterity must admit that we hold the moral
high ground? What we hope and pray for is a return to normality.'

'I agree Alex, that so far the Cameronian position has been
essentially one of self defence. But if we are to raise a regiment, it must
be prepared to take offensive action in support of a new king. Where do
you stand on that?'

'I don't want to get too theological, for I know you are only a simple
soldier.'

' *"Honi soit qui mal y pense!"* I have degrees from both St Andrews
and Leyden in medicine and law, my poems have been published in
Edinburgh, also my Latin *Disputatio* in Utrecht, Alex. *"Quis custodiet
ipsos custodes?"* '

'Ouch! Sorry, Will!'

'Just wanted to make the point that not all soldiers are uneducated
louts!'

'Point taken! So if I may continue…?' Will nodded his assent. 'The
Westminster Confession of 1642 is subscribed to by the Scots Kirk.
Chapter XXIII charges a people to obey the lawful commands of their
king, and gives him the right to wage war, *"upon just and necessary
occasions."* We Cameronians have held that by their tyranny, the House
of Stewart has abrogated its own right to rule, and that their laws about
how we must conduct our worship are unlawful, as conflicting with our
consciences as free men. Therefore we have not had freedom under God
to serve such a king, including serving in his army.'

Will nodded his understanding.

'However,' Alex continued, 'if we were to get a king whom in conscience we could submit to, we would be free to serve in his army, for soldiers serve as an instrument of the State. Romans 13: 4 says: *"...for he beareth not the sword in vain, for he is the minister of God, an avenger to execute wrath upon him that doeth evil."* In such circumstances I would be honoured to serve in a regiment under your command.'

'I am relieved to hear it! Of course I still may not get a regiment, but if I do, I will certainly ask you to be our chaplain. That's assuming you are still alive of course, for I hear you are homeward bound once more, and you will both be hunted men from the moment you arrive.'

'Well in that case, don't be too long before you arrive with Prince William and his army!'

CHAPTER FIFTEEN

"AN EVIL DAY'S WORK"

December 1687. Scotland.

WHEN THE SHIELDS BROTHERS REACHED SCOTLAND once again, it was to discover that King James had not been inactive. In February, June and July of 1687, he had offered three religious tolerations which had the unintended and surprising effect of virtually uniting the Scots nation against him. Whilst the great majority of moderate covenanters had taken advantage of these tolerations, non-roman catholics amongst the ruling class began to realise that their days of influence were numbered. *The Revocation of the Edict of Nantes* by Louis XIV of France in 1685 had given protestants throughout Europe serious cause for concern regarding the intentions of all catholic monarchs, and James was now revealing his plan for Scotland.

The Cameronians were undergoing a particularly trying time, for the tolerances, whilst offering relief to moderate presbyterians, catholics, and quakers alike, specifically excluded the Cameronians. Meetings '*in the open fields, for which... there is not the least shadow of excuse left:... we do herby strictly prohibit and forbid, against all which we do leave our laws and acts of parliament in full force and vigour.*'

By the time that Michael and Alex had reached James Renwick in Galloway, the pressure was worse than ever. Claverhouse and his troops carried out no less than fifteen intense cordon and search operations to seek out Renwick, breaking into cellars and through roofs in their pursuit of the most wanted man in the kingdom. His narrow escapes became legendary, once hiding in a hollow under a rock virtually in sight of his pursuers, once being nearly taken at Peebles as he waited for his horse to be brought. His escapades were so nearly miraculous, that his enemies began to put about a story that he was in league with the troops who sought him, or even in league with the devil! By the end of 1687 he was so exhausted and weak that he could not sit a horse, but had to carried in a litter to preach at conventicles.

♣

Renwick had just preached at Bo'ness, where Donald Cargill had ridden the day the Queensferry Paper was seized. From there he made his way secretly to the home of John Lookup on Castle-hill in Edinburgh.

'Mr Renwick, we are honoured to have you under our roof, and want to take full advantage of your visit to us. Will you lead our family prayers?'

'Gladly, my friend. Come, let us all pray together...'

But unknown to Renwick, Lookup was a trader in contraband goods, and had attracted the attention of the customs authorities. Exciseman Thomas Justice was outside in the street with his ear to the door! He flapped his hand in silent command to his men to be quiet! 'I ken that voice,' he thought. 'That's young Renwick, my life upon it!' As the sun set he silently withdrew down Castle Wynd with his men following him.

Before dawn next day Justice returned with a stronger body of officers and surrounded the house, stationing three men at each door. He then hammered with his baton on the stout street door, which was cautiously opened by none other than Renwick himself. Seeing the excise uniform, he slammed the door in Justice's face, locking and bolting it on the inside.

'I have the traitor Renwick here!' roared the exciseman down the Wynd. 'Aid me, all good citizens! Help me carry this dog to the guardhouse!' Being early morning there were few people abroad, and Justice was alarmed by the sound of a pistol shot from the back of the house. Renwick and two friends had attempted to break out of another door, and James had cleared the way with a shot from his pistol. But as he broke through the cordon, he was almost felled by a blow from the cudgel of one of the officers.

Dizzy from the blow, he half ran, half staggered, down the Castle Wynd towards the Cowgate, his hat blowing off as he ran. He fell twice, pursued by the cries of the excisemen. The second time, a passer-by grabbed him by the scruff of the neck, and held on to him until Justice and his party caught up. 'Drag him to the guardhouse!' he gasped, as he fought to get his breath back. As they manhandled James into the city guardhouse, Captain Graham of the Guard demanded to know what was going on.

'This here is Renwick,' cried Justice. 'We have just taken him!'

'What? This wee bit laddie? Don't tell me this is the Renwick who has been the scourge of the nation? He's nothing but a boy!' replied Graham. At that point Baillie Charters came in, and on learning who the prisoner was, ordered him to be manacled and locked up, until he could appear before the Court. Two days later Captain Graham delivered him to Viscount Tarbet, the Chancellor. 'Now I have delivered Renwick up to justice, let's see what they make of him!'

'You are here,' Tarbet intoned, 'because you deny the authority of the King's Majesty, denounce the cess tax, and maintain that bearing arms to conventicle meetings is lawful!' When James had been searched after his arrest, two pocket books had been found in his possession, containing notes of sermons and initials of a number of people.

'My Lord, these are notes for some sermons already preached by me, therefore I am happy to answer your queries. Firstly, I do indeed reject the authority of James Stewart over me and my people, since he rejects the authority of Almighty God over his life. He professes the fear of God, but his actions belie his words. We have been persecuted far too long!

'As for the cess, it is a tax designed to equip and sustain those who hunt us down. We are required to finance our own tribulation. Pray tell me, where in the world is that accepted as a just law? As for bearing arms at conventicles, self-defence is always legal. That statement was made by Rev Thomas Douglas when the conventicle at Drumclog was attacked by Claverhouse. It still grates with the authorities that we defeated him that day! We bear arms as free men in defence of our inalienable liberty from God above!'

'What about all these initials in your pocket book?' asked Tarbet? 'Some secret code?'

'No, my Lord. They are merely the initials of my correspondents.'

'Well, I must ask you to identify them, for your correspondents are like to be badly wanted men. And what did you correspond about?'

'We corresponded about our suffering as the people of God. You already know all their names. The first two are Alexander and Michael Shields. The rest are well known to you by repute. I break no confidence by telling you who they are. They are already hunted men. But the last I would keep secret, for it is a lady.'

The advocate spoke up: 'If I give my solemn word that she wlll not be harmed on your account, and that if you reveal her identity to us you shall be spared the torture, will you reveal her?'

'You already know that she is one Mrs Millar of Glasgow, and that she is well out of the country and safe. But I would be glad to be spared the torture.'

Renwick's helpful attitude did much to reduce the anger of his interrogators. In fact, from this point on, he got the feeling that they were trying to exculpate him, or even to provide a way of escape. Directly after Viscount Tarbet completed his questioning, James was taken to the Court of Justice where the indictment against him was read out:

> *"You, the said Mr James Renwick, having shaken off all fear of God... and having entered yourself into the society of some rebels of most damnable and pernicious principles and disloyal practises, you took it upon you to be a preacher to these traitors, and became so desperate a villain, that you did openly and frequently preach in the fields, disclaiming against the authority and government of our sovereign lord the king,... asserting that he was a usurper, and that it was not lawful to pay cess or tax to his majesty; but that it was lawful and the duty of subjects, to rise in arms, and to make war against his majesty."*

Then followed the names of jury candidates and the hostile witnesses testifying against him. When he heard that George, Viscount Tarbet was to be a witness, James protested. 'I have already been examined by my Lord!' he exclaimed, but when the name of Major-General Graham of Claverhouse was read out, he merely looked down at his boots. He was returned to the guard house still in shackles.

♣

'There's a leddy tae see ye,' said the jailer, unlocking the door of his cell. None other that James' mother, Mrs Elizabeth Carsan, entered.

'Mother, how came you here? They will not even let any of my friends visit me, but you are welcome above them all!'

'How are you, my dearest boy? Are they treating you right? Are you getting enough to eat? Are you keeping warm?'

'You are like every mother that ever was! Food and warmth are not my main concerns right now. But I can hardly get to praying!'

Elizabeth was greatly disconcerted. 'How so, James? At a time like this you must be constantly in prayer!'

'No Mother, you misunderstand me. I am so full of joy, that I am quite overcome with praise which continually bursts out spontaneously.'

'Well, that is certainly evidence of the Holy Spirit in great measure, but I greatly fear that if they put your head and hands up on the Netherbow Port, along with Cameron and Cargill's and so many other godly men, I will never be able to thole it!'

'You will not have to face that trial, I feel sure Mother, for I have a great peace that my body will not be abused after death.'

On 8th February he appeared again before the Court of Justiciary to answer to the indictment. 'Do you admit the charges brought against you?' demanded the clerk of the court.

'All but where it is said, "I have cast off all fear of God"; That I deny utterly, for it is because I fear to offend God, and violate His law, that I am standing here to be condemned. You brought the same false charge against the Rev Donald Cargill, when all the world knew him to be a man of God.'

James was found guilty and sentenced to be executed in the Grassmarket on the following Friday. 'Do you desire a longer time to prepare for your death?' asked the Justice-General.

James shrugged. 'It matters not to me. My Master's time will be the best time.'

Episcopal clergy were now allowed to visit him, but not his own friends. Some, like Bishop Paterson, showed real concern, whilst others merely wanted the notoriety of leading this high profile covenanter into the episcopal, or even catholic way. Despite many attempts to get him to retract his testimony by offers of leniency, or even pardon, he withstood them all. On the morning before his execution the chief jailer told him he might still save his life, if he merely signed a petition for mercy. The fact was, that Renwick's execution was going to have a profoundly bad effect on public opinion, for the populace now began to realise the injustices they all suffered under. The authorities would have been glad to find any excuse to pardon James, but he did not give them one!

He was summoned before the Privy Council on 14th February, and cross-examined about the *Informatory Vindication*, copies of which by now had appeared in Scotland. He was told of the Council's leniency in delaying his execution for a week without even so much as an appeal from him. Again he replied that it was all one to him when he died

♣

Execution morning, 17th February 1688, was a mist of greyness. A sea-haar had drifted in from the Forth, and all Edinburgh was cold and dank. James' mother and sisters had been permitted to visit him at breakfast time, but although he was firm and cheerful, they were full of tears. At length the drums could be heard and the jailer summoned him from the cell.

The place of execution, the Grassmarket, was packed with a silent and sullen crowd. The common people surrounded the gallows, and the gentry sat in the upper windows of the houses overlooking the market. The gallows was ringed by the city guard, with a path kept clear for the condemned man. The drums ruffled continuously.

'Just look at his face!' exclaimed Tarbet, who had a window seat. 'Do these Cameronians have no fear of facing eternity? He looks at peace, even joyful! King and Kid, Cargill and Boig, and so many others! They all had this same peace and joy on their faces at the scaffold! What is it with these people? Never have I had such evidence of joy on *my* face, I'll warrant! I fear to meet my Maker, but these men positively exult at the prospect!'

'Maybe they have the right after all, my Lord?' quietly responded Sir John Dalrymple, the king's advocate.

Renwick climbed up onto the platform. The drums continued.

'May I not have some quiet to address my last words, as is customary?'

'You are to say nothing!' responded the hangman, as the drums rolled louder.

'I *will* say what the Lord has given me! You have no authority over me but what He allows!' He turned to the crowd. 'Spectators, I am come this day to lay down my life for adhering to the truths of Christ, for which I am neither afraid nor ashamed to suffer... I am this day to lay down my life for disowning the usurpation and tyranny of James Duke of York, for preaching that it was unlawful to pay the cess expressly exacted for bearing down the Gospel and for teaching that it was lawful for people to carry arms for defending themselves at their meetings for the persecuted Gospel. I think a testimony for these is worth many lives; and if I had ten thousand, I would think it little enough to lay them all down for the same.'

'Enough! Be silent now!' The hangman was truculent!

'I have near done. Ye that are the people of God, do not grow weary of maintaining your witness, for there is a storm coming that will try Scotland to its foundations.'

'Up the ladder, ye blatherskite! Right the noo!' The drums rolled yet louder.

James Renwick paused with his feet on the ladder. To the one friend who had been allowed to accompany him at the end, he turned and said: 'Tell my people not to be weary or discouraged.'

With that the ladder was kicked from under him, and he swung free. The drums fell silent as his body convulsed in his dying throes. A great groan went up from the crowd and many wept.

'I think perhaps we have done an evil day's work here today,' said Tarbet to Dalrymple.

James Renwick was the last person to be formally executed for his faith in Scotland. He was 26 years and two days old.

CHAPTER SIXTEEN

"PRELUDE TO INVASION"

May 1688. South Queensferry.

'**Y**OU'RE SURE WE ARE SAFE TO LAND HERE, CAPTAIN?' Dr William Blackader was nervous being put ashore so close to Edinburgh, having already spent time immured there after the Argyle expedition of 1685.

'Och Doctor, dinna fash yersel'. The watchers on the coast are few and far between now, what with the country in the stramash it is. Even the excisemen go to bed at night for fear they will be attacked if they try to intercept contraband. The Hawse Inn is in good hands, and you will be well received there.'

'Better than Donald Cargill was?'

'Of course, Doctor. Do you think we are still in the "Killing Times?" Dinna play clever wi' me!'

Dr Blackader, and his companion Captain William Cleland, were even able to step ashore at the slipway, and walk comfortably up to the Inn. No sign of any patrol!

'This is a lot easier than Druridge Bay,' said Cleland. His companion raised one eyebrow quizzically. 'Before Argyle in 1685,' answering the unspoken question. 'The last time I came home.'

'Well, I certainly hope it turns out better than my experience in Orkney on the same expedition! I ended up in a dungeon in Edinburgh Castle!'

'How did you escape?' asked Will.

'My companion Spence was brutally tortured with the boot, but fortunately, as I was being taken up to the Castle, I saw my sister, and was able to warn her by signs that she must destroy the hat in my baggage. It had incriminating letters in it, but fortunately she twigged on. Then I managed to smuggle a letter out to Pensionary Fagel in Holland, who persuaded Prince William to champion my case—with good results.'

'It surely won't happen again!'

But of course it did! Blackader found himself back in the same dungeon within the month, this time accompanied by Captain Aenaes Mackay, one of the General's nephews.

But by that time, Cleland was well on his way to the south-west.

♣

A few days later William slipped through the postern gate at Cambusnethan and stood under the rowan tree. The house was dark and silent. Expertly he threw a piece of gravel at a window, to be immediately answered by the cry of a baby. He desisted.

'Who's there? Show yourself!' The blunderbuss sticking out of the window looked as big as Margaret herself!

'Wheesht, woman. You'll wake the bairn!'

'Will?... Will!... Oh, Will!' There was no doubt by now that the bairn was well and truly awake, as Margaret rushed down the stairs and met her husband at the back door. Their tears mixed as they embraced, and it was a long time before either spoke.

They sat at the kitchen table upon which young William slept in his basket. 'He's wonderful,' breathed Will senior, gazing admiringly at his son.

'I am glad to see that you are not so much of a soldier that you cannot be a father too!'

'Aye! He'll make a grand soldier!' Margaret threw a ripe pear at him!

Next morning Will took stock of his situation. 'I will have to travel far and fast as I did in '85, to assess the situation and report back to Pensionary Fagel, so he can brief Prince William in good time.'

'I might have known it! Here for one night and then off into the blue! I feel more like a kept woman than a wife! Can you not stay a few days at least?'

'Dear wife, there will come a time when I can stay at home. But not until all our friends are freed from prison or exile, and Scots are free to worship as they choose.'

Margaret sighed a resigned, but weary, sigh!

Three days later. Castle Dangerous, Douglas.

'My Lord, things are come to a very close pass. Since I last visited you here in '85, the climate in Holland has changed radically. Prince William is now ready to lead an invasion upon England, with a diversionary move on Scotland if necessary. Once more I am here to scout out the land, for time spent in reconnaissance is seldom wasted.'

The Marquess of Douglas was pacing up and down the gallery. James, Earl of Angus sat on the fender seat by the fire. 'You are quite correct of course, Will. The situation is very different now. Few are left in any doubt as to King James's intention to make Scotland a Roman Catholic country. In which case the persecution since the Restoration will seem like nothing, especially here in covenanting country. This time all Scotland save the highlands is ready to rise, nobles and commons alike.'

'My Lord, I have a delicate matter to raise.'

'You were always a straight talker, Will. Out with it!'

'You are aware how the Cameronians are looked down upon by most of the nobility, as being from common stock, and of little influence?'

Douglas nodded.

'You are also aware that had they risen in arms in '85, the story might have been very different. In Scotland we have always held that every man is as good as another, whatever his blood?'

Douglas nodded again.

'But the reality is that such a position is only recognised by the bonnet-lairds and the like, while the nobility still cling to their superiority. But the nobility hold their titles by courtesy of the king, and we have witnessed a monumental struggle between the divine right of kings and the rights of man, since the Stewarts took over the English throne in 1603.'

Another nod.

'And the fact is that the rights of man will triumph in the end, because that is indeed the right! And the only people in the kingdom who have never resiled from that position are the Cameronians. The kirk caved into the Indulgences, in the highlands the rights of the clan take precedence over individual rights, (not a bad system!), and the nobility spends its time "trimming" from one regime to the next. Which leaves one with the Cameronians as the only group in the country who have steadfastly held their ground.'

At last Douglas spoke: 'I can't fault your reasoning Will, but I don't see where you are going?'

'My Lord, now is the time for those of the nobility who truly believe in a free Scotland to stand up and be counted. The Cameronians have the potential to be a brilliant fighting force, but they need a noble leader to give them credibility. Will you not give your name to such a regiment?'

The Marquess took another turn or two up and down the gallery, lost in thought. Suddenly James burst out: 'Father take me, I beg of you! You are too old to go campaigning, and I am still but a boy! Let me show the world that the House of Douglas still has the blood of the Black Douglas in its veins! Let me lead the Cameronian Regiment!'

His father looked him in the face. 'Jamie, you are but seventeen years old, and your education is not yet complete.'

'The Black Douglas joined Bruce when he was only twenty!'

'Well, when you are twenty you can become a Colonel, not before!'

'My Lord, there is a way round this.' Cleland looked embarrassed.

'And what might that be, Mr Cleland?' The Marquess did not look pleased at the interruption.

'The Earl could become Colonel of a regiment now, but take command only when he is twenty years old. It the meantime the regiment would be commanded by its Lieutenant-Colonel.'

'Who would be you, I suppose?' He paused! 'Will, you have been like a son to me, growing up in my house, and mentoring Jamie here since he could walk. I know of no-one more worthy to command a regiment of Cameronians, and if I have your word that you will not call Jamie into active service before he completes his education, I will give the scheme my blessing.'

James Douglas, Earl of Angus, let out a most unbecoming whoop of joy!

'There is just one small problem,' said Will.

'What's that?' asked Jamie.

'We have to overthrow the House of Stewart first!'

♣

By early July Cleland had made his way by night marches over the high moors to Wood of Earlston, Galloway.

'Man Alex, you are as hard to track down as was Renwick!'

'Of blessed memory,' rejoined Alexander Shields.

'Yes indeed! And you still live in the wettest place on the face of the earth!' Will took off his dripping hat and drenched cloak, and let them fall in a sodden heap in the corner.

'Well, at least this hideout has remained secure through the years, and Lady Earlston keeps us well supplied with victuals. That's when she's not on the Bass or Blackness with her husband of course!'

'We live in crazy times Alex. I suppose she is pregnant again?'

'Need you ask?'

'And now that you have assumed Renwick's mantle, you will be as hunted as he was, I'm sure!'

'That's true, but Clavers, now a Major-General by the way, has been much in London with the King, or at his estate in Fife. The Stewart power is on the wane and many who have been brutalising innocent people now go in fear of their lives. Things are changing.'

'The whole situation is changing and our stance will soon be justified! Not that that will help the dead!' he said bitterly. 'How is Janet?'

'And it's you that is the great fool, Alex! She is to marry James Scot as soon as the country is settled! I don't want to talk about it!''

One could have cut the atmosphere with a knife!

Later, strengthened by a bowl of good broth, the old friends were finally able to get down to business.

'You are aware that I have but recently arrived from Holland?' Alex nodded.

'I am doing what I did in '85, going up and down the country, talking with rich and poor alike, and discovering that King James has sunk his own ship by turning much power over to papists.'

'And it's going to get worse Will.'

'Yes, it's going to get much worse!'

'But?'

'But this time Prince William of Orange will lead the expedition in person! He has a good claim to the crown, which is reinforced by his wife Mary, daughter of James Stewart. This is a properly planned invasion; fifteen thousand strong, with Hugh Mackay and his brigade in the van. His old comrade in arms, General John Churchill, is rumoured to be ready to change sides, and of the Scots' army, only Clavers' Horse, The Royals, and Buchan's Greybreeks are likely to remain loyal to James.'

'Then you don't need us!'

'But we do! We need you desperately! We need the Cameronians to provide some stability for Scotland until Mackay sorts out the English situation and gets up here.'

'You think we would provide stability? You may be seriously mistaken! I have been having the greatest difficulty keeping the Societies in check!'

Before their October meeting at Wanlockhead, the United Societies had discussed *ad nauseam* the problem of whether or not they should support William of Orange if and when he landed. Everybody was thoroughly fed up with the subject! The argument had been going on since July, and here they were already in October, with every indication that the Prince of Orange would land within a month or so. A definite course of action must be decided upon!

Finally Alexander Shields had, for the umpteenth time, drafted a paper for submission to the General Meeting. In this he endeavoured to set out a clear intention for the Societies, but the excessively independent-minded covenanting spirit made this task virtually impossible.

However the paper had finally been drafted, and Michael Shields as the clerk, read out the proposal:

> *'It is hereby resolved that duty and safety require us to assume a posture of defence, for it would be a reproach against us if we, who have so far borne arms in the cause of liberty and religion, were not to continue to do so.*
>
> *We will not take the field if the invasion is only against England. But if the expedition includes Scotland, we will muster to the place in the kingdom closest to the Dutch, and some of our number should be stationed in Edinburgh for the purpose of providing intelligence to all quarters, once the Dutch reach Scotland.*
>
> *It is agreed that we may co-operate with the Dutch against the common enemy, to supply them with intelligence, to accept ammunition from them, and to accept training in the art of war. However we are not prepared to accept Dutch officers over us, or to come under Dutch command.'*

As so, as often before, the meeting erupted into a cacophony of angry voices, some refusing to take part in any insurrection whilst others were willing to lead it! Finally, the Moderator, after much banging on the table and shouting, managed to regain some semblance of order.

'We all know what we have endured during the half-century since our National Covenant was signed? Surely we can agree on a course of action so that those who follow our decided course of action, may know that they do so with the formal approval of this meeting?'

The place erupted worse than before! The Moderator rolled his eyes at Michael, who shrugged his shoulders and holding up his hands, looked despairingly at Alex.

Alex jumped to his feet, then jumped on to his seat. 'Friends! Friends! The future of our nation may depend on the decision we make now! We have been persecuted and abused! Our friends, our leaders, and even some of our women and bairns have paid with their blood, so that one day we may be free! That day is upon us! No one is forcing anybody to take up arms! It is the free choice of each individual! But we resolved long ago that we would do nothing on an individual basis, but that we would strive to act as *United* Societies. So Moderator, I move that the resolution we have just heard read is put to the vote, and that we abide by the outcome.'

Further uproar!

The Moderator, shouting above the din, yelled out, 'If you are for the motion say "Aye!" Who is for the motion?'

A great roar of "Aye!" went up. Many waved their hats and some even threw them into the air.

'And who is against the motion? Who is for "Nay?"'

Another shout went through the meeting. "Nay!" "Never!" "Not for us!"; could all be discerned. But this shout was clearly taken up by far fewer than those who had cried "Aye!"

'Very well! The "Ayes" have it! Clerk, mark it down so!'

Late October 1688. Den Haag.

'His Highness will see you now sir.' The equerry stood aside for Cleland to enter the audience chamber.

Seated behind a table in the centre of the floor was William, Prince of Orange, Stadtholder of the United Netherlands. He was flanked by Pensionary Fagel, Rev William Carstares, and Major-General Hugh Mackay.

Cleland bowed.

'Ah Captain Cleland, you are newly returned from Scotland I hear?'

'Two days ago, Your Highness.'

'We know you for a keen military observer and an accomplished spy. What is your view of the current situation there, pray?'

'I have traversed all the southern and border counties, and I can inform Your Highness that matters are very much improved for your cause than they were in '85. Not only are the supporters of the Covenant prepared to rise for you, but this time the nobility and the lairds as well. I believe the reason for this change of heart, is because King James's intention to declare Scotland a catholic country is now finally out in the open.

'So what do you advise?' asked Fagel.

'There are two factors likely to harm your cause, sir; the tolerations of last year, and the birth of the Prince of Wales. Whilst the tolerations may seem at first glance to promote religious freedom for all, in fact thay are intended to promote catholics to positions of authority and force out the protestants. Clergy who accept them are severely restricted, under continual threat of being ousted and replaced by unlettered episcopal curates.'

Carstares broke in: 'We have reports from London that if Your Highness desires support in England, you will be obliged to retain the Church of England as anglican, and that in gratitude for this support, you must guarantee continued entrenchment of episcopacy in Scotland.'

'I am not used to being dictated to, neither will I submit to blackmail!' William of Orange was his own man!

'Your Highness, your Calvinist background is well known, as well as the moderation shown by your lady wife in matters ecclesiastical. Your kindness to Scots exiles, such as Lord Cardross, Sir Duncan Campbell of Auchinbreck and others, has been noted with approval over the water. If it were known that you propose to end epsicopacy as the established religion in Scotland, and that you are not prepared to countenance a catholic heir, the majority of nobles and commons alike will declare for you. Of that I am certain!'

'You speak with great authority sir,' cut in General Mackay.

'General, like you I am a soldier. I speak as I see it.'

'Hmm...You are not afraid to speak your mind!'

'I very much hope not, sir!'

'And what of strategy? Does that fall within your purview, Captain?' The Stadtholder was clearly wanting to draw William out.

'I consider that simultaneous attacks on Scotland and England would prove effective. But, unlike the ill-conceived expedition of 1685, you must strike at the heartland and not the periphery. Claverhouse has about 600 mounted troops; horse, dragoons and guards: the Castles of Edinburgh, Stirling and Dumbarton are strongly held, and there are nineteen companies of foot spread out from Leith to Ayr. A surprise dawn raid on Leith should quickly bring the capital under your Highness's control, and we have irregulars such as the Cameronians ready to march on Glasgow and Ayr. This time mounts from Northumberland are already guaranteed. Scotland should speedily be yours!'

'It seems Captain, that you have been privy to our secret discussions here in den Haag?'

'Not so, Your Highness. Just good common sense.'

'And so it is Captain, a good clear mind.' Hugh Mackay was clearly impressed. 'Nevertheless we have decided to concentrate our force, and to invade England first. Then only will we deal with Scotland. Do you think your Cameronians might be able to hold the breach, until regular troops can be spared from the south?'

'They are not my Cameronians... yet! And they are of an excessively independent spirit. Nevertheless, I believe that a holding action is possible, providing you are not too long arriving in Scotland.'

'If we do not take England we will have failed altogether! So we must put our trust in you and your folk to hold the line in the north.'

With that Cleland withdrew, and went to seek out his old friend James Henderson for a drink... or two!

CHAPTER SEVENTEEN

"INVASION!"

5 November 1688, Torbay, England.

'**GET THE BRIGADE ASHORE THOMAS,** and deploy them immediately!' General Hugh Mackay was feeling really ill, but his Brigade was to be the first of the invasion force to land, and he was keen to get it into position to cover the disembarkation of the rest of Prince William's army.

Sir Thomas Livingstone, Brigade Major, did not need to be told twice! He was glad to get ashore, having endured a tempestuous voyage from the Netherlands, which at one stage saw the whole expedition back in Hellevoetsluis port. Very few in the brigade had not been sick, and the horses aboard had suffered badly.

As Livingstone stepped ashore, a young officer doffed his hat to him. 'Sir Thomas? Captain William Cleland at your service, sir. The Prince desires me to inform you that there will shortly be a Service of Thanksgiving on the beach, and bids me ask you to secure the area from surprise attacks.'

Livingstone considered Cleland with a querulous eye! 'I think Captain, with your conventicle experience, you might be better at this job than me! Can I ask you to site our outlying picquets, while I hold the main body to cover the perimeter?'

Soon the beachhead was secured. There had been no resistance to the landing, and all looked quiet enough. At a given signal, Prince William and his entourage came ashore in small boats. Once they were assembled and surrounded by the troops who had already landed, a short service was led by Rev William Carstares, the Prince's personal chaplain and adviser.

'Interesting that it's a Scot who takes the first service on English soil!' said Livingstone in an aside to Cleland.

♣

King James, shattered by the defection of many he trusted, including General John Churchill, and even his own daughter the Princess Anne, with her husband the Prince of Denmark, ordered the disbandment of his army on 11th December 1688.

Claverhouse, who had been elevated to the peerage as Viscount Dundee when the Scots troops still loyal to James reached Salisbury, wept with frustration and chagrin!

♣

Claverhouse, (or Dundee, as we must now call him), had led his regiment north to Watford and waited. He did not have to wait long! A despatch rider galloped up to his temporary headquarters.

'Urgent message for My Lord Dundee!' he called out, as he reined in violently.

'That would be me,' said Dundee, as he stepped out onto the balcony. 'But of course, you would know that Major Elphinstone, or rather I see you are Colonel now. I suppose turncoats can expect to be promoted!' he continued with extreme sarcasm.

Dougie Elphinstone coloured, but made no rejoinder. Silently he drew a parchment from inside his coat, and handed it to an equerry, who ran upstairs to hand it to his commander.

"My Lord Dundee,
I understand that you are now at Watford and that you keep your men together. I desire that you may stay there until further orders, and upon my honour, none in my army shall touch you.
William, Prince of Orange."

Silently Dundee let the parchment slip from his fingers. It fluttered down and fell in a muddy pond before the door.

'That Colonel, is my answer!'

♣

King James was still in London but he was in an intransigent mood. 'Your Majesty, I beg you! Issue orders to remuster the army and defend London from this usurper! I can raise 20000 men by tomorrow!'

'General, I know you for a true friend, but I have not enough of your like to turn this tide!' King James was finally facing up to reality. 'My Lords Balcarres and Dundee, will you walk with me?

The three men strolled down The Mall in the sunshine, quite unprotected!

'I would ask you gentlemen, now that all the world has deserted me, why you still remain with me?'

Dundee replied vehemently: 'I own you as my rightful liege, Sire. Though I have served others, King Louis of France, and even William of Orange, you have my enduring loyalty as my true and rightful King. Whatever may befall.'

Balcarres also replied in the same vein. King James was visibly moved! 'Louis of France has offered me refuge and I will accept. But one day the House of Stewart will return to these shores. My Lord Dundee, John, I make you my Commander-in-Chief for Scotland as Lieutenant-General. Go and do what you can, and may God go with you.'

'Sire!'

♣

Francis Fordyce, Episcoplian Curate in Cumnock was looking forward to his Christmas dinner. His womenfolk had been in the kitchen all day, and an appetising aroma permeated the manse. Gradually however, his complacency was disturbed by a loud noise from the street.

'That sounds like quite a crowd,' Francis remarked to his wife. 'Could it be carol singers, do you think?'

The noise grew louder and nearer, and it gradually dawned on the curate that this was no well intentioned gathering. The shouts were angry and loud, and could soon be discerned as threatening.

'Throw the 'Piscies out!'

'Death to the malignants!'

'Burn them out!'

'Restore our own minister to us!'

Suddenly a stone crashed through a window, followed by several others. Fordyce and his wife cowered by the fireplace as the front door shook to heavy blows. Soon it smashed inwards, to reveal the crowd outside, led by a man with drawn sword in his hand.

'Francis Fordyce! Your hour has come! No longer will you persecute and mislead the good people of Cumnock!' So saying he entered, followed by a number of men who dragged Fordyce into the street.

'Spare me! Spare me!' he shrieked, falling to his knees.

'As you spared so many others in the Grassmarket?' acidly responded Daniel Ker of Kersland, the leader. 'Robert Hamilton, and others like him, have been calling the likes of you to judgement since Rutherglen. Fetch his clerical gown from the house, and find his prayer book.' A few men rushed to obey.

Putting his gown on him, the crowd led Fordyce down the street to the Mercat Cross, dragging him along with a noose about his neck. His prayer book was mock-ceremoniously carried on a pillow behind him. Arriving at the Cross, he was tied to it, and Kersland stood before with his naked blade in hand. Fordyce was near fainting!

'Don't faint on us, Usurper! The people you betrayed to the gallows, flogging, branding and mutilation, did not faint. Not to mention those imprisoned to die in the black hole of Dunnottar, or drowned on the way to slavery!'

'But... but I never hurt anyone!' squealed the Curate.

'No, you didn't have the guts for that! Fortunate for you we are not in the Grassmarket! But you betrayed old men for possessing a bible, and wives and children for hiding their own men to Clavers and Lagg and others. And they did your dirty work for you!'

Fordyce was silent. A damp patch at his feet showed that he had lost control of his bladder. Some in the crowd were baying for blood!

'This for your clerical authority!' said Kersland, as he expertly cut Fordyce's gown to shreds with his razor-sharp sword. The curate flinched, but Kersland never as much as nicked him. 'Now burn this gown and this Prelatic prayer book! Here in Scotland we do not need a bishop to tell us how to talk with God! Jenny Geddes taught us that!'

That having been done, Kersland led the crowd to the banks of the Lugar Water, which was frozen over. 'Get out of the bounds of this parish—and never return! Ever!'

'But its frozen…'

Planting a boot in the Curate's backside, Kersland propelled him onto the ice, which promptly broke, immersing him up to the waist in the icy water. 'It's not deep and you will not drown or die, unlike some of your victims. Now begone!'

♣

By 8 January 1689, Prince William of Orange was safely ensconced in the Palace of St James, and had summoned all the influential Scots currently in London to attend him. He was attended by Rev William Carstares, now his closest and most trusted adviser. Thirty peers and about eighty landed gentry attended.

'My Lords and gentlemen, here in England all has quickly fallen into place, and it is Our intention to retain the Episcopal Church, as is the will of the majority. But We seek your views about how to proceed in Scotland, and We would ask the Duke of Hamilton to lead a discussion, and for you to return to Us with your best counsel as soon as you can.'

For the next three days the Ship Tavern in St James's Street rang with angry Scots voices. All the nobility and gentry who could manage had flocked to London to seek the favour of the new monarch, and everyone hoped to turn the king to his point of view. Each had his own agenda, but William was his own man, and was going to make his own decisions.

Viscount Dundee did not attend. He had sent a letter with Gilbert Burnet, a relation of his wife's, to ask the king *"what security he might expect, if he should go and live in Scotland without owning his (William's) government?"* The king assured him that if he lived quietly, he would be protected. However a quiet life was not what Dundee had in mind!

At length the Duke of Hamilton sought another audience. 'Your Majesty, we have finally concluded that you should call an urgent meeting of the Convention of Estates in Edinburgh, with a view to forming a Parliament to carry out the necessary reformed legislation, and to ensure the security of your northern realm.'

'H'm!' In an aside to Carstares, William muttered, 'Mayhap Our views on what is *necessary* legislation may differ somewhat?'

Carstares merely nodded.

22 January 1689. Sanquhar.

'I don't like what I hear, Daniel! We have always comported ourselves with extreme correctness in the hope of counteracting some of the spurious lies that are put about regarding our behaviour.' Alex Shields was very angry, and Daniel Ker was on the receiving end.

'We have rabbled about 200 curates out of their manses, and not one has been seriously injured! Compare that to what our people have had to endure!' Kersland was unrepentant.

'It's not about comparisons! It's about doing it right! Richard Cameron declared a war by prayer and fasting, which we are about to win in the most glorious fashion! If we resort to violence, will just be what they accuse us of!'

'No-one was hurt!' said Kerland in a defensive tone.

'No-one was hurt? Who are you trying to fool? In Govan, Russell's wife and daughter beaten, and we are accused of stealing the communion plate! In Cathcart, Finnie's wife and five chidren ejected into the snow! In Galston, Simpson made to wade through the frozen river Irvine!'

Kersland looked embarrassed.

'Let me go on! In Ballantrae, White hit in the face with a musket butt and wounded by a sword. His wife gave premature birth! In New Galloway, Brown tied to a cart in the snow at 4 a.m., and left there! In Renfrew, Ross beaten, and his wife and child of three days ejected into the snow! If there have been no deaths or serious injuries, it's certainly not your fault!'

'But...'

"But nothing! In one fell swoop you have undone years of patient and quiet suffering! This is not Christian! We are not it the business of revenge, we are in the business of healing!'

'Don't tell me we have not suffered enough?'

'I absolutely grant you that our people have been tried beyond bearing! But that is why we have to show that there is a better way. Forgiveness!'

Sir Alexander Gordon of Earlston, just released from Blackness Castle, rose to adress the General Meeting being held at Sanquhar. 'I desire to place before this Meeting my opinion, that the Rev Mr Boyd, a clerical leader of our Societies, was the reader of a Proclamation from the Prince of Orange in Glasgow and has thus, by implication, associated us all with that Prince's views. This was done without the common consent which we have required from all our members since 1682.'

There was a general murmur of approval. 'Your point is well noted, Sir Alexander,' replied the Moderator.

The Meeting then went on to discuss the "Rabbling of the Curates." The general opinion was that, at last, an opportunity had arisen to shake off the yoke of prelacy under which the south-west had suffered for so long. Although the Cameronians had been in the forefront of this action, they had harmed no-one and stolen nothing, albeit some items, such as prayer books and surplices, had been burned at Mercat Crosses. At last the hated curates, who feared neither God nor man, were now in fear of the people whom they had so despised and betrayed, and many were in fear of their lives.

Alexander Shields rose slowly to his feet. 'We are not being honest with ourselves. Ever since these Cameronian United Societies were formed, we have been denigrated and lied about. We have become pariahs in our native land. Even when we take action in complete sincerity and with an earnest desire for peace, we are pilloried and labelled as sanctimonious. But that puts us in a good place, for Our Lord Himself was despised and rejected of men. However the times are changing, and we who have been the dregs of society, now have the ear of the new rulers of our land. All the more vital, therefore, that we do not destroy our own witness during the "Killing Times," that we continue to exercise Christian forbearance as our policy, even though many of our people have been tried far beyond what is humanly bearable. We are not striving in our human strength, but in the fear of God.'

There was a mixed response from the Meeting, some calling for Shields to have done and sit down, and others calling for him to continue. It took some time for order to be restored.

When the gathering fell silent, Alexander went on: 'I therefore propose that a letter be issued to the people of each parish, addressed to the curates that remain, warning them to desist and remove themselves, so that those ministers who were "outed" from 'way back in 1662, may receive their pulpits back again.'

Andrew Rigg from Carrick jumped to his feet. 'I second that proposal!' There was a general call of 'Aye' from the Meeting, and Alexander Shields was called upon to draft the letter to the curates.

'I have already done so,' he replied. 'Here it is:

"We, belonging to the Parish of............, having suffered a long continued tract of manifold and cruel oppressions and persecutions for many years, upon the account of not owning and submitting to instruction of Episcopal Curates; ...Do therefore... warn you............ to surcease and desist from preaching and all other ministerial exercises in the kirk of..............., and to depart from the cure and benefice of the said kirk, and to deliver the keys of the same, under certification that if you refuse, you shall be forced to do it."

There was a silence when he finished reading, and then a general babble broke out. Gradually remarks such as, 'well said,' 'good paper,' 'just what's needed,' began to emerge, and the letter was unanimously agreed to without a vote.

Because the times were so perilous and events were happening at such an alarming rate, the Meeting also decided to muster the armed men into companies, each with its captain and lieutenants. These companies had no formal authority beyond being an adjunct of the Societies.   It was further resolved that the officers should meet separately from the ministers and elders, as did the commissioners. Each group was then to bring its salient points to the Meeting, so that all might be dealt with expeditiously.

♣

The Borland hillside was crowded with people listening to the Rev Thomas Lining reading the Covenants.

> *"And... we declare before God and men that we have no intention nor desire to attempt anything that may turn to the dishonour of God, or to the diminuition of the greatness and authority of the civil magistrate, but to the contrary we promise and swear that we shall to the uttermost of our power, with our means and lives, stand to the defence of the civil magistrate's person and authority, in the defence and preservation of the foresaid true religion, liberties, and laws of the kingdom..."[1]*

'Whit happened tae the King? The meenister read out the *civil magistrate,* but in the original Covenant it said the King! Hoo can we hae been true to that?' whispered Andrew Semple to his companion, Willie Gibbs from Lesmahagow.

'Wheesht!' Those in his vicinity were not amused!

---

[1] Original wording of the National Covenant was changed on this occasion to exclude "the King" and replace him with "the civil magistrate."

'But hoo can we have been true to that?' insisted Andrew. 'We have rejected the King!' Willie drew him quietly aside from the crowd.

'Can ye no' see that the Stewarts rejected us first, Andra'?'

'That disnae mak' it right!' he stubbornly replied.

For Andrew, in his simple, homely way, had put his finger on the sore which had troubled the theologians of the Covenant. However sincere, they had certainly rejected their king, and the original Covenant had promised to support and protect him! It was therefore to be a great relief that soon Scotland was to get a new king in William of Orange, who was prepared to defend the protestant religion, and to whom they could submit with a clear conscience.

In a curious way, the Covenants were about to become *de trop*, just as they achieved their purpose!

CHAPTER EIGHTEEN

"THE CAMERONIAN GUARD"

13th March 1689. Edinburgh.

THE CAPITAL WAS IN AN UPROAR! Since the sacking in December of the Chapel Royal by a mob, the city train bands had not proved effective in maintaining law and order. The Cameronian clergy, and a watching committee from the western shires led by Patrick Walker and Michael Shields, made their way through the unruly streets to Castle Hill. Several hundred Cameronians had arrived in the capital on their own initiative, and sought quarters with friends. Great events were afoot!

When the Convention of Estates assembled on 13th March it was remarkably representative of the nation: Nine bishops, forty-two peers, forty-nine county and fifty burgh representatives attended. But the battle lines were immediately drawn over the matter of electing a president. The two candidates were the pro-Jacobite Duke of Atholl, and the Duke of Hamilton, a political opportunist. Hamilton was elected by a majority of forty, and twenty members promptly crossed the floor to the Whig side. Hamilton was not the only opportunist that day!

'My lords and gentlemen, we have therefore resolved that the Duke of Gordon must surrender the Castle to Prince William's authority, and that the Earls of Lothian and Tweeddale be entrusted with the task of bearing the order of the Convention to him!' The motion was carried by acclamation!

♣

'Get yourselves a place to stay, and let us foregather at noon,' said Alexander Shields, the leader of the Cameronian deputation. 'Find out what you can before we meet up again.'

Once they had entered the city, they had seen many whom they recognised as society people. Jacobites were notably absent from the streets that day. Yet there was an air of caution and expectancy abroad, for the Duke of Gordon still held the Castle for James. His guns commanded the town and would wreak havoc if they opened fire.

At noon the Cameronian "watching committee" foregathered again. 'So, what's your news?' asked Alex.

'There's a right stramash!' reported Patrick Walker. 'The Earl of Crawford, Lord Cardross and Sir Patrick Hume have all had death threats. They would seem genuine enough, but we also hear that Mackenzie and other supporters of James are going about in fear of their lives, for the town is full of our people. The town guard is virtually toothless, and of course there are no army units in Scotland, all having been called south by James.'

'Seems the report is of mobs all over town, pillaging and destroying! Students and rabble for the most part, though as usual we are being blamed for much of the uproar. The rumour is that they are going to march on the parliament building itself, and break up the Convention,' chipped in John Muir.

At that point a knocking was heard at the door, and it being opened, William Cleland and Daniel Ker entered. 'Goodness,' said Alex, 'a real clutch of Cameronians! Where did you come from, Will?'

'Prince William sent me north soon after he landed. I travelled with the Earl of Leven, who is currently my commanding officer. I was intended to go to the south-west counties and assess the military potential there. Kersland seemed the best man to seek out, for though you clergy might not like his methods of "rabbling", at least he got something done! He also exercised enough discipline to prevent any loss of life, a not inconsiderable achievement! I hear you and he were despatched by the General Meeting to see the Prince, but that events have overtaken you? And our old friend Clavers is here in town, making waves in the Convention!'

'What sort of waves, Will?'

'We'll know soon enough!'

♣

'Gordon, you cannot yield this Castle! You'll ruin everything, and gain nothing! Where is your loyalty, man? You know that we catholic nobles will count for absolutely nothing under William. We need King James! And you need me!'

Although Gordon was a duke, and Dundee a mere viscount, there was no doubt who was in charge of the meeting. Gordon was a nervous and indecisive man, who had already decided to accept the Convention's terms for surrender of Edinburgh Castle. They were meeting in the early hours of the morning. Dundee had come secretly through the town, and been let in at the postern door.

'Why would I need you? You have only fifty troopers at your back, not even a full squadron!'

'And how many did Bruce have at his back at Glen Trool? His brothers, the Black Douglas and just a few others! But he ultimately won all Scotland! Balcarres and I have an authority from His Majesty to hold an alternative convention at Stirling. The Earl of Mar is Governor there and displays more determination than you! My Lord of Atholl, and others of note, are with us.'

'Very well, I shall continue to hold here!'

Dundee left while it was still dark, and the following day assumed his seat in the Convention Hall. As he sat down, a grubby piece of paper was thrust into his hand by an usher, who promptly disappeared. *"There is report of a plot to murder you and Mackenzie."* He handed the paper to Sir George Mackenzie who sat in front of him. Mackenzie went pale!

'Sir George, you wish to speak?' The Duke of Hamilton was quite enjoying the goings on. He felt sure he could manipulate matters to his own advantage.

'Your Grace, I do. There are reports of threats on the lives of members of this body, myself and Viscount Dundee amongst them. I move that the Convention provide security for those who are thus threatened.'

'Sir George, the entire city is in an uproar. We cannot postpone public affairs, to consider personal matters. We must proceed...'

♣

In the early morning light Dundee and his fifty troopers clattered down the Royal Mile to the house where Balcarres was staying. The Marquess of Atholl had agreed to meet him there, and to ride with him to Stirling.

Balcarres appeared at the top of the steps.

'Where's Atholl?' demanded Graham.

'He's changed his mind. He is going to stay one day more.'

'Damn him for a fool and a coward! I have a vital rendezvous on the Stirling Road. I must ride!'

'Won't you stay one day longer?'

'I have stayed too long already. Troop, follow me!' and the furious Dundee led his men under the Netherbow Port, glancing up at the shrivelled heads of Cameron and others, as he went. "There will be some fresh heads there soon!" he thought. Pursued by the jeers of the crowds who thronged the streets, a few of whom threw stones and filth at him, Dundee rode on with head up and hand on hip, heading for the Nor' Loch.

Once beyond the Loch, and free of the crowd, he reined in beside the towering rampart of Castle Rock. Throwing his reins to a trooper, he leapt from the saddle and, to the amazement of the few onlookers, began to scale the rock face. Soon he reached a little known postern gate, which opened for him. Inside stood the Duke of Gordon.

'Everyone is wavering,' seethed Dundee through his clenched teeth! 'Bunch of cowards and turncoats! Disloyal traitors! You must hold this castle, or I shall have *your* head off! Do you take my meaning, Gordon?' One did not normally address a duke thus!

Gordon merely nodded, speechless!

♣

Alex and Michael were also up early. They had arranged to meet with a small group at the Netherbow Port, to pray about the general situation. The dried out heads of many of their friends impaled above them, added extra vehemence to the prayers!

When Clavers rode through the port he practically rode them down. The Cameronians scattered as the troopers filled the whole way with scant regard for any pedestrians. 'Bluidy Clavers!' exclaimed several as one man.

'Looks like he is leaving in a hurry.' Thomas Lining had joined the group. 'We had better warn Will Cleland urgently. Whereabouts is he?'

'He was going to attend the Earl of Leven at the Convention House this morning. Just up here.'

Sure enough, Cleland was standing at the entrance to the Parliament Close. He had around him a group of nearly fifty Cameronians, all well armed. 'I have been getting our people organised into proper sub-units under their own officers. If we are needed, it will happen suddenly! We must be prepared for instant action! We have a group already blockading the castle entrance. Kersland, you must go there now and take command!'

Daniel Ker needed no second bidding. 'Right sir, I'm off!'

♣

Inside the Convention Hall, William Duke of Hamilton flicked the report from the Committee for Securing the Peace across the table at Sir John Dalrymple, the Lord Advocate. 'This recommends that Leven be authorised to raise a regiment for the defence of the city, and that all the cannoniers be mustered under command of Capt Sledzer, providing he swears fealty to the Convention.'

Just then an usher came up and whispered into Hamilton's ear.

'What!!' The Duke exploded, going scarlet in the face. 'Dundee and Gordon spoken together! We'll have the cannon about our ears any minute, and that bloody man Graham is likely to attempt a *coup d'etat*. Lock the doors, and put the keys here on the table before me! Let us see who is on whose side!'

The entire Convention Hall burst into furious babel, some going white with fear, some going red with fury, and few remaining calm at the new threats which had developed in the last hour. One such was the Earl of Leven.

'Gentlemen! Gentlemen!' he shouted to be heard above the noise. 'Listen to me, I beg you!'

Gradually the noise died away. Leven was known for a soldier, and many felt he might well be the man for the hour.

'I will be honoured to raise a regiment for the purpose of defending the city. But right now there is a greater need to defend this Convention! The greatest harm the followers of James Stewart can do us, is to prevent us from legislating. This is one of the most momentous days in Scots history! Do we take a new king or not? Our most vital need is to protect this Convention, so that what we resolve to do has legal standing. You need protection right now! Today!'

The place erupted once more! Some made for the door seeking to escape, only to be confronted by Cleland and his men, standing just outside with drawn swords in their hands.

'Stay in your places and sit down! Sit down, I say!' Hamilton roared. As he continued raging like a bull, gradually some order was restored. 'Hear Lord Leven! Else we may all be dead men before the next dawn!'

Leven went on: 'Your guard already stands at the door! Captain Cleland and his men will protect you until we have regular troops to do so. Mr Cleland, bring in your men!'

William Cleland and about twenty of his officers filed in. The Duke of Atholl and the Earl of Balcarres, both of whom had tried to slip out, looked very worried indeed! 'You can't bring this rabble in here!' shouted Balcarres.

The point of David Gemill's sword was just two inches from Balcarres' throat!

'Murdering swine!' he grunted through clenched teeth. 'Your kind have ravaged my people for the last time. I should run you through now!'

His sword was forced aside by Cleland's upward swing. 'I *will* have order and discipline in my Guard, or you are no part of it!' he spat. 'Get out!' Turning to Balcarres, 'I am sorry, my Lord. Your judgement will find you out soon enough, but not this way!'

Balcarres collapsed onto his seat!

'Put up your swords!' ordered Cleland. The Convention visibly relaxed as the cold steel was sheathed and the Cameronians silently filed out.

'I'm not sure that the danger of a *coup* lies only with Dundee,' whispered Atholl to Balcarres, as the doors were locked and the keys laid on the table before the President.

♣

'Whom have you in command here, Captain? And what are his orders?' asked Lord Leven, who had arrived to inspect the entrenchment before the Castle

'Capt Daniel Ker of Kersland, my Lord. His orders are to prevent any communication between the Castle and the townfolk. There are many still well disposed to James Stewart who are keen to let the Duke of Gordon know what is happening in the Convention Hall.'

'Kersland, I can count on you?'

'You can that, my Lord! We have suffered too long to throw away this chance to right it all!'

'And what measures have you taken for the city, Cleland?'

'We have set a night watch on the lodgings of the Earl of Crawford, Lord Cardross and Sir Patrick Hume. They have all had death threats. We have a standing guard at the Parliament House, day and night. Any member who fears for his life may ask the guard commander for an escort. That applies to all, Jacobite as well as Whig. I feel there is as more likelihood of finding the bodies of some of our late persecutors cold in the morning, than those of our friends.'

'Very well! You seem to be well in control here. I am off to find a drummer and raise my Regiment!'

'And how long will that take, my Lord?'

'Oh, about four hours, I should think!'

And so it did!

♣

The Privy Council was in session:

'We are greatly relieved to welcome you, General!' The Duke of Hamilton sounded greatly relieved! He had spent an anxious week, fearing that the Cameronian Guard might try to take over the city and force their leaders on the Convention. However, Cleland and his men had behaved with the utmost discretion, and the city had remained both quiet and secure. 'What troops do you have with you?'

'Only three very understrength Scots Regiments from Holland. I was forced to leave the rest of my best troops in England.'

'But you will assault the castle?'

'No, we'll starve 'em out. What troops have you got here?'

'Leven's Regiment, just one week old. Some artillery. That's it!'

'So how did you keep order?'

'We've had a mob of wild westland Whigs! A real rabble! I'll be glad to see them go!'

'Perhaps you should be grateful for them Your Grace?'

'Oh, we are! We are! But now, thank God, we can dismiss them with our thanks and a week's pay! We'll be glad to see them go! See to it, Major Buntine!'

When the Muster Master-General tracked down Cleland, he was with his command group, overlooking the approaches to the castle.

'A week's pay! A week's pay! You think we did this for pay?' Daniel Ker of Kersland was spitting blood! 'We have saved the Convention; we have saved the city; we have probably saved the kingdom! And you seek to pay us! What price do you put on martyr's blood? You insult us, sir!'

Hugh Buntine, gentle soul that he was, coloured, but remained speechless.

'At least we have done our duty here,' said Cleland. 'Come, let's go home!'

The Cameronian Guard quit the capital that very night, but their "watching committee" remained.

♣

William Cleland and Alexander Shields were chatting in Greyfriars Kirkyard at the end of a momentous day in the Convention. Both were weary to the point of exhaustion.

'Well Alex, it looks as though we may actually have won!'

'Yes, King James deposed and William and Mary offered the Crown! Praise the Lord! Everything Cameron declared at Sanquhar has come to pass!'

'Just one small problem!'

Shields eyed his companion quizzically.

'Dundee!'

♣

'General Mackay, you are empowered to recruit your three Dutch Regiments up to strength, but we also propose to issue commissions to raise another seven regiments for Scotland.' William Douglas-Hamilton, Duke of Hamilton and leader of the Privy Council was much concerned.

'That would help, my Lord, but what I badly need are well trained troops if I am going to deal with Dundee.'

Hamilton shrugged. 'We have none! But the Laird of Blackwood had advanced the suggestion that we should raise a regiment from among these Cameronians who provided our Guard before you arrived. They are an ill bred and troublesome bunch, but I must admit they seem to make good fighters. They also have a bare modicum of discipline. I would support the raising of such a regiment if, and only if, they had a gentleman to lead them.'

'Has Blackwood proposed a Colonel?'

'He proposed the Earl of Angus, but he is still in his minority, and from what I hear, has a head full of the notions of these religious minded Whigs. I'm not sure he can be trusted. Also they want that man Cleland as Lieutenant-Colonel. Can we trust him?'

'I have met him several times, and he has done good service since he landed with me at Torbay. He is a sensible, resolute man, though I think not much of a soldier.'

'Nevertheless he was a very useful spy for us, both in '85, and before William invaded. And the Cameronians seem to trust him. He did a good job before you arrived, and I hear Angus defers to his judgement. Trouble is, he's not really a gentleman!'

'If I could get one of the the nobility to stand patron for the Earl, would that help?'

'It would.'

'Then may I propose Lord Cardross? You have given him a regiment of horse, and he was with Cleland's brother-in-law in the Carolinas. I trust him, and he's a good soldier.'

'Very well, General. Go and ask him! And seek out Mr Cleland as well, sound him out. I gather the Earl of Angus is at his studies at Utrecht University. Better leave him be.'

Blackwood and Cleland were anxiously waiting in the anteroom as the General emerged. 'His Grace is prepared to support the raising of of a Regiment of Cameronians, but only on certain conditions.'

'Which are, sir,' queried Cleland?

'I think he is nervous that you are more committed to the Douglas camp than to the nation. The Marquess is well known for his covenanting predelictions, and you Blackwood are his factor, whereas you Cleland, are the son of his previous factor.'

'In other words we are not to be trusted?' William sounded bitter!

'Not so! Not so!' Mackay was immediately placatory. 'But the council have asked for a patron from the gentry to take the young Earl under his wing.'

'And we are not gentry enough?' asked Blackwood angrily.

'I fear not, Mr Laurie. But what would you say to my Lord Cardross?'

'There is no-one I trust more,' replied Cleland.

Mackay raised his eyebrows at Blackwood.

'We will need to consult the Cameronian clergy. No-one will enlist without their approval. We had best go and seek out Mr Shields.'

'Nevertheless, I intend to issue commissions today to the Earl of Angus as Colonel, and to you, Cleland, as Lieutenant-Colonel, to raise a regiment of 1200 foot within fourteen days!'

♣

Blackwood and Cleland found Shields sitting morosely on a gravestone in Greyfriars Kirkyard where so many covenanters had languished and died after Bothwell Brig.

'Cheer up Alex, we bear good news!' Will recounted in detail their recent meeting with General Mackay. 'What think you of that?'

'I think it's what we hoped for so long ago in Holland. But it must be approved by the General Meeting for the decision is not ours to make. The next meeting is in ten days at Douglas.'

CHAPTER NINETEEN

"A REGIMENT IS RAISED"

29 April 1689. Douglas.

S T BRIDE'S KIRK REVERBERATED with angry voices. The debate over whether or not to raise a Cameronian Regiment had resurrected the sort of jangling debates the likes of which had not been heard since the days of Bothwell Brig!

'Cleland's not one of us! He cannot be trusted not to introduce licentious officers to command our men!'

'To have a regiment of our friends under government pay would be a most sinful association, since there are still many murderers of our folk still serving in this army, and our officers will have to consort with them in their councils of war. Also this man Mackay who now commands in Scotland, what sort of man is he? We know nothing of him or his religious position!'

As so often before, the meeting erupted into furious babel.

Alexander Shields was quickly on his feet! 'Friends! Friends! Hear me I pray!'

Shields, as the successor to James Renwick, was generally held in high regard throughout the Societies. Gradually the noise died away, and Alex began.

'We have endured half a century of persecution as a result of our support for the Covenants. The ten years since Bothwell have been particularly brutal, and most of our leaders were either killed or exiled. In 1680 Richard Cameron, from whom we take our Cameronian name,

193

declared a spiritual war on the House of Stewart which steadfastly sought to enforce its royal will on our consciences.'

There was a growl of agreement.

'This very month our Convention of Estates stripped James Stuart of his crown, and the reasons given were exactly those set forth by Cameron at Sanquhar. Few will accept that the most effective type of warfare is spiritual, but no-one can deny that what we stood for has been vindicated up to the hilt!'

Another growl from the assembly!

'And had it not been for our guarding of the Convention, Dundee and his cronies might well have attempted a *coup d'état* from within, rather than being forced to lead a rebellion from without! Therefore surely we are under an obligation to defend our new found freedom with every means at our disposal, including taking the field under arms against those who would remove it from us?'

This time some dissenting voices were heard. 'We are weary of conflict! We want no more fighting! We would live in peace!'

Alex pitched his voice up, to be the better heard. 'We are all weary! We all want to live in peace! But if we want our bairns to live in peace, we had best defend King William's cause. He has vowed to defend a presbyterian kirk in Scotland and not be a tyrant to anyone!'

'Aye, but can we trust him? *"Put not your trust in princes!"*'

'So would you rather have us return to the old regime? Back to the killing times? For be assured, if they do return, what has happened in the past will seem mild compared to the avenging wrath of the Stewarts!'

No-one in the meeting wished to return to the past, for they knew that Shields spoke the truth. A silence fell over the kirk.

'I have prepared a paper to be submitted to Lieutenant-Colonel Cleland and his officers, setting forth the conditions under which our members are willing to serve in a Regiment under King William's authority. Here it is!'

♣

The next day Michael Shields, scribe to the Meeting, read out his brother's paper which had been tabled the night before. It had generally been well received, and the meeting now resolved to call Cleland in to give his response to the conditions set forth.

Rev Tomas Lining, in the Moderators's chair, enquired: 'Mr Cleland, (for I cannot yet call you Colonel), you were provided with a copy of Mr Alexander Shields' paper to discuss with your military council?'

'I was, Moderator!'

'And may we enquire as to your reaction?'

'There are some conditions which are within my power to grant, and others which are not. I have authority to choose my own officers, but I will undertake to appoint none against whom you have a justifiable objection. As for where the Regiment is called upon to serve, and power to impeach former persecutors, such matters lie within the purview of His Majesty, and I can give no guarantees there.'

The meeting erupted yet again! Alex Shields took his friend by the elbow and escorted him out of the church. 'They are in no mood to listen to anything but their own bigoted voices. Best you leave us to our deliberations, if they can be dignified by such a description!' Cleland left to return to the Castle and report to Polwarth and Blackwood.

As he left, he was rudely brushed aside by two men who had just dismounted from badly blown horses, lathered in sweat. As they burst into the kirk one yelled, 'The Irishes have landed in Galloway!' The other shouted, 'And the highlanders have flocked to support Dundee and are already marching south!'

The meeting really had no option but to erupt yet again!

8th May 1689. Cambusnethan Parish Church.

'Do you, Janet Cleland, take this man James Scot, to be your lawful wedded husband, to have and to hold…?'

Janet whispered, 'I do,' as a tear rolled down her cheek.

'I am sorry my dear,' said the minister, 'I can't hear your reply.'

'I do! I do!' screamed Janet, and throwing her bouquet in her groom's face, she turned and fled from the church.

'This may turn out to be a tricky marriage to finalise!' remarked the minister mildly.

James Scot looked sick!

12 May 1689, Douglas.

Alexander Shields was preaching up a storm! His text was "*Curse ye Meroz,... because they did not come to the help of the Lord, against the warriors,*" and there was little doubt where he stood in the matter of raising a regiment.

His congregation was about ten thousand strong, from every covenanting county. The military captains who had mustered their companies were present with their men, and the atmosphere was more explosive than at any time since 1638, when the National Covenant was signed.

The congregation was visibly moved, some to tears.

♣

Since the previous meeting, Alex had given deep thought to the papers he had been asked to produce and had had many discussions with both clergy and laity. He had had no opportunity to discuss the problem with his friend, Will Cleland, but realised his greatest hurdle was overcoming objections from the General Meeting. Approval by the military would just have to wait!

'Moderator, I have drafted two papers. The first contains the conditions under which those who decide to enlist in the Cameronian Regiment desire to serve. The second is a declaration to be subscribed to by those who enlist, as to the principles which bind their consciences.'

'Will that aspect no' be covered by an oath of fealty to the king?' enquired John Matheson. There were angry growls from all over the church.

Alex burst out: 'You are all bitterly aware of how the *Test Act* and the *Oath of Abjuration* were forced on our people, leading to immense suffering, even death, for many who objected. We will therefore, whilst promising loyalty to king and state in defence of the new found liberties, continue to submit ourselves to God before any earthly monarch.' There was now a murmur of agreement all round.

'A copy of both papers is posted on the kirk door for those who wish to read the full text, but I propose, with your permission Moderator, to read the headings.'

'Pray proceed, Mr Shields.'

Alex bowed his head in acknowledgement. 'I have some points which I consider desirable to be accepted by our brethren who wish to serve:

> '"*That all officers and soldiers make profession of their soundness in religion, and are in harmony with the approved principles of the Church of Scotland.*
>
> *That all officers and soldiers concur in advancing the reformation of church and state.*
>
> *That we... have the right to impeach such as have persecuted us without mercy these past years...,*
>
> *That we may choose our own officers, and that none are to command without our consent...,*
>
> *That we may have a minister of our own choosing, and an elder in every company.*
>
> *...that those off duty may meet for prayer, fellowship and Christian conference as convienency will allow.*
>
> *That there be severe punishment for fornication, lascivious talk, swearing, drunkeness and the like.*" '

'That's it?'

'That's it, Moderator!'

'I think, Mr Shields, that you and a deputation from this meeting need to go to Castle Dangerous, to present these papers to the military council.'

Accordingly the Shields brothers, Rev William Boyd, and five others plus Blackwood, made their way to where the Castle stood brooding over the Douglas Water. They found Cleland and Polwarth ensconced in the dining room, the table before them strewn with papers and maps.

Polwarth read the papers first: 'Personally I have no problem with the tenor of these, but I cannot say the same regarding their attitude to military discipline. We cannot have private leagues between soldiers and officers. What happens if your officers are killed, and you come under the authority of someone you mislike in the heat of the battle?' The deputation remained silent.

Cleland now read the papers! 'I cannot go along with these proposals,' he said angrily! 'No-one under any sort of military discipline could allow private soldiers to choose their own officers! Some of these proposals are like the ordination vows of a minister! The result would be chaos! Also the chaplain and elders to be allowed to call the commanding officer and others to answer to charges of morality?'

'That has always been one of the duties of a chaplain,' responded Alex quietly. 'We answer to God before we answer to you! We guard the conscience of the Regiment!'

William Cleland was highly incensed! He saw his long-held dream of leading a regiment of covenanters against his long standing enemy Dundee evaporating before his eyes! All the sacrifice, all the blood, all the freezing nights on the moors—all gone for nothing! Did these sanctimonious ministers not realise that this was a time for action? Would he have to eat humble-pie and ask Leven for a captain's commission in his regiment after all? What's the use of it all, he thought?

The deputation, sensing it was at an impasse, withdrew and returned to report back to the General Meeting. James Howie of Lochgoin, a recognised leader from Fenwick, stormed out shouting: 'This is no way to serve our God, consorting with malignants and traitors!' He was followed by several religious extremists who had refused to accept any king who would not subscribe to the Covenants. General gloom reigned, but Alex, still not prepared to give up, offered to draw up yet another two new papers, one for officers and one for soldiers, to be read at the head of each company on the morrow.

Unbeknown to them, Polwarth was doing the same thing at the same time!

♣

Early next morning, Cleland and Blackwood came to St Bride's Kirk, where the ministers had gathered for prayer.

Cleland was still angry: 'We are breaking off negotiations with the Societies! The position is clearly untenable, and I am simply not prepared to raise a regiment under the strictures which you have laid down! I bid you good day, gentlemen.'

As Cleland stormed out of the kirk, Alex Shields quickly got to his feet and followed him outside. 'Will, don't do this! After all we have been through! After all we have suffered! Remember how we discussed a Cameronian Regiment in Utrecht way back in '85?'

Whilst he had been speaking, Cleland still continued to walk away. Alex grabbed him by the shoulder and swung him round, confronting him face to face. 'You have no right to treat the men who wish to serve in this way. They have endured unbroken suffering here, while you and I have been much in Holland. They have seen their homes ravaged and their families destroyed. Now they finally have a chance for freedom! What right do you have to deny them the right to fight for it?'

'Let them join Leven's or one of the other regiments being raised!'

'Are you mad? What other formation would allow them to fight whilst maintaining their moral convictions? These men may be considered religious bigots, but they are honourable and courageous men who, unlike the rest of the world, have endured all that the Stewarts could throw at them! They deserve a chance to serve with their own ilk. Not the drunken, whoring, blaspheming sort one normally finds in the ranks of any army!'

Cleland paused. 'So what do you propose?'

'We drown ourselves in words! I have drawn up two short and simple papers, designed to cut through all the prevarication and bigotry. I hope they may fill the bill?'

'Even better,' said Cleland. 'Polwarth has produced a one-pararaph paper, setting out what we fight for. If you will support it, I know the men will enlist, for they trust you.'

'As I trust you, Will. So let us go forward together! Come! The companies are already drawing up under their captains on the Holm. Let's go and raise *our* Regiment!'

Cleland's horse was tethered to the kirkyard railing, and he now swung himself into the saddle. He looked every inch a soldier. 'I'll need a chaplain, Rev Shields.'

'That you will, Colonel!'

With that Cleland rode, with Alex walking beside him, down to where the troops were mustered. Riding up to the company commanded by his brother-in-law, Captain John Haddow, he removed his hat in acknowledgement to John's salute.

'Captain Campbell of Moy, would you be kind enough to read this paper to the company?'

John Campbell took the scroll, and began to read:

> *"You declare that you engage in this service,... to resist Popery and Prelacy,... and to recover... the work of Reformation in Scotland..."*

As the paper was read, Cleland looked at the faces of the men. Good strong faces, which looked at him without any shifting of the eyes or self consciousness. He noticed here and there a missing ear, cropped by the likes of Claverhouse. Some even had a brandmark on their faces. But all seemed steadfast.

Once Campbell had finished reading, Shields spoke out: 'We engage in this Regiment, the Earl of Angus's, to defend the freedom of conscience for which we have struggled so long. Make no mistake, evil men are seeking even now, to take it away from us, and to return to the times we have endured. Until now we have not been free to fight for the crown, but now we have a king in William, who has declared he will protect our presbyterian faith in Scotland. Also you serve under a Commander-in-Chief, Major-General Hugh Mackay, described by Gilbert Burnett as "the most pious soldier he ever knew." Our officers are indeed men whom in conscience you may submit to. Will ye serve?'

Sixty voices echoed a deep 'Aye! That we will!'

*The first Cameronian: Sentinel John Thomson in the dress and
equipment of The Cameronian Regiment 1689.*
Courtesy of the Regimental Trustees of the Cameronians (Scottish
Rifles) and the Dow Family.

'Good then,' said Lieutenant-Colonel William Cleland, 'I am pleased to have you serve with me. Captain Haddow, record the names, and then have Lieutenant Ballantin march your company to the rendezvous at Rigside for the night. I will need you at my council-of-war in Douglas later.'

'But sir!' John Haddow had drawn close to his brother-in-law, and spoke quietly. 'Is there to be no oath of fealty?'

Cleland replied just as quietly: 'After what these men have suffered there will be no oaths in this Regiment! These are sworn servants of God. Their yea is their yea. Their word is better than twenty oaths.'

'Sir,' quietly acquiesced Haddow.

This procedure was repeated at the head of all twenty companies drawn up. At the company commanded by Captain George Monroe, Shields murmured in his ear: 'George, you know there was an objection to you at the Meeting yesterday? I trust you to give no occasion for it to be sustained?'

'Hardly likely, Mr Shields, since you perceive my Lieutenant is a son of Dalzell, that curse of covenanters. I have had to endure much suspicion on his account, but I will stake my life on his commitment to our cause. I can hardly do less for myself!'

After the document had been read out at the head of the 15th Company, whose Captain was Daniel Ker of Kersland, Cleland spoke after Shields. 'I know that many of you served under Capt Kersland in the "rabbling of the curates". I also know that no-one suffered lasting injury or death, and that you have been commended for your restraint after years of provocation. But I *will* have discipline in this Regiment! I will not tolerate any behaviour other than the most immediate and complete obedience to orders! If you accept this, you may enlist. Otherwise not! What do ye say?'

Sergeant Abraham Oliphant spoke out: 'We have already discussed this with our officers and amongst ourselves, sir. We are resolved to be the finest company you have! You can rely on us!'

'Well said, Sergeant. Do the rest of you concur?'

A single unified shout of "Aye!" rent the air. Cleland and Kersland both visibly relaxed.

♣

Later the Lieutenant-Colonel convened his council-of-war in Douglas. The companies had departed under Major James Henderson to their overnight bivouac at Rigside. All the company commanders were present, as was Blackwood, in his role of regimental agent, and the chaplain, Alexander Shields.

'I welcome you gentlemen as the leaders of this new regiment. Leading our men will require considerably more courage and tact than is usually found in an army. Our men are of an excessively independent frame of mind, and it will take committed leadership to make them follow you. Be aware of their sensibilities. Many of you officers take a drink, most of our men are teetotallers. Be circumspect and they will respect you. Be of loose morals and they will despise you.' He looked slowly round the room, searching every face.

Every officer met his eyes. None looked away!

'Well gentlemen, we are posted to quarters at Dunbland and Doune. We collect our weapons as we pass through Stirling.' Turning to Blackwood, 'What news of uniforms?'

'I have arranged for 1200 coats and hats to be provided from Edinburgh. We will get them at Dunblane. For now the men's own shoes and boots must suffice.' Cleland raised his eyebrows. 'And officers must of course provide their own uniforms. William Jardine's on Forth Steet has the pattern, and I have your's and the Major's uniforms here now.'

'And the officers wear black hackles?'

'They do indeed sir!'

On the line of march through the covenanting country of Lanark and Cambusnethan, family members and the public turned out to cheer the new Regiment as it passed. Young William Cleland, now four years old, was supported on the garden wall by his mother. As the Lieutenant-Colonel drew level, he reined in, and catching the boy up, set him before him on the crupper.

'I suppose you think that's funny? Turn him into a soldier when he is still only a child!' said Margaret.

'Perhaps it will be the only time he sees his father in uniform,' replied Will senior.

'Don't make jokes like that, my husband! Just see you come home safely to us!'

♣

'Matchlock muskets! You are going to fob us off with these ancient things? Where are our flintlocks?' Major James Henderson was really angry!

The Governor of Stirling Castle was immediately on the defensive. 'There's none left! We have had to equip Leven's, and there are another five regiments being raised. You are lucky to get these four hundred muskets.'

'Four hundred! We have 1200 men to arm! What about the rest?'

'There are another hundred muskets coming. And I have orders to issue you with 400 pikes, and 40 halberts for your sergeants.'

'You are going to send these totally untried troops against the rebels armed with pikes?'

'What can I do? It's all I have! I have no favourites.'

'Well, what about powder, ball and match? We need to be able to fire these things?' Henderson was nothing if not acerbic!

'We do have these for you,' said the Governor with obvious relief. 'We also have your uniform coats and hats here.'

'At least we'll look like soldiers! Maybe the rebels will run away when they see us!'

'I doubt if Dundee will!'

♣

The Cameronians had been in quarters in Dunblane for the past three weeks. Cleland and his officers had kept them hard at work with weapon handling and company tactics. The fiercely independent-minded men struggled to submit to military discipline, but gradually they were being welded into an effective fighting force.

On 7th July, Alexander Shields had drawn up a petition addressed to the Privy Council at the request of the soldiers, to the effect that many officers who had persecuted them during the killing times were still serving in the army, and had not been disciplined in any way. Also that they had not yet received any pay! When they showed this to Major Henderson he approved, and Cleland did not object. But when the papers reached the Privy Council, the Duke of Hamilton was visibly upset, and issued a directive for Angus's Regiment to be remustered, and for this to be supervised by the Lieutenant-Colonel of Leven's Regiment. Blackwood was also ordered to attend. Lieutenant-Colonel William Arrot of Leven's Regiment, and Major Hugh Buntine the mustermaster-general, had arrived the previous night to draw up new muster-rolls for the Regiment.

'I'll start with the Lieutenant-Colonel's company if I may?'

Lieutenant John Stewart marched his men up to Buntine's table.

'The Lt-Col's Company is present for muster, sir. Three officers, including the Colonel, two sergeants, two drummers, three corporals and fifty-seven sentinels on parade, sir!'

'Thank you Mr Stewart. I have the Lieutenant-Colonel's details. May I ask your first name?'

'It's John, Major.'

'Oh! You were one of those banished to Barbados in 1687, I think? You did very good work freeing your fellows from the plantations there.'

'How do you know that?'

'In my position you have to be well-informed. I'm sure you have a lot of interesting people in your company.'

Maj Buntine recorded all the non-commissioned officers and drummers. The first Sentinel to be registered now stood before him.

'Name?'

'Peter Christie, sir!'

'Where you from, laddie?'

'Old Machar, sir.'

'An Aberdonian? Not quite covenanting country, is it?'

'No, but I am a Covenant man sir.'

'Good for you, Peter. Next!'

Once the company had been registered, the Mustermaster-General annotated the bottom of the paper:

> '*I, Lt Col William Cleland, do hereby declare upon my parole of honour that I mustered the above company without fraud or deceit, as witness my hand at Dunblane this tenth day of July, 1689.*'

'Kindly sign this Colonel, if you accept what I have written?' Cleland expressed himself satisfied, and signed the roll. Buntine countersigned in his official capacity.

During all this going-on, Lieutenant-Colonel Arrot remained inconspicuous, somewhat embarrassed by having to check up on an officer of equal rank. He was clearly relieved once the new muster rolls were finalised.

♣

'Major Henderson, I want you to take the companies out and get on with some real training. Since we don't even have proper weapons for all our men, and half are armed with pikes, we are going to have to get down to some serious work, to ensure that the musketeers are protected by the pikemen whilst reloading. I want companies to learn how to form an arrowhead *schiltrom,* with the sergeants at the apex. Pikemen in the front rank, musketeers in the second rank.'

'But Colonel, that is very unusual! I've never seen it before.'

'Nevertheless, these are my orders! It's like a human demi-lune. It puts a great deal of pressure on the sergeants to stand fast, but means the initial shock of a charge is reduced over a broad front. Worked for Bruce at Bannockburn, so why not for us now? It also means that all the musketeers have a clear shot at the gaps between companies. Better than if they are simply in extended line. The highlanders do not fight as sophisticated armies do. They discharge their firearms, then throw them away and charge right in with claymore and targe. Volley fire does not deter them, they just keep coming until they close. Perhaps it may turn out to be a blessing there were not enough muskets for us all. Pikes will keep the enemy at arm's length if we use them properly!'

'Pretty original, if I may say so sir.'

'Thanks! What would you call it?'

Henderson paused to think. 'What about interlocking arcs of fire?'

'Not bad, though I doubt if it will catch on!'

Cleland continued: 'We'll use your company and mine as guinea pigs. Use the other companies as enemy, until they pick up the idea and we get the whole lot working together. We may show these old soldiers a thing or two!'

'I trust we are not going to do anything which might be construed as ungentlemanly? We have enough trouble with the powers-that-be, as it is!'

'James, I know you have been involved in continental wars and served in actions where opposing commanders invited each other to fire the first volley, thereby having a number of their own men killed for no other reason than etiquette. I am not about to have any of my men killed for etiquette! Maybe for honour, but not for etiquette!'

Henderson looked doubtful.

Turning to the Major's company, Cleland called out, 'Sergeant Bell! Step forward!' A grizzled veteran stepped out. 'John, you were with me at Drumclog, were you not?'

'I was indeed, sir!'

'How many casualties did we take?'

'Only one in the bog. John Morton, as I recall.'

'And why was that?'

'Because he lifted his head to see what was going on, when you had ordered us all to lie down.'

Turning to Major Henderson, 'Would you consider lying down to receive enemy fire an ungentlemanly act?'

'On the continent, I would! But against irregulars, I'm not so sure.'

'Well, take note Major that I will not permit any of our men to be killed for no good purpose. I expect them to fight and I have no doubt many of them will die, but they should die fighting, not for some misplaced conception of honour!

'Now let's get on with it! We have been ordered to join the Earl of Argyle with his own Regiment and Glencairn's at Inveraray, and to deal with the rebels at Lochaber. We must be very fit to cope with the forced marches we will face.'

♣

'Gentlemen, the news is very bad!' Argyll had called his commanding officers together in Inveraray for an urgent briefing. 'I have within the hour received an urgent dispatch from Edinburgh to the effect that General Mackay has been defeated by Dundee at Killiecrankie. Dundee himself is killed, but his army is heading south, and there is a real possibility it may take Perth! If it reaches Stirling the Privy Council plan to flee to England! Pretty gutless bunch, but they are politicians after all!'

The assembled officers expressed their concern, but Argyll cut across the conversation. 'We will return by forced marches to our quarters in the Stirling area. Be prepared to march within the hour!'

There was a chorus of 'My Lord!' and the commanding officers wasted no time in getting back to their units to issue orders for the move out.

'Colonel Cleland, if you would, kindly remain behind for a minute.' William looked worried. 'Your Regiment is double the strength of all the others, and while we require to get back to central Scotland as quickly as possible, I cannot leave Argyle completely at the mercy of the rebels. I therefore propose to detach seven of your companies to remain and police Kintyre. You have two companies commanded by Campbells. I would appreciate if they might be included?'

'My Lord, I also have two companies commanded by Stewarts! Would you like them too?'

'Cleland, your reply borders on the insubordinate!'

'Nevertheless my Lord, I must insist on my right to select which companies I will detach. I believe you will find them all effective, and perhaps you might be able to arm them up to scale? Captain William Greive will be in overall command of the detachment. Captain Campbell of Moy I wish to keep under my command, as his lands are close to Ruthven Castle which appears to be a vital point in the current campaign. Now with your leave sir, I must go!'

The weather was so bitter that two men died on the march back to Dumbarton, but by 10 August, the main body of Cameronians was once again at quarters in Dunblane.

CHAPTER TWENTY

"A PYRRIC VICTORY?"

Midnight 26/27 July 1689. Dunkeld.

MAJOR GENERAL HUGH MACKAY, Commander-in-Chief in Scotland, had spent a frustrating two months chasing to and fro after Dundee in the highlands. He had received information that a rendezvous of potential Jacobite supporters was planned for 29 July at Blair Castle. Dundee was expected to reach the castle on the night of 26/27 July. Mackay was advancing to intercept him with a force of 3000 foot and two troops of horse. A significant number of his infantry units were newly raised and untried, but he had three understrength regiments from his Anglo-Scots Brigade who had considerable experience of continental warfare.

However what had not been taken into account by most of his officers was the fact that the highland style of warfare was radically different to that which they had experienced on the continent. Also, whilst his infantry was equipped with the new flintlock musket, the bayonet which was issued with it had to be screwed into the muzzle before use, thus making it impossible to reload or fire the musket with the bayonet fixed.

Despite the non-appearance of six troops of horse which he had expected from Stirling, Mackay decided to march with the troops he had mustered. By nightfall on 26 July he had reached Dunkeld where he bivouacked. At midnight he was still working on his orders for the following day.

'Despatch from my Lord Murray, sir.' Captain Bruce Elphinstone ushered a mud-bespattered rider into Major General Mackay's presence.

Mackay quickly tore open the package and read the contents. 'He says that Dundee showed up at Blair yesterday, and he was forced to withdraw. He left a picquet at the north end of the pass and is withdrawing to join us.' Mackay looked worried. 'I doubt if his men will hold the pass for us. Ask Colonel Lauder to attend me immediately.'

'You wanted me sir? '

'Yes Lauder, I want you to take two-hundred of your fusiliers, and march immediately for the Pass of Killiecrankie, to picquet the north end and enable our main body to get through safely.' Within 30 minutes Lauder and his fusiliers were marching out of Dunkeld.

By daybreak, the rest of Mackay's force was already moving out on the road to Killiecrankie, but before reaching the pass, Lord Murray met up with the general. He had a very small group of horsemen with him. 'General, I regret to tell you that most of my men took to the hills when Dundee appeared, and I have doubts about the fortitude of the picquet I posted at the north end of the pass.'

'Did you not see Colonel Lauder on your way down?'

'I did sir, but I thought it best to report to you in person.'

'Hm!' Turning to the Earl of Leven who rode with his command group, 'My Lord, be good enough to detach Lieutenant-Colonel Arrot and two-hundred men to move forward and reinforce Colonel Lauder at the north end of the pass, and report back when they get there. They must keep the pass clear until the main body is through!'

'Very good, General!'

At noon, having received a report that the road was clear, Mackay's army commenced its march through the Pass of Killiecrankie. To their right, the rock rose sheer above them, and below them the River Garry thundered along in raging flood. The column was severely restricted to the narrow road, and the potential for ambush was very evident. A few men on the heights above could have stopped the entire column by the simple expedient of rolling rocks down the cliffside. Mackay rode near the head of the column, immediately behind the vanguard, Balfour's Regiment.

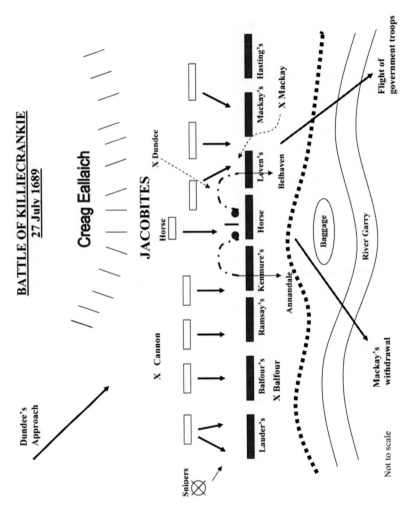

Battle of Killiecrankie 27 July 1689.

Emerging from the pass, Mackay saw to his relief that there was no sign of the enemy. Unbeknown to him Dundee had been waiting for the Irish levies to join him before advancing from Blair Atholl. However he had detached 400 men under Sir Alexander Maclean to attack Lauder's advance guard by the most direct route, whilst his main force of 2000 was approaching by a flank march around Creag Eallaich and was about to debouch onto the steep slope rising above Mackay's position.

Mackay seeing the danger, having sent Lauder's advance guard to clear Maclean's 400 from the ridge, ordered his battalions to right form, and ascend to an area of flat ground, suitable for deployment and further away from the river where his baggage train had halted.

His extreme left flank was held by Lauder and his fusiliers, with Balfour's and Ramsey's Regiments next to them. Balfour himself was in overall command of the left wing. This wing consisted mostly of veterans of the Anglo-Dutch brigade, who could be expected to stand fast in the face of severe assault, although the regiments also contained a large percentage of recently recruited Scotsmen. Kenmure's, newly raised and unblooded, was deployed as two half-battalions in the centre. Mackay himself commanded the right wing, consisting of the newly raised Leven's Regiment, Mackay's own Regiment from Holland, and an English Regiment under Col Fernando Hastings. In the centre were two troops of horse under Lords Belhaven and Annandale.

Riding along the front of his extended battleline, Mackay stopped before each unit to say a few words of encouragement. 'Stand fast and we will prove ourselves men today! Do not let our line be broken, or we are all in trouble! We depend upon each other, and we have the advantages of discipline and training!' As he rode slowly along the line, some enemy snipers who had moved forward to have a better view, took potshots at him. Although the General was unharmed, several men close to him were brought down, so he detached his nephew Captain Robert Mackay with some skirmishers, to drive them off. This was achieved successfully.

Hugh Mackay was greatly concerned about the danger of a night attack or forced withdrawal after sunset. Darkness favoured irregular units such as the highlanders, and his many untried troops had little experience of night movement. It was now getting to be about six o'clock in the evening, and although the sun was low, it still shone into the eyes of Dundee's men. For two long hours, the two small armies faced each other.

'Come oan! Come oan,' muttered the young soldiers through gritted teeth!

'Stand fast! Dammit, stand fast there!' growled the sergeants, as the line began to sway. 'You'll huv tae be real soldiers th' day.'

The men sweated in their heavy scarlet coats, and looked anxiously uphill at the highlanders resting on their weapons, clearly waiting for the word to charge. The anticipation was manifest, and for those who were in their first battle, nerves were stretched to breaking point.

'Aye, yonder's Black John of the Battles! I hear he canna' be killed!'

'Don't talk nonsense man!' retorted his officer. Nevertheless he was concerned about the growing unsteadiness among his men, and the mystic charisma surrounding Dundee did not help!

The sun sank lower and lower, but still glinted on the highland claymores. Only when it had finally sunk behind Ben Dearg, did Dundee, clearly visible by the great white plume in his hat, draw his sword and wave his men forward.

'Charge for King Jamie, your rightful king!'

With a great cheer the highlanders advanced at a run down the slope. There were some personal grudges to settle. The Macdonalds facing Mackay's Regiment, and Clan Ranald and Glengarry on the left-wing, had officers who had served under Mackay in Holland. The full weight of Dundee's left flank was directed against Mackay's own Regiment, which received them with three well aimed volleys, blowing wide gaps in the charging line. Despite this, the attackers closed ranks and continued to advance with unabated pace. Though the highlanders discharged their muskets too early and to little effect, they then threw them away and closed in with the steel. The highland charge was indeed an awesome sight.

The officers of Mackay's Regiment stood their ground and were virtually wiped out! Their men broke and fled down the hill towards the river! Such was the force of the charge that it missed most of Leven's Regiment to the right, which was able to pour a devastating volley into the highlanders from an enfilade position. Fernando Hastings quickly wheeled his battalion, only to see the enemy pour past him and disappear down towards the baggage, before he had time to open fire.

The Battle of Killiecrankie 27 July 1689 by Terence Cuneo. Courtesy of The King's Own Scottish Borderers HHQ and Museum

Mackay's left flank hardly fared any better! Kenmure's Regiment had withstood the attack of the Glengarry men with an effective volley, but any further hope of holding their ground was destroyed by their own horse, which had been ordered forward by Mackay, suddenly panicking and galloping back through their ranks. The same happened with Annandale's troop, which instead of attacking Lochiel's men, suddenly wheeled back through Leven's battalion, breaking it in half. Everywhere men struggled to reload, or to screw in the awkward plug bayonet. Disaster stared Mackay in the face!

The cavalry officers had rallied to the General as their troopers fled. 'Follow me!' cried Mackay as he spurred directly into the thickest part of the enemy. But only one man followed him, young Davie Semple, who promptly had his horse shot under him and was hacked to death while lying on the ground. Mackay, alone, broke through the thick of the enemy unscathed, and wheeled to survey the battlefield.

'My left-wing's gone!' he exclaimed to himself. 'It looks like I have the field to myself!' Where his centre had stood was a pall of smoke. Looking around the broad sweep of the plateau which, until a few minutes ago had been held by six regiments of infantry, he spotted one small group of redcoats. Riding towards them he found them to be the remainder of Leven's Regiment, under the command of the Earl. 'Well done my Lord! You have done better than most today! I suggest you get yourself into a state to receive any further attack. I am going to check out Colonel Hastings, for I see his Regiment still stands fast!'

As he rode forward he was joined by his nephew Captain Richard Mackay, who although wounded in several places, remained in the saddle. 'Ritchie! You are still alive! Are you badly wounded?'

'I can still ride, sir. What are your orders?'

'I want you to go after these cowards who have fled. Round them up and get them to come back to muster at the river! And tell Hastings to join up with the Earl of Leven and prepare to withdraw!' Captain Mackay rode off towards Hastings' Regiment.

'Withdraw? Withdraw, sir! I am not about to quit this field while my Regiment is still in good order!' remonstrated Colonel Fernando Hastings.

'Very commendable attitude Colonel, but your Regiment and Leven's are probably the only hope we have of getting off this field with any of us still alive!'

The surviving officers of Mackay's own Regiment gathered around him as he returned towards the centre of the field. 'Did anybody see what happened to Dundee?'

'I saw him disappear into the battle smoke at the head of his cavalry, but I have no idea what happened to them after that,' replied Bruce Elphinstone who had miraculously survived, although two horses had been shot under him. Just then Belhaven and Annandale together with their surviving officers rode up. The atmosphere was icy to say the least!

'Gentleman, we have lost the day and it behoves us to save as many lives as we can. Our main danger is pursuit by Dundee's cavalry, so we will march cross-country to Strathtay, and then head for Stirling via Drummond Castle. We must survive, consolidate, and prepare to return and fight another day.'

The mixed group of horse and foot followed their General downhill to the river. Many were wounded and many more shamefaced. Two miles after they crossed the river they overtook Ramsay with a hundred and fifty of his men. Most had lost their weapons and were in utter disarray. Ordering them to fall in behind him, Mackay plodded steadily forward into the darkness.

Coming to a crofter's cottage with a light on, the General asked directions. To the surprise of his retinue he did so in Gaelic. *'A bheil sinn air an t-slighe cheart a Shrath Tatha?* Is this the correct route to Strathtay?'

'Didn't know you spoke the language sir,' said Leven.

Mackay raised one eyebrow as he responded, 'Mither tongue, my Lord! I am a highlander, after all!'

As the day began to dawn they were approaching the small town of Strathtay. The residents, seeing an armed force approaching out of the darkness, took fright and ran to and fro in a panic. Ramsay's men were so broken in spirit that they started breaking away up the hillside to avoid passing through the town.

Drawing his pistol, Mackay shouted to his officers to stop the men deserting. 'If these men leave us now, they will be murdered in the hills. Shoot any man who steps out of line! You will be doing him a favour! We must maintain military order, otherwise none of us will reach Stirling alive.'

Despite these measures, about a hundred of Ramsay's men managed to slip away, and it was discovered afterwards that they had all been killed and stripped by the men of Strathtay. The march continued with the half battalion of Leven's Regiment leading, and Hastings' as rearguard. The few horse still with them proved useful as scouts and to cover their flanks, but to Mackay's considerable surprise, no pursuit was encountered. As the sun set on Monday 29 July, Mackay led his weary remnant into Stirling. He had been in the saddle for nearly sixty hours, and during that time most of his men had had no sleep.

As he swung wearily out of the saddle, he remarked to the Governor of the castle: 'I cannot understand why we were not pursued. I can only think that Dundee was killed in the action, and that his troops dispersed after plundering our baggage.'

'You may well be quite right, General!   We've had fugitives straggling in for the past twenty-four hours, and their reports are very confused. One man said he saw Dundee on the ground and that he appeared badly wounded. We have another who reports that he saw Dundee's body being stripped by his own men. He himself was quite badly wounded, but was able to crawl away without being spotted. I think you will find your command is stretched out all the way from Killiecrankie to Stirling! Many died on the way and some of them were finished off by the locals.'

'I would ask you to see to the care of my men, especially the wounded. Meanwhile, before I rest, I need pen and paper to write a report to the Duke of Hamilton and Lord Melville.' That night Hugh Mackay slept the sleep of complete exhaustion, but in the morning he was up with the dawn, checking on his troops, and re-forming those units which had not been totally broken.

During the course of the morning, Major-General Sir John Lanier rode into the castle. 'Well, am I glad to see you, Sir John! I have a lot to tell you!'

'I have a great deal to tell you also. May we go somewhere private to discuss?'

The two generals were shortly closeted in Mackay's chamber, pleased to discover that hot coffee was one rare luxury still obtainable in Stirling Castle. Mackay still looked exhausted, and Lanier was most concerned.

'I'm sorry to be the bearer of more bad news Hugh, but I have to tell you that Edinburgh is in a state of total confusion! I have been sent here because of rumours that you had been killed, and that Dundee survived and already is marching upon the capital! We have had only panic reports about Killiecrankie. The greatest cowards run the fastest, and the capital has received very confusing news.   The Privy Council is considering withdrawing to Glasgow or even to England, and it has been decided to evacuate all troops from the highlands and allow the Jacobites free rein benorth the Tay. I took it upon myself to refuse to obey such an order, and undertook to defend Stirling, Perth, and such other towns as we still hold.'

'These politicians do not improve, do they? Even now I wonder where Hamilton's loyalties lie! These nobles are continually "trimming", and King William's cause is far from secure in Scotland. There is still a real chance that we'll finish up with an episcopal or even catholic Church of Scotland! Maybe even a Stewart King back on the throne! I'm going to muster whom I can, and march for Perth today!'

♣

Lord Belhaven strode into the Privy Council chamber early on 1 August, jubilantly brandishing a despatch!

'Well, that's better news at least!' The Duke of Hamilton had been in a foul temper since he had received the news of the Killiecrankie defeat three days ago. The members of the Privy Council looked mighty relieved, for they had all been operating on a short fuse, continually under the threat of having to remove themselves at short notice to Glasgow, or even England.

'Why? What's happened?' asked Sir John Dalrymple, for the Duke had not shared the contents of the newly arrived despatch.

'Mackay has met with some Jacobite rebels outside Perth and killed 120!'

'Goodness! That's an improvement!' Sir William Lockhart began visibly to relax. 'So we are back in business, are we?'

'Seems like it,' said the Duke. 'But we had better gather all the troops we can muster, because the prospect of booty will surely draw reinforcements to Dundee's army. By the way, who commands it now?'

Belhaven responded, 'We have no reports of any significant chieftain coming to the fore. Cluny MacPherson and Lochiel have withdrawn to their own lands, and no one of like calibre has emerged. In fact, it seems that Cannon, who led the Irish at Killiecrankie, is now in command of what remains. In retrospect we did not come off too badly! Latest estimates are that one third of Dundee's men killed, and a third wounded. That does not leave very many able-bodied men to carry the war into the lowlands.'

'Hm! Argyle should be reaching Glasgow in a few days with his three battalions.' Hamilton sounded pleased with himself. 'We also have two regiments of horse due to join Lanier from England, and Livingstone's dragoons are marching to Aberdeen already.'

'I think his Majesty would be glad to have this news,' said Lockhart.

'I have already sent a dispatch to London. Thank you, my Lord,' said Hamilton, dismissing Lord Belhaven with a nod.

♣

The Duke of Hamilton was closeted with the acting Chancellor, Lord Crawford, and Lord Stair, President of Session.

'Look at this letter I just got from Argyle. The man's after money again! He says that Angus's and Glencairn's have mutinied for lack of pay. Apparently Angus's issued a mutinous declaration before they left Dunblane, complaining that the army had not yet been purged of those who had persecuted them in the covenanting days, and that they have not yet been paid! I thought we had already dealt with this?'

'These Cameronians are a real headache!' said Crawford. 'They have got such an inflated opinion of themselves, we don't even know yet if they will be any use in battle. Bunch of religious fanatics!'

'Argyle suggests that Angus's Regiment should be reduced to the same size as other regiments. You'll recall they mustered twenty companies, instead of the usual ten? He reckons half of them might be of some use, but the other half, both officers and soldiers, are quite mad, not even to be governed by Rev Shields whom they regard as their oracle! So the Earl detached seven of their companies to police Lochaber. Means Cleland will not really have the strength for independent action!'

'They just can't be trusted! They are so bloody-mindedly independent that it would need the Archangel Gabriel to get them to toe the line!'

'The real problem is that their officers are not gentlemen! When they showed the declaration to Major Henderson he approved, and Cleland did not object. You can't trust them! I hear Cleland is teaching them most unusual tactics. Not the sort of things a gentleman would do! Like lying down to receive a volley!'

'Well, their men certainly trust them, which is the only reason we have such a regiment under arms. Whatever one may say about them they are not hypocrites, and have withstood persecution for many years. You might be surprised how well they fare in battle,' replied Stair. 'Mind you, lying down would not have done Mackay's men much good last week!'

'How right you are!' sneered Hamilton. 'But we might find an opportunity to get rid of them. That Regiment is a loose cannon and will give us much trouble in the future! Mark my words! Perhaps we could send them on a forlorn hope, so that they either cover themselves with glory, or disappear? Either way we score!'

CHAPTER TWENTY-ONE

"TRUST IN GOD..."

12 August 1689. Dunblane.

W ILLIAM CLELAND AND ALEXANDER SHIELDS were chatting together, when an urgent knock was heard. The door opened and Captain Bruce Elphinstone came in with the inevitable despatch in his hand. 'Direct from the Privy Council, Colonel. I was told it was very urgent.'

'Thank you, Bruce. Your family seems to spend its entire life bearing despatches!'

'That's pretty well it, sir.'

'Go and get some food and rest. You look like you need it!' Cleland opened the despatch and read it carefully. He then read it again. Thoughtfully, he passed it over to the chaplain. 'What do you make of that, Alex?'

Alex read the paper carefully:

Lord Angus's Regiment.

The Lords of his Majesty's Privy Council do hereby ordain Lt Col Cleland to march the Lord Angus Regiment under his command from Doune and Dunblane where they are now quartered, to Dunkeld, and upon their arrival at that place appoint said Lt Col to acquaint Major General Lanier and the commanding officer of his Majesty's forces at Perth, and to receive and prosecute such orders and directions as Major

General Mackay, the said Major General Lanier, or the commanding officer of the forces at Perth, shall give or send him.

He looked doubtful. 'There's more to this than meets the eye. Mackay is up north and General Lanier is somewhere off to the east. Why would the Privy Council issue a direct order to you, rather than to one of the generals? Doesn't make sense!'

'Unless they wanted to land us in trouble!'

'What sort of trouble?'

'Dunkeld is at the south end of a pass. Not as dangerous as Killiecrankie, but a defile nevertheless. It controls the road to Perth. If Dunkeld falls, Dundee's army will have a clear run to Perth, and if *that* falls, Stirling and the lowlands lie open to them!'

'But if we don't hold the pass, they could merely bypass the town.'

'They won't do that! '

'Why not?'

'Because these highlanders hate covenanters! Particularly me! You remember I published a mocking poem about the Highland Host of 1678? That still rubs them raw! We are like a pot of honey to bees. Also we stand for a presbyterian kirk, whereas they want to stay episcopal, or even catholic! If we hold Dunkeld we will have saved Perth, and perhaps Scotland. If we are destroyed, that will be one thorn the less in the side of the Scottish parliament. Do not fool yourself Alex, we have enemies on both sides of the fence!'

'But we are going anyway? Even though we may be wiped out?'

'Of course! Even though we may be wiped out!'

♣

The Cameronian Regiment reached Dunkeld on 17 August as dusk was falling. For the last few miles they passed inhabitants of the town who were not keen to see the battle, fleeing in the opposite direction!

'We'll lie to our arms tonight, James. Better base ourselves on the Cathedral and Dunkeld House. The perimeter walls give us a reasonably firm base,' ordered Cleland of his second in command. 'It's a great pity we have only 800 men with us! We could do with the 400 we detached to Kintyre.'

'Right-ho, sir! I'll see to the picquets for the night, and the rest can bivouac in company groups.'

'Get your advance picquets to reconnoitre at least half a mile ahead before taking up their positions for the night!'

'Sir!'

Next morning the Lt Col called his command group to Dunkeld House for orders, and set his men about improving the defences of Dunkeld.

'We must make this town as secure as possible for defence. All the breaches in the dikes need to be repaired and any ditches with thorn hedges on the enemy side must be strengthened and deepened. Anything which will slow down the impetus of the attack! The Cathedral and Dunkeld House will be our inner perimeter. Major Henderson, take the two Campbell companies and make it as impregnable as you possibly can. But leave entry points to the town and on the west which can be quickly barricaded. We may have to withdraw to our inner perimeter in a hurry.'

'Captain Lindsay, you will establish a strong picquet under an officer on the east side of town, with a clear retreat to the next line of defence. Captain Monroe, same for you at the town cross. Take your company and erect the highest barricade you can to prevent their horse attacking us along the street. Captain Steel, you're on the west side in the open ground outside the perimeter. Captains Campbell Dhu and Campbell of Moy, you each command one half of the inner perimeter under Major Henderson.

'The rest of you follow me! I will allocate each a sector, and I want patrols to a depth of two miles to your fronts. Report on the going and any enemy activity.'

Soon breaches in walls were being repaired, barricades set up, and trenches dug in positions where a good field of fire was possible. The town was a hive of activity. Supplies began to arrive from Perth; barrels of powder and boxes of shot; coils of slow match and sacks of rations.

'What in the name of goodness is this?' as Sergeant John Moore opened a barrel of what he expected to be gunpowder. 'Just look at this!' he said to the corporal assisting him.

'Looks like dried figs, Sergeant!'

'That's exactly what it is, laddie! Look at this, sir!' he called out to Ensign Lockhart.

'Hm! Someone in Perth is trying to keep us regular!'

♣

'About eighty highlanders reported to the north of the town at 3 p.m., sir.' Ensign Andrew Dennistoun was very excited! This was the first time he had been in action, and he was nervous!

'Who is keeping an eye on them, Andrew?'

'Captain Haddow has his company out there, keeping them under surveillance. He thinks they are about to send in a flag of truce. If they do Lieutenant Ballantin will conduct it through our outposts to the town cross.'

'Flag of truce coming in now, sir,' called out Campbell of Moy.

'Right! Let's go and join George Monroe at the Cross. Please accompany me, Maj Henderson.' The Lieutenant-Colonel and his second-in-command arrived at Monroe's picquet just as the Laird of Ballanchin reached the barricade with a white cloth tied to a halbert. He looked around uncertainly.

'I command here,' said Cleland. 'What is your business with us, sir?'

'I bear a missive from the gentlemen of Atholl mustering to resist your occupation of this town.' He held out a sealed parchment which Cleland took and tore open.

"We, the gentleman assembled, being informed that you intend to burn the town, desire to know whether you come for peace or war, and to certify you, that if you burn any one house, we will destroy you."

'H'm, very interesting. Wait, and I will write a reply! Meanwhile there is something I would have you hear.' With that he signalled to Lt Charles Dalzell, who began to read out loudly and clearly from a paper which he had just been handed by Major Henderson. The paper was a royal indemnity for such rebels as were prepared to lay down their arms. It guaranteed them safe conduct and retention of their property, as well as protection from future Jacobite reprisals, but the messenger gave no indication of listening with any degree of interest.

Meanwhile William was penning his answer.

> *"We are faithful subjects to King William and Queen Mary, and enemies to their enemies, and if you, who send these threats, shall make any hostile appearance, we will burn all that belongs to you, and otherwise chastise you as you deserve."*

'Here, take this to your leader, and tell him what you have heard read. I defeated Dundee once, and I will defeat his army the more easily now that he is dead!'

As the truce bearer left, Cleland and Henderson returned to their headquarters at Dunkeld House. 'It looks as though the fiery cross has gone out and the Atholl men are mustering in considerable numbers. I don't think Cannon has yet arrived with his main force, but it can only be a matter of time! I'm going to send to Perth for some cavalry. You know how the highlanders fear cavalry, especially if they can be cut off from their mountains!'

♣

'Cavalry coming in sir,' quietly called out a sentry at the ford. 'Looks like dragoons.'

Lieutenant Nathaniel Johnston, the forward picquet commander squinted through the early morning light. 'Looks like it might be Cardross's Dragoons. Stand-to quietly. Sergeant Richmond, inform the Colonel cavalry are coming in.'

As the cavalry splashed across the ford of the River Tay, Johnston was pleased to see that it was indeed Lord Cardross at the head of his dragoons.

Cleland was no less enthusiastic. 'Well, you are a very welcome sight, my Lord! What strength do you have?'

'Well met indeed, Colonel! I have three troops of my own dragoons and two of horse, Eglinton's and Grubit's. Where would you like us?'

'If you would station one troop of horse inside our perimeter by the western entrance, and the other between the Cathedral and the cross, to repel any attack by enemy cavalry, I'd like your dragoons to reconnoitre as far forward as they can. Bring in reports of how the enemy mustering is proceeding. I know it seems unlikely, but it appears that Cannon has actually got more men than Dundee had at Killiecrankie. We've had some reports from locals saying up to 5000 strong, but I think that is excessive. The only reason I can imagine that he has managed to raise so many, is that Atholl has finally declared for the Jacobite cause, and other clans are following suit. There's also the possibility of plunder. If they can knock us out of the way, Perth lies open before them.'

'Good! I would like to get a good feel of the land before we go into action. A proper reconnaissance is my immediate aim.'

'Perhaps we could dine tonight, my Lord?' asked William.

'As long as it's not porridge!'

'No, we can do a lot better than that! We can even give you figs for dessert!'

♣

Cleland and Cardross were whiling away the time after supper.

'Looks like the fiery cross has been very effective, Will. We took a few prisoners this afternoon and one of them was very talkative. We learnt that the Athollmen are flocking to Cannon's banner, plus several other clans, including the Macleans and Stewarts of Appin. He estimated Canon's force to be about 4000 strong.'

'Yes, I'm getting continual reports of campfires and movement of large bodies to our front. I think tomorrow will be an interesting day.'

'Tell me, how is your brother-in-law Thomas Steel getting on? He and I were exiled to the Carolinas together and then managed to get back to Holland. But he somehow contrived to be allowed to settle back at home long before I could. I only got back with the Prince of Orange!'

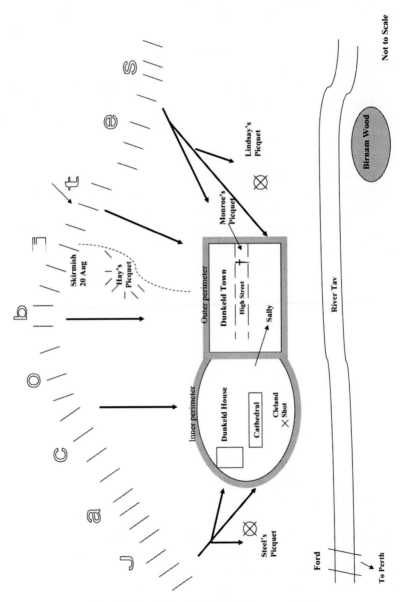

The Battle of Dunkeld 20/21 August 1689

'Just like me,' responded Will. 'The last time I saw Thomas, he was doing well in Jedforest. His cousin Ninian is one of my captains here. Not sure if you ever met him?'

'No, can't say I ever came across him. Well, I will just check my troop commanders and then try to get some sleep. Tomorrow promises to be a very heavy day. Goodnight, Will! Hope you get some sleep.'

♣

By first light the vanguard of forty musketeers and fifteen pikemen under Capt George Monroe, supported by fifty horsemen under Sir James Agnew and Cornet Livingstone, was almost out of sight. Ensign Alan Lockhart followed up with thirty pikemen.

'Right! Captain Monroe has the vanguard well in hand. We'll move out in thirty minutes,' ordered the Colonel. 'Just to remind you! Order of march will be: Captains Campbell (the younger) and Hume with a hundred musketeers, followed by Borthwick and Herries with two hundred musketeers and pikemen mixed. Then the main body, led by myself, leaving one hundred and fifty men under the second command to hold the town.'

The cavalry deployed as scouts and flank guards. As Monroe advanced over a crest he saw a group of three hundred enemy in the open ground before him.

The enemy opened fire at long range, managing to wound Cornet Livingston in the leg and bring down a few horses. The cavalry withdrew behind the infantry as Captain Monroe continued his advance, firing by half companies as he went. The highlanders withdrew under this disciplined fusillade, but rallied on the forward slope of a small hill, until a volley, followed by an uphill charge by the pikemen, cleared them off.

Just then Cleland rode up and drew Monroe's attention to a house on the left flank which he had seen some rebels enter. 'Captain Monroe, send a Sergeant to clear out that house on your left. They have you in in enfilade!

'Sergeant Anderson, take six men and clear these vermin out!'

Sergeant Anderson and his men made for the house at the double, but as they approached about twenty highlanders debouched from it and opened fire.

'Mr Sandilands, take twenty men and get Sergeant Anderson out of there!' Cadet Willie Sandilands needed no second bidding, but was off like a scalded cat, followed closely by his men. As the enemy saw him advance they retreated over the crest of the hill, and when he caught up with the sergeant's party, they all withdrew to the main body, carrying three wounded with them.

Capt Hume advanced to a small dike with his half company. When they reached the dike, they were heavily attacked by a large group of foot who came on very briskly. The Cameronians were forced back by superior numbers, and withdrew from dike to dike, keeping the enemy at bay with volley fire from each position.

'Very well Captain. It's clear the enemy are present in strength, hidden in the woods. We will withdraw to the town and make ready to defend it in the morning. Send a runner to Lord Cardross to inform him.'

'Very good, Colonel!'

♣

At 4 p.m. Colonels Cleland and Cardross sat their horses within the Cathedral perimeter. It was clear that Lord Cardross was deeply troubled.

'What do you think of this?' he said as he handed over a paper to Cleland.

Cleland read the paper and went white in the face. 'This cannot be right!' he exclaimed. 'Ramsay is ordering your immediate withdrawal to Perth! We cannot possibly spare you! You are essential to the defence of this town!'

'I am vitally aware of that,' replied Cardross. 'I didn't tell you earlier, but I had already received an order to withdraw before we went out this morning. I took it upon myself to reply that this was an impossible order for me to obey, saying we are in actual contact with the enemy, and my presence here was vital to the success of your mission.

This is the reply I have just had! What would you have me do?' Cardross threw his hands up in disgust.

'My Lord, you are aware that your men, of all the cavalry in Scotland, are the closest to our way of thinking. Most of your troopers have suffered as we have from persecution. To lose your support will severely damage the morale of my men. But you have no choice! The order is clear and peremptory, and so you must go, as I must stay. My orders are to hold, and even if I'm left on my own, I must stand fast!'

'I cannot say how distressed I am. And to get the order from Ramsay of all people! He did not quite cover himself with glory on the retreat from Killiecrankie! Perhaps he is trying to prove himself now. When I get to Perth, I will do everything in my power to be allowed to return immediately to your support. May God be with you!'

'And with you, my Lord. We would covet your prayers.'

With that Cardross turned to his aide. 'Jamie, how's that wounded leg?'

'I can still ride my Lord,' responded Coronet Livingston.

'Good. Go tell my troop commanders to report to me here immediately!'

Within a few minutes the five troop commanders had mustered to their leader. 'Gentlemen, we have orders to retire to Perth.' Seeing the startled reaction of his officers, Cardross continued, 'Our orders are quite clear and I have already questioned them. We have no choice but to obey. I want you ready to march in fifteen minutes. Is that clear?'

'Sir!'

♣

As the cavalry formed up and moved out in formation towards the ford over the Tay, the Cameronians began to gather inside their main perimeter, and watched them go with falling hearts.

'Where ye gaen, Wullie?' John Gibson called out to his cousin riding past.

'Been ordered back tae Perth, John! What sort of glakit sumph ordered that?'

The infantry was very restive, and as more and more men crowded into the Cathedral area, the noise grew! Men began to shout at Cleland.

'Have you brought us all here to die?'

'Whit'na use is it for us to hold this toon? Even the folk here loath our guts!'

'S'aa right fir you'se officers! We hiv'nae ony horses! You'se can get oot if it gets too hot!'

Suddenly the whole Regiment was shouting, and men were beginning to shoulder their packs with the obvious intent of following the cavalry.

Cleland stood in his stirrups and shouted for quiet! His officers and some of the sergeants also shouted for him to be heard. Gradually the hubbub died away and silence fell over the assembled multitude.

'My orders are to hold this town, and I intend to do that if I have to stand and die alone! But to show you that your officers are totally committed to you, I am ordering them to bring out their horses and to shoot them all!'

There was a stunned silence!

'Gentlemen, have your horses brought here!' Cleland swung himself out of the saddle and stood by his horse's head. He drew and cocked one of his pistols, and held it to his mount's forehead. 'I will not give an order that I am not prepared to obey myself. I will shoot my own horse first!'

'No! No! Don't shoot the horses!' a general cry went up from the whole gathering.

Sergeant Thomas Lyon, the senior sergeant, stepped forward. 'Sir, I was with you at Drumclog, and I was with Major Henderson at Muirdykes. I am fully convinced that our officers would never desert us in any time of danger. I will stand with you, even if no one else does!'

'Thank you Sergeant Lyon! Is there anyone else with me?'

There was a silence, and then the assembled Regiment erupted with cheers. Many took their hats off and waved them at their commanding officer.

'Well that's better!' muttered Will to himself. By this time all the officers' horses had been led out. 'Gentlemen, mount yourselves!' and they all swung up into the saddle. Cleland held his hand up for silence and an expectant hush fell over the assembly.

'Cameronians! This is a grievous day for you! We may say that this is a grievous day for Scotland, as we are about to be attacked by our own countrymen. But be of good cheer, the Lord our God is with us!

'You may think our presence here will have no significance beyond Dunkeld. I must tell you that the battle we are about to fight will be critical to the future of Scotland. If we fail, and the Jacobites reach Edinburgh, there is every probability that the Stewarts will return to the throne. You all know the suffering which you have endured during the *killing times*, and you must be aware that a Stewart restoration would bring these evil times back, especially in our home counties. Episcopal curates or maybe catholic priests will be enforced upon us again, and your new won freedom of worship will be denied once more to you and to your bairns. How we comport ourselves tomorrow will affect, not only us, but future generations!'

Turning to Alexander: 'Reverend Shields! Will you give us a word of prayer before we disperse to our several posts?' Alexander Shields removed his hat and the entire Regiment followed suit.

'God of our fathers and Lord of our battle line! You have brought us to this dangerous pass. But we come of a people that has always turned to You in times of danger! We ask that on the morrow, You might makes us strong and of a good courage, that we be neither afraid nor disheartened, but that we may face our foe in the certain knowledge that the Lord of Hosts is with us! Amen.'

The entire fighting congregation echoed the Amen.

'Now lads, to your posts!' Cleland stood in his stirrups. 'Whatever the outcome tomorrow, let us carry ourselves like men, for win or lose, we are fighting for liberty as much as our forefathers did at Bannockburn. The great sadness is that tomorrow we face our brother Scots!'

Silently the Regiment moved to take up their battle stations.

'Come on padre, let's go round the posts and see how our men are faring. It's always a long night before a battle!' It was 11 p.m. as Cleland buckled on his sword, clapped his hat on his head and made for the door of Dunkeld House. Alexander Shields grabbed his hat and cloak and followed. As they came down the front steps Cleland cast his eye over the guard at the front door. 'Orr! Christie! Bring a lantern and escort us!'

'See's a haud o' yer lamp Wullie!' demanded Orr. The two soldiers hurriedly grabbed their weapons and ran to catch up with their commanding officer and chaplain, who were already striding out of the gap in the perimeter wall leading to the town cross.

'Jings! Does'nie gie us much time, does he?' said Peter Christie to his friend Tom Orr. Despite the speed of their walk, Cleland and Shields moved quietly and surprised the picquet at the town cross. Lieutenant Charles Dalzell quickly scrambled to his feet when he saw Cleland, who signalled him to be quiet.

'Don't disturb those who are sleeping,' ordered William. 'They have need of all the rest they can get!' Dalzell nodded. 'Charles, I can't say how pleased I am to have you under my command here! Your father, I believe, would have been very angry if he had ever heard that you were going to serve with us?'

'He would indeed! In fact, he would be furious! He cut me off without a penny, but I didn't expect anything anyway! My mother was only handfasted to him, so he never really accepted me as his son. In any case, there is no way that I could in conscience continue on his way. He was a brutal and cruel man, and I hope that my service with Angus's Regiment many repay some of the hurt and damage he did to so many.'

'There's no doubt that you will. Each of us must live with our own conscience. That's what all this fighting is about anyway!' Turning to Lieutenant Stewart of his own company, he remarked, 'Not quite as hot as Barbados, eh John?'

'And am I grateful for that!' The mark on his face where he had been branded still looked red and sore. 'There are quite a few who were banished to the Americas who got back home and are with us tonight. Look at Macphie over there, minus an ear, cropped off before he sailed! How good God has been to bring us home from that terrible slavery and allow us to fight as free men once more. It makes all the suffering worthwhile!'

'Where's your captain?'

'Here, sir!' said George Monroe as he stepped forward into the firelight.

'Make sure your men get some hot porridge into their bellies before first light. We'll need to have a full stand-to then. It may be a long time before they get anything else to eat.'

'All in hand, sir!'

'Good, George! Come Alex, we'll go and see Jimmy Lindsay next.' The two friends walked along the north bank of the river, closely followed by their escort, until they reached the eastern picquet furnished by No 16 Company. 'Evening Jimmy, everything in order?'

'Very quiet sir! There is quite a lot of movement on the forest edge, and some campfires deeper into the hills, but so far all quiet.' Captain Lindsay was not one to be bothered by the proximity of the enemy.

'That's good!' Turning to his nephew Lieutenant Thomas Haddow, 'Tom, how do you feel about your first battle?'

'It's surely a far cry from Douglas, but I would prefer to fight here than in my hometown where my mother and sisters live!'

'What news of your Janet?' he asked Ensign John Kirkland. 'It seems that in this company everyone is related to everyone else! Your wife is your company commander's sister?'

'Well, blood *is* thicker than water, sir! We fight all the better for having our family alongside us.'

'How right you are, John! This Regiment really is a family, for we have all shared the same perils, and now we have a chance to put things right. You've been around since that conventicle at Kyle in '82, so you're certainly no novice to persecution. I seem to remember you've had a few run-ins with the dragoons over the years too?' Kirkland nodded. 'But tomorrow will be tougher.'

The Ensign grimaced. 'Aye! It will that!'

Shields pointed in the dark to the barely discernible loom of a wood on the south side of the river. 'You know what that wood is called, Will?'

'Sure! It's Birnam Wood. Oh, I see what you're getting at Alex!'

'Well, it should be an encouragement to us. If *"Birnam Wood can come to Dunsinane,"* then beating the foe tomorrow is definitely a possibility.'

'Please let us not get into a competition to see who can quote the most Shakespeare! We have weightier matters in hand!' Cleland turned to the picquet commander: 'Can you furnish us with a guide to William Hay's position?'

'Absolutely!' answered Jimmy Lindsay. 'Sergeant Spence, take two men and show the Colonel to Captain Hay's position.' The Sergeant led off into the night, with Orr and Christie bringing up the rear, but keeping close so as not to get lost in this unknown area.

'Halt! Who goes there?'

'Commanding officer and padre,' called out Sergeant Spence.

'Well, at least one picquet is properly alert. Good for Will Hay!' muttered Alex.

'Advance one, and be recognised!' called the voice from the darkness.

Cleland advanced alone.

'Halt! S*otto voce* from the sentry; *"The Sword of the Lord!"*'

'*"And of Gideon!"*'

'Pass friend!'

As soon as their group reached the light of the fire round which the off-duty picquet members were gathered, everyone scrambled to his feet. 'Stand-to!' Sergeant Robbie Robertson, in charge of the sentries, took his job seriously!

'How's the fishing Robbie?' asked the padre quietly.

'We have'nae ony time tae fish here, meenester!' Robertson was indignant.

Looking at several trout grilling on the open fire, Alex remarked, 'Is that so, Robbie!'

'You are the most exposed picquet we have.' The commanding officer spoke quietly to Captain Hay. 'If you see the enemy start to gather on that hill in front of you tomorrow morning, I want you to force them back, and then withdraw in bounds to the town perimeter. You've got a good man in Alan Lochart. He can be relied upon to exercise initiative and courage.'

'Yes, I know! He's been invaluable already patrolling our front and bringing back sound information about enemy movements.'

The small party made its way back to the town, checking on sentries as it went. Back at Dunkeld House Cleland found that Major James Henderson had allocated perimeter positions to companies previously uncommitted, whilst holding the pikemen of the 5th and 6th companies in reserve ready to repel any attackers who might breach the perimeter wall.

'James, one more task before you lie down. Please ensure that the quartermaster has supplied food to every position, so that our men may have something hot before we fight. I see you have already prepared to resupply powder, ball and match for the forward positions. Well done!'

'Thanks, Col. I hope you're going to get your head down for an hour or two?'

'Right now, James! Right now!' Cleland wearily climbed the stairs, and found his orderly, James Graham, waiting for him at the top. 'There's a letter for you by your bedside, sur. It came this efternoon with the dispatch for Lord Cardross.'

'Thanks Graham, I hope it's not more bad news! Make sure I am wakened at 3 a.m. A cup of tea would be nice, if you can find any! Goodnight!'

'Night, sur!'

William was weary to the bone, but knew that the next day would be even more demanding, and it was imperative he should get some rest if possible. As he walked over to the bed he saw a letter propped up against the candlestick. It smelt of lilac! With great trepidation he tore it open and read:

"My beloved husband,

I have no idea where you are, for I hear you have left Dunblane, but there is no news of where you are proceeding.

I fear you are about to be exposed to great danger! That is my wife's intuition, and I truly hope that I am wrong. However I want you to know that you have always been my one true love. Although I have been jealous of your love and commitment for our native land and your search for freedom for future generations, I know that you love me too.

As I write, our little Will is safely tucked up in his bed, dreaming of being a soldier like his father.

May the Lord keep you safe, and bring you home to me soon.

Your loving wife, Margaret."

William Cleland sat lost in thought for a long time!

CHAPTER TWENTY-TWO

"...AND KEEP YOUR POWDER DRY"

6 A.M. Wednesday, 21 August 1689.

LIEUTENANT COLONEL WILLIAM CLELAND had been on the go since before 4 a.m. He had used the time before dawn to good effect by getting his men to build up the perimeter walls even further, using stones from the ruins of cathedral housing between the wall and the river.

He stood by the northern wall with Captain John Campbell Dhu, and observed the surrounding hills as dawn broke.

'There's lots of movement the morn' sir,' remarked Campbell. 'Looks like they're all around us!'

'Yes, they clearly consolidated their force during the night. We're going to have an interesting day ahead!' Turning to his second-in-command, Cleland ordered runners to be sent to each outlying picquet to bring back up to date news of the current situation.

The entire Cameronian Regiment was standing to. Each company, or half company, under its officer, had taken up a defensive position behind whatever barrier was available. While the inner perimeter had stout stonewalls and the town had some garden walls, the more outlying posts depended on ditches and thorn hedges. However no sub-unit was in a totally exposed position, as had been the case at Killiecrankie.

'There's a body of horse moving across our front,' said Sergeant Andrew Forrest to Ensign Campbell. 'Looks like they are heading for the ford.'

The town of Dunkeld. (The Cathedral is at top left.There was no bridge in 1689.) Courtesy of Dr Patricia McDonald.

'They are obviously planning to cut off any withdrawal across the river,' responded his officer. 'Good thing we're not going anywhere!'

As the day dawned bright and clear, the entire Regiment could see movement on the heights above. The early morning sunlight glittered on broadswords as the highlanders massed in their clan groups. The soldiers, muskets primed and ready, or with pikes sticking through the barricades, waited silently. Most of the town's inhabitants had already fled, but the few who remained, and who did not side with the Jacobites, came in dribs and drabs, seeking shelter in the Cathedral. 'Get inside the kirk and stay out of the way,' they were ordered!

James Lindsay, whose company was covering the approach along the riverbank from the east, observed a large baggage train of packhorses some distance to his front. 'They travel rather heavy for a guerrilla force,' he remarked to Ensign Kirkland.

'At least they have not used their baggage horses to increase the size of their cavalry,' John replied. 'Not that they'd probably be much use!'

'Look! Hay's picquet is going to see the first action today.'

As No 16 Company looked northward to the small hill where No 12 Company was stationed, there was a surge of highlanders over the crest beyond. Pausing to fire a ragged volley, they threw their muskets to the ground and came charging down on the Cameronian position with a cheer. Echoing shouts resounded all round the hills and the eight hundred Cameronians knew they were heavily outnumbered!

The Cameronian musketeers fired a volley, but as the attacking Macleans wore body armour, (unusual for highlanders), the initial volley did not do as much damage as was expected. The highlanders pressed their attack home with all the vigour of mountain men, but despite many of them wielding two-handed broadswords, they were unable to close with the Cameronians due to the determination with which they used their pikes. As the pikemen kept the Macleans at bay, their musketeers were enabled to reload and fire a second volley,which this time drove the highlanders back.

'Up and at 'em, Mr Lockhart! We'll give you covering fire from the right flank. Musketeers move fifty paces right! At the double! Fall in on Sergeant Robertson!'

Before the highlanders knew what was happening Ensign Lockhart and his half company of pikemen had leapt over their redoubt and advanced at the run and with a cheer! They took up position behind a small dike at the bottom of the hill. The musketeers fired a further volley from the flank and advanced to join them. But the enemy now attacked in greater force and they noticed some cavalry moving to their flank with the clear intention of cutting them off from the town.

Captain Hay took over. 'We will withdraw as planned, holding intermediary positions as long as possible!' he shouted above the battle noise. 'Bounds as planned!' As Alan Lockhart led his half company back to their next prepared dike, the other half company fired a volley.

'Withdraw!' As Hay stood to wave his men back, his foot caught between two stones and his leg twisted badly. Unable to rise, he told his men to go on without him.

'We'll no' leave ye here, Captain,' responded the burly Sergeant Alex Hamilton, who unceremoniously hoisted his company commander over his shoulder, and made for the fallback position at a lumbering run.

♣

Highlanders now began to pour down the gap between Hay's hill and the east side of the town, heading straight for Lindsay's outpost. 'Here they come, boys! Soon as you've fired, reload and fire at will. Pikemen, dig in! They must not get within arm's length!'

'May God defend the right!' breathed Sergeant Spence, the company elder.

The crash of muskets and the clash of steel rang throughout the valley. Try as they might the highlanders could not get to grips with the Cameronians due to their excellent pike work, and the musketeers were enabled to reload, although under extreme pressure. The training on the march to Inveraray was now bearing fruit. The highlanders, with fury in their eyes, yelled and spat as they hacked at the barricades, but the Cameronians, grim faced, sweating and determined, stood fast!

However numbers eventually told, and Lindsay was forced to withdraw his company to the edge of the town. The east side of the town was now under continuous attack at all points, and despite the walls, a few highlanders managed to get over, only to be cut down by the pikemen waiting in reserve.

As the defenders were forced back from house to house, they fired the thatch of those they vacated. The fog of war began to billow thick and black, shrouding Dunkeld, as the attackers withdrew in some confusion to consolidate before coming on again.

Meanwhile there had also been action on the west side of the town, where Lieutenant John Forrester was stationed. Two troops of enemy horse started to move up from the ford towards the Cathedral, supported by infantry. Forrester's men opened fire as the cavalry came at them at a canter, but it was clear they could not hold the small dike behind which they took cover for very long. So he withdrew his men to the perimeter, and the gap at the western end was quickly closed up by willing hands.

The western half of the main perimeter around the Cathedral and Dunkeld House was now manned by a ring of steel, half pikemen, half musketeers, with two half companies of pikemen in reserve under command of Captains Borthwick and Steel. With the withdrawal of Forrester's picquet, the musketeers on top of the Cathedral tower now had a clear field of fire to the end, and being able to reload under protection of the parapet, made good practice against the enemy assaulting their comrades below. The as-yet uncommitted companies were used to resupply those soldiers in action with powder, ball and match. The order was given to keep only one end of the slowmatch alight, to reduce use.

Cleland had remained mounted throughout the initial stages of the battle. He appeared to be everywhere at once, checking on the forward picquets, encouraging the men on the outskirts of the town, and keeping an eye open for enemy groups forming up which might give some indication of a fresh attack. The highlanders were by now up to the edge of the town and beginning to infiltrate the ruined buildings between the Cathedral and the river.

The Cameronians were completely surrounded and virtually the whole Regiment was engaged in close hand-to-hand combat. The highlanders yelled their slogans as they came on, hacking, kicking, and even biting at any flesh they could see, but the soldiers, with fierce determination kept them at arm's length with their pikes, thus allowing the musketeers to keep up a continuous, if sporadic, fire. At such short range every shot told, and the ground in front of the barricades began to fill up with dead and wounded. The few Cameronians who were injured were carried to Dunkeld House, where Surgeon Gideon Elliot did his best with the limited medical supplies at his disposal.

'Hold them boys! Hold them! More powder and shot here! Quick!' John Campbell the Elder was right up in the heat of the battle with his men, hacking over the wall with his own claymore. Campbell pulled some of the walking wounded off the wall and ordered them to distribute the powder and ball which had been brought up. The musket barrels were getting hot with the continual rate of fire, and men wrapped neckerchiefs around their left hands, in order to be able to continue firing. The walking wounded also brought up buckets of water.

'Well done lads! Well done indeed!' The Colonel was right up at the perimeter himself, leaning out of his saddle, wielding his Andrea Ferrara to good effect at every opportunity. Suddenly he slumped in the saddle as he took a shot in the liver, and immediately afterwards was thrown to the ground by another shot which hit him in the head.

The chaplain who had continually exposed himself to enemy fire while assisting the wounded, rushed forward to aid his friend. Captain Borthwick commanding the reserve pikemen did the same, and together they raised Cleland up.

'Get me into the House quick! I don't want the men to see me like this!' Taking an arm each over their shoulders, Shields and Borthwick half carried their commander round the Cathedral and into Dunkeld House. The hall was filling up with wounded and the Surgeon was up to his elbows in blood, trying to staunch some fearful wounds. His surgeon's assistants were in the same case. 'Get him upstairs where he is out of this carnage,' ordered Elliot. 'Here you two, give these officers a hand!'

Borthwick returned to his company, as Shields and two soldiers bodily carried Cleland up to the room where he had spent the night. 'Put me on that couch by the open window!' ordered Cleland. 'I can see out of it, and I want to know how the battle progresses.'

'The battle is very severe, though I believe that it is God's will that we should pull through,' replied Shields. 'We have nowhere to withdraw to anyway, so we must stand fast! Now you lie down and take some rest!'

'All right! All right! Surely having once defeated Claverhouse with pitchforks, we can defeat his army with proper weapons and good discipline? And anyway Dundee is dead, his army is weakly led, and today must be our day of vindication for all with the scorn that has been poured on us over the years!'

As Captain Borthwick ran down the steps of the House, he was horrified to see Major Henderson fall back from the western wall, obviously badly wounded. He ran to him, only to find that Henderson had been shot in the chest and groin. A piece of his upper leg had been blown away and the artery was pumping out blood in spurts. Borthwick realised that Henderson had but a few minutes to live unless something radical was done. In desperation he thrust his fist into the cavity, forcing it against the pulsing artery, and held the blood back until Sergeant Hutchison and two men came to his aid, staunching the flow with their shirts which they had ripped off.

'Get him into the House quick!' Borthwick was under no illusion that the almost simultaneous loss of their commander and second-in-command could prove disastrous for the day. Grabbing Ensign Huie by the shoulder, he hissed into his ear: 'John, I have an urgent mission for you!'

'Right Captain! Order away!'

'It's bad! It's really bad! I need you to get down to the town cross and tell Captain Monroe that he is now in command.'

John Huie looked at him blankly.

'The commanding officer and second in command are both badly wounded and unable to continue. Monroe is the next senior. We need him here to take over command! Get the men in the rectory to cover you down the street and take a couple of your own men as escort. Now go!'

♣

The enemy had now broken through the eastern part of the town which was burning furiously. The barricade at the cross was under serious attack. Capt George Munroe and his men were very busy indeed! The press of attackers against the barricade was so great that parts began to give under the sheer weight of human bodies.

'What's that you say?' Monroe was annoyed by the distraction.

'Captain! You are needed back at the Cathedral!'

'Are you mad? Can you not see that I am totally extended here and cannot possibly retire?'

'The Colonel and the Major are both down sir. You are in overall command! You are needed at the command centre!'

'What? Both down?'

Huie merely nodded.

Monroe went to stand beside Lieutenant Henry Stewart, fighting at the barricade. 'Henry,' he shouted into his ear, 'you are in command here! I have to take over at the Cathedral. Colonel and Major both down!'

Stewart wiped the sweat from his brow, rolled his eyes and merely said, 'Aye!' as he thrust at another hairy figure.

'Hold on as long as you can and then withdraw to the inner perimeter!' Turning to Huie, 'Warn the men in the rectory to be ready to cover a withdrawal from the cross!'

'Sir!'

♣

As they carried James Henderson into the main bedroom and laid him on the bed, William Cleland grimaced. 'You look pretty bad, James!'

'I feel pretty bad, William!'

They both lay silent for some time.

'There's something I want to say to you before it is too late,' said James Henderson. Cleland merely raised one eyebrow. 'I know you have been slated by the nobility, who have continually questioned your right to command this Regiment. I want to say that I consider you to be one of the truest gentlemen I have ever met! You also are the only officer I know who always puts the welfare of his men absolutely first!'

'So you think I'm a gentleman, James?'

'I do! In addition to that, I consider you to be an outstanding soldier. It's because of your leadership and training that our Regiment will win today, even if neither of us lives to see it.'

'That's one of the nicest things anyone has ever said to me!' Cleland tried to raise himself up to look out of the window but fell back with a groan.

♣

George Monroe stood anxiously by the gap in the perimeter wall leading to the cross. He watched Stewart's men fire one final volley, and then run for the gap. The pikemen withdrew more steadily, but the enemy immediately swarmed over the barricade and were upon them! Vicious hand-to-hand fighting ensued, and George saw Henry Stuart go down under a tremendous blow from a lochaber-axe. He was promptly trampled underfoot by the rampaging attackers. Two pikemen went down, but by now the rest were within range of covering fire from the rectory, and reached the gap safely.

'Get this gap sealed up on the double!' shouted the Captain. Stones had been laid in readiness for that very purpose, and as the perimeter defenders fired disciplined volleys down the narrow street, the enemy was forced to a halt. This however was only temporary, as with a cheer, the highlanders, led by an officer wearing a breastplate, fell afresh upon the defenders of the wall. But by this time the pikemen were well-positioned, and try as they might, the men with claymore and targe could not come to grips.

Suddenly men at the wall began to be shot down! Captain James Caldwell standing beside Ensign Huie, threw up his arms and fell back, his shirt front blossoming red. John peered anxiously through the dense smoke to see where the shots were coming from. Suddenly the smoke cleared as if by a miracle! It seemed as though the wind was blowing away from the Cameronian position in different directions at the same time, giving a clear field of fire all round, enabling the defenders to see that the shots were coming from some houses overlooking their position. The conflagration had not yet reached them and enemy snipers in the windows were firing with surprising accuracy.

'Captain Steel! Report to me on the double!'

'Sir!'

'Ninian!' You see what's happening here? I want you to burn these snipers out! Take your men! Tie burning torches to the end of their pikes and set fire to the thatch. Seal up any doors you can, and burn them out! We'll give you covering fire from here!'

'Right boys, get these faggots tied onto your pikes! We will sort out these snipers and give them a taste of their own medicine!' Steel's men stood in a circle igniting their torches from a small fire. 'Right boys! Remember Bothwell!'

The gap in the wall was opened, and as two volleys rang down the narrow street, the pikemen advanced upon the occupied houses with a cheer. Thrusting their flaming pikes into the thatch, the houses were soon ablaze. Some doors had keys in them which were promptly locked, leaving the inhabitants unable to escape. As the fire swept through the sector, the screams of those trapped echoed throughout the area!

'This is a very hard day's work,' said Willie Cathcart to Captain John Campbell Dhu. 'I wonder if we'll ever see the end of it?'

By 9 a.m. the Cameronians had all withdrawn to the inner perimeter. Highland leaders continued to gallantly lead their clansmen into the attack, frequently at several points simultaneously. But the Cameronians had learned their drills well, and few got within striking range of the defenders on the wall. Here and there, a particularly fierce attack drove the defenders back as some attackers managed to scale the wall, only to be immediately repelled by the reserve pikemen under Borthwick.

After each assault the attackers withdrew taking their wounded with them when possible. The dead were left to lie!

'Is there is no end to these people!' exclaimed Monroe from his position between the Cathedral and Dunkeld House. 'We can hold them for now, but there will come a time when we run out of powder and ball, and then we will be unable to drive them back as we can with volley fire.' Turning to Captain Cranston, commanding the Earl's Company: 'Got any suggestions, James?'

'The gutters of the House are lead,' he responded. 'We can tear them down and melt them for slugs. Did it in the covenanting days! But once we're out of powder we are really stuck!'

'Very well! Get a party busy making slugs and I'll pass the word that any musketeer who runs out of powder must fix his bayonet and fight with cold steel!'

'Sir!'

The battle continued unabated! There seemed to be no end to the Jacobite reinforcements as their officers led them against the wall time and again. Both sides began to be very weary, and a grim determination was evident on all faces.

The chaplain was much in evidence, continually encouraging the defenders of the wall and praying with the wounded, while more practically attending to their hurts. Periodically he would disappear into Dunkeld House to encourage the Surgeon and his mates and to check on Cleland and Henderson.

'Howzit going James? You must be in a lot of pain? I think the surgeon still has some laudanum left.'

'I think he's gone!' James said, gesturing towards the couch and biting back his pain. 'He's fought his last battle!'

Alex walked over to the couch by the window and looked down on the face of his friend. 'He looks so peaceful! He certainly fought the good fight! We'll all miss him.'

'We will that! Alex, you must help me get up and back out to the battle. I need to take over command!'

'I know you would crawl back to the battle if you had to James, but you can't even sit up! You're losing blood at an alarming rate! Just lie there and try to be at peace in the certain knowledge that you have more than done your duty and trained these men superbly. No unit ever fought better, and despite the massive odds against us, I'm sure we will carry the day!'

Henderson slumped back with a groan and passed out!

♣

'Getting very low on powder, sir!' Sergeant John Dalrymple's hands and face were blackened. 'Enough for another three volleys I think, but we are right out of ball!'

Just then Sentinel John McFarlane came round the corner carrying a bucket. 'Here's slugs for you'se yins. No very roond, but they'll dae the job!' He walked down the line handing out misshapen slugs to each man. At the same time others were resupplying the rest of the perimeter.

'Make every shot count!' shouted Lieutenant Nat Johnston. 'And only half-shot your muskets! We can still fire effective volleys at this short range.'

'Jings, Wully. These heathen are still coming!' James Cramond peered through the smoke in the hope of seeing some cessation of the attack, but if anything the assault was renewed more vigorously than before. The defenders licked their dry lips, gritted their teeth, and hefted their weapons as determinedly as ever. The dead bodies of the attackers continued to pile up before the wall.

Dunkeld was now a raging inferno with all but three houses ablaze. After the pikemen had burned the snipers out, the attack centred on the riverbank and the north-west perimeter. After each attack the highlanders had to drag more and more wounded with them when they retired, and the casualty station in Dunkeld House was a fearful scene, with men dreadfully wounded by battleaxes, clubs and two-handed claymores.

'Pray for us padre, pray for us!' Captain George Monroe was under no illusion that his men could hold out much longer! 'If they break through, we will make a last stand in the House, and if need be burn it down over our heads. There will be no surrender! But we could use all the help we can get, from any source!'

'We fight as we pray and pray as we fight,' responded the Rev Alexander Shields! 'If we stand fast today Scotland will be a better place for our children! Remember the words of Richard Cameron whose name this Regiment bears: "*They may take away our lands, but they can never take away the right that remains to our children, and our young ones shall possess the land.*" We call upon the Lord to witness that we are in the right, and to give us victory in this day of battle.'

As he prayed the noise of battle continued all round. The groans of the wounded mingled with the clash of steel, but the cries of the attackers were now silenced, for all throats were bricky-dry. Men fought with each other in a grim silence as both sides grew weary with the struggle.

♣

'The attack seems to be slackening.' It was 11 a.m. as John Orr looked at his friend Peter Christie through bloodshot eyes.

'Ah wouldnae' bank on that!'

But indeed it was true! The highlanders had drawn off to reorganise, and charged yet again, but this time their numbers were noticeably fewer and although their leaders led right up to the wall, their followers were noticeably less enthusiastic than before. Gradually the action was discontinued right round the perimeter, and the attackers withdrew out of sight.

'They've gone!' Sergeant Lyon looked down the burning street to the cross. There was no sign of the enemy! Sergeant John Dalrymple on the western wall scanning the body-strewn ground before him, saw no movement save for seriously wounded who had not been evacuated by their fellows. 'They've gone!' he said to no one in particular.

'Don't count on it!' said Captain George Monroe. 'They'll be back! We must use this time to good effect and strengthen our defences. Get the pews out of the kirk and use them to shore up the breaches in the wall. I want fire steps inside the church so that we can fire out of the windows if need be, and barricades in all the ground floor windows of Dunkeld House. Now get cracking!'

The soldiers were slow to respond to this last order. They were weary to the point of exhaustion, and many collapsed where they stood, and lay with their backs to the wall, eyes closed, just breathing!

'Come on! Come on!' shouted the sergeants with parched throats. Slowly and painfully the weary men got to their feet and, as buckets of water were carried around, slaked their raging thirst. Gradually discipline, which had come perilously close to breaking down, was restored.

'Company commanders to me!' This was the first chance Monroe had had to talk to his commanders, and the opportunity might be very short! Several officers were wounded. The Major's company was now commanded by its Ensign, for Henderson was mortally wounded and his lieutenant had been killed at the cross. Captain James Caldwell, of the 6th Company, was also mortally wounded, so Lieutenant Robert Stewart commanded his company.

'I want all companies which patrolled on the night we arrived, to patrol forward five hundred yards on the same axes as before. But be careful! Any indication of an enemy rally and I want you back here on the double! No more heroics! We have had quite enough for one day! The rest of you keep on working on the defences! What's the ammo situation?'

'Virtually out of powder, sir, but still some slugs from the guttering. Lots of match left!'

'Right! Captain Cranston, you're appointed second-in-command. Take over here. I'm going to check on the wounded.' As Monroe entered the hall of Dunkeld House, Surgeon Elliot approached him, wiping his hands on a bloodstained sheet.

'What's the bill, Surgeon?'

'Two officers dead, the Colonel and Henry Stewart; Henderson and Caldwell unlikely to recover. Quite a few others wounded, Borthwick and Steel quite badly, but all returned to their posts after treatment. Another fifteen killed, and thirty wounded, most of whom will survive!'

'Quite a price for our first battle!' George wearily climbed the stairs and entered the main bedroom. Cleland's body lay on the couch, his face covered with his cloak.

'Well Major, how are you faring?'

'I doubt I will ever rise from this bed again. But more to the point, how goes the day?'

'I think we may have won!' said George Monroe cautiously. 'The enemy has withdrawn and I have sent out patrols to see if they are really gone. I think it's just possible that we have defeated five times our own number!'

'God be praised!' James Henderson fell back wearily onto the pillows.

♣

As the patrols returned, all reported that the area was completely clear of enemy. Some wounded prisoners were brought in and questioned in Gaelic by Captain John Campbell of Moy.

'*Dh'fheuch ar n-oifigearan ri toirt oirnn ionnsaigh a thoirt a-rithist. Tha sinn deònach strì an aghaidh fhireannach ach chan ann an aghaidh dhiabhlan!* Our officers tried to get us to come on to the attack again. We are willing to fight against men, but not against devils!'

'Not very complimentary for an avowedly Christian regiment!' remarked Moy.

As it gradually dawned on the defenders of Dunkeld that their enemy had indeed withdrawn, with great shouts of joy they threw their hats in the air. The drums ruffled, the colours were unfurled, and the atmosphere changed dramatically! Someone struck up a psalm of victory:

> *Now Israel may say and that truly,*
> *If that the Lord had not our cause maintained,*

If that the Lord had not our right sustained,
When cruel and men against us furiously
Rose up in wrath to make of us their prey.

...

Ev'n as a bird out of the fowler's snare
Escapes away, so is our soul set free;
Broke are their nets, and thus escaped we.
Therefore our help is in the Lord's great name,
Who heav'n and earth by His great power did frame.

♣

Lieutenant John Blackader was writing to his brother. He sat on a stone and used his saddlebag as a desk. The battle was barely over, but he wanted to get his thoughts down on paper while they were still vivid in his mind.

Dunkell, Wednesday, August 21, 1689

Dear Brother,
    I have taken this first opportunity to show you I am in good health, because I believe many false reports will, by this time, be come to your ears anent our engagement, which was this same day; ... The highlanders came swarming in on all sides, and gave a desperate assault in four places all at once, first firing their guns, and then running in on us with sword and targe ... In this hot service we continued about three hours, the Lord wonderfully assisting our men with courage, insomuch that our old soldiers said they never saw men fight better ... The Lord's presence was most visible, strengthening us so that none of the glory belongs to us, but to His own great name: the enemy retired as we hear to the Castle of Blair; we expected

still they should assault us again, but word being sent to
Perth... we expect speedy help from thence.
    This in haste from,
    Your affectionate brother,
    J Blackader.

The civilians who had taken shelter in the Cathedral slowly started to venture out, only to be confronted by the devastation of their town! Some picked through the charred remnants of their homes to see if anything might be salvaged, but the majority stood numbly around the fires where the soldiers were brewing up.

'Here lassie, here's a wee bit hot parritch fir ye. There's no' much, but it will warm ye a bittie.' Little Lucy Anderson ate greedily, nearly burning her tongue.

Lieutenant William Cathcart was already in the saddle. 'We need to let the outside know how things have gone here. Ride hard, Willie!' George Monroe handed him a despatch for the officer commanding in Perth. 'Make sure this gets to the most senior officer. I earnestly hope by now General Lanier or Mackay may be in Perth! They are more kindly disposed to us than Ramsay!'

'Wait, Willie!' John Blackader came running up as Cathcart was about to put spurs to his horse. 'Put this letter in your bag. It's for my brother. He is doctor to the King, and it may be good if His Majesty were to hear about this action from one of us, rather than one of his ministers of state!' Cathcart took the letter and spurred off towards the ford.

The remainder of the daylight hours were spent getting things back into order. The soldiers concentrated on dressing wounds, cleaning weapons, cooking, eating and resting, while the Surgeon and his assistants continued to toil ceaselessly among the wounded.

♣

'Forasmuch as it hath pleased Almighty God to take unto himself the soul of our brother William Cleland, here departed, we now commit his body to the earth: earth to earth, ashes to ashes, dust to dust...'

The flaming torches flickered against the walls of the un-roofed cathedral nave. The stars shone down upon the Cameronian officers and sergeants, gathered to bury their commander. Many wore bloody bandages. Some sat on the pew set against the wall, unable to stand long due to their wounds. All were exhausted, yet there was an atmosphere of victory tinged with sadness. As the chaplain stood at the head of the grave, the body of Lieutenant-Colonel William Cleland in full uniform, his soldier's cloak covering his face and his hat with its black hackle on his chest, was lowered slowly into the lone grave.

Captain George Monroe, standing at the foot of the grave, carrying Cleland's own sword, raised the hilt to his lips and arced the blade gracefully down in salute.

Alexander Shields spoke. 'We have won a great victory today. This was due in large measure to the courage and leadership of the man whose body lies here. Let us ensure that he, and the others who have laid down their lives today, did not do so in vain. We may have won today, but there will be more battles ahead! Had we not stood firm here at Dunkeld, the future of church and state in Scotland might well have been different. Many will continue to misunderstand us, and we ourselves probably will misunderstand others, but I pray that the blood spilled today, by both sides, may become a healing sacrifice for our nation!'

Someone began quietly to sing a well known psalm. Others took it up:

> *The Lord's my shepherd, I'll not want,*
> *He makes me down to lie*
> *In pastures green: He leadeth me*
> *The quiet waters by.*

While the funeral service had been going on, the entire Regiment, save for the sentries, had silently gathered between the Cathedral and the river, where the other Cameronans who had died were buried at sunset. Standing in the light of the flickering torches, they took up the strain:

Yea, though I walk in death's dark vale,
Yet will I fear none ill:
For Thou art with me; and Thy rod
And staff me comfort still.

Eight hundred voices rose into the still air above the shattered town. They had more than justified the raising of their Regiment, and though they had been plotted against and had their support withdrawn, they had emerged victorious!

Goodness and mercy all my life
Shall surely follow me:
And in God's house for evermore
My dwelling place shall be.

Last Post. Cameronian officers guard the regimental communion table upon which lies the sword of Lt-Col William Cleland. Courtesy of Soldier Magazine and MOD ((c) UK MOD Crown Copyright 2010).

EPILOGUE

"LAST POST"

14 May 1968. Douglas.

'*C*AMERONIANS, THIS IS A GRIEVOUS DAY *for you and for all of us here! We may well say that it is a grievous day for Scotland, seeing that your roots have been so closely intertwined with the history of church and state in this land!'*

The Very Rev Dr Donald MacDonald, former chaplain to both 1st and 2nd Battalions of The Cameronians (Scottish Rifles) was preaching at the disbandment conventicle of the last regular battalion of Cameronians.

The picquets had been posted and the picquet officer had reported to the chaplain. The two wings of the Battalion stood under arms, forming a "V", with the regimental communion table at the apex. On it was the regimental cross and the sword of William Cleland. A congregation of several thousand attended. Behind stood the ruin of Castle Dangerous. Nothing much had changed since 1689! The Regiment had come home to die!

It had taken almost 300 years for the politicians to have their way! The thoughts of many were verbalised by General Freddy Graham, Colonel-Commandant of the Scottish Division. *'You have never yielded yet to enemy swords. You have to yield now to the stroke of a pen in Whitehall!'* Despite having been betrayed and deserted at Dunkeld, the Cameronians had gone on for nearly three hundred years to make a name for themselves as exceptional fighters.

Not a bad heritage for someone whose general once described him as:

"NOT MUCH OF A SOULDIER!"

♣

Would you approve of how the tree has grown?
I like to think so. You bequeathed your own
Love of a harassed land and honest cause,
Love which without advertisement or pause
Inspired a hundred Clelands less renowned
And warms platoons of Thompsons in the ground,
Men who have walked this road and shared this view.

Campbell and Lindsay forged the sword with you.
Lit by your pride they handed on the text,
Each generation shaping up the next.
Lindsay and Campbell finish it today.
Axed lies the tree. Now put the sword away.
No old forgetful age will end our story.
Death cuts our days, but could not stain our glory.

Written to Lt-Col William Cleland the first
Commanding Officer, by Lt-Col Leslie Dow the
last Commanding Officer, at Douglas 1968.
(Courtesy of the Dow family).

AUTHOR'S NOTE

THIS BOOK RECOUNTS THE HUMAN STORY behind my DTh thesis (Stellenbosch University 2008), *Bible and Sword: the Cameronian contribution to freedom of religion*.[2] Whilst the thesis is a dry theological dissertation, the human story behind it is both exciting and dramatic. As far as I know the whole story has never been told, so I hope this background to the origin of the Cameronian Regiment may fill a gap.

Although most of the characters and events in this book are historical, I have taken some licence, particularly with regard to meetings. My aim has been to tell the story, rather than to record a sequence of events. It is unlikely that Cameron and Cargill met in Holland, whilst Alexander Shields was not present at the Battle of Dunkeld, having been called away very shortly before the action to take a petition to the King. It is still not known which lady helped Shields escape from prison. His love affair with Janet is entirely conjectural! But in general the events occurred as set forth, and the people involved were there!

---

[2] http://hdl.handle.net/10019/1576

Cleland was indeed a tactical innovator well before his time! When no less a person than the future Duke of Wellington ordered his infantry to lie down during enemy bombardment more than a century later, it was considered a "controversial, possibly pernicious, innovation!"[3] Certainly the concern of Cameronian officers for the welfare of their men endured! When Sir Rory Baynes joined in 1908, he wrote: "The importance of looking after the welfare of the troops... was the first thing that had been impressed upon me when I joined the Cameronians."[4]

1689 was a pivotal year for Scotland, and the Cameronians played their part! Had the Cameronian Guard not provided some stability in Edinburgh, the probability is that Parliament would not have been able to pass the legislation declaring King James to have forfeited the Crown. The Cameronian victory at Dunkeld broke the back of the Jacobite rebellion and ushered in a period of comparative stability. It is noteworthy that the outcome of this battle was contrary to the expectation of virtually all parties, from Gen Mackay down to the common soldiers themselves.

The Cameronian Regiment amalgamated in 1881 with the 90th Perthshire Light Infantry to become The Cameronians (Scottish Rifles). Ironically the 90th had been raised by a Graham!

An indication of the importance attached by the Kirk to reconciliation with the Cameronian United Societies is evidenced by the fact that the General Assembly's first substantive business in 1690, after a gap of 37 years, was the reception into the Kirk of the three Cameronians ministers: Alexander Shields, Thomas Lining and William Boyd. Approximately two thirds of the Societies' members followed their ministers back into the Kirk, so the Cameronian heritage lies more within the Church of Scotland than within the Reformed Presbyterian Church of Scotland. This fact has been largely ignored by history. Only about one-third of the Societies' members went into religious *laager* with Sir Robert Hamilton and his remnant, cutting themselves off from virtually everyone and retaining only the most extreme aspects of

---

[3] Hastings, Max 2005. *Warriors,* p xiii.
[4] Baynes & Maclean, 1990. *A Tale of Two Captains*, p21.

United Societies' behaviour. In 1743 this group formed the Reformed Presbyterian Church of Scotland.

From 1689 the majority of the people of Scotland, including the most radical Covenanters, were free to worship according to the dictates of their conscience, for religious freedom in Scotland set a new course from that year. Thenceforth no-one was executed for his religious views. However, complete religious freedom was not yet established: The Episcopal Church of Scotland only became truly free from 1792, and the Roman Catholics from 1793. But 1689 was a turning point!

At the disbandment conventicle of the last regular battalion of Cameronians, the Roman Catholic soldiers, (about 40%), who had always fallen out from regimental religious parades, asked if they might remain and worship together with their Presbyterian brothers-in-arms. Alexander Shields would have been pleased!

Shields was finally ordained into the Kirk in 1691 and accompanied the Regiment overseas as its chaplain. At the Battle of Steenkirk... But that is another story!

CHRONOLOGY

1679	May	3	Archbishop Sharp murdered
	May	29	*Declaration of Rutherglen*
	Jun	1	Battle of Drumclog
	Jun	22	Battle of Bothwell Brig
	Jul/Aug		Richard Cameron ordained Rotterdam
1680	Jun	3	*Queensferry Paper* seized
	Jun	22	*Declaration of Sanquhar*
	Jul	22	Cameron killed at Aird's Moss
	Sep	12	*Torwood Excommunication*
1681	Jul	27	Cargill executed
	Aug	31	*Test Act*
	Dec	15	First United Societies General Meeting
1683	May	10	Renwick ordained in Groningen, Holland
1684	Nov	8	*Apologetical Declaration* published
	Nov	25	*Abjuration Oath* framed
1685	Jan	11	Alex Shields arrested in London
	Feb	6	James VII and II succeeds to the throne
	May/Jun		Argyle Rebellion
1686	Oct	22	Alex Shields escapes and joins Hillmen in Galloway
1687	Jul		*Informatory Vindication* published
	Dec		*Hind let Loose* published
1688	Feb	17	Renwick executed
	Nov	5	William of Orange lands in Torbay, England
	Nov	23	James II and VII flees London
	Dec/Jan		Rabbling of the Curates
1689	Mar	3	Covenants renewed at Borland Hill
	Mar	14	Cameronian Guard in Edinburgh

Mar	25	Scots Regiments from Holland arrive in Edinburgh
Apr	4	Convention of Estates declare James VII forfeits throne
May	11	William and Mary take Coronation Oath
May	14	Cameronian Regiment raised at Douglas
Jul	27	Battle of Killiecrankie; Claverhouse killed
Aug	21	Battle of Dunkeld; Cleland killed

LIST OF CHARACTERS

Principal Characters in Bold
Fictitious characters in italics.

Characters mentioned merely *en passant* not included.

à Brakel, Rev William. Dutch minister, supporter of the Cameronians.
à Marck, Prof John. Prof of Divinity, Groenigen University
Anderson, Sgt James. 7th Coy Cameronians
Arrot, Lt-Col Wm. Lt-Col of Leven's Regiment.
Balfour, John of Burley. Covenanting leader.
Balcarres, Lord. Pro-Jacobite statesman.
Balfour, Col. Commander of left wing at Killiecrankie.
Bass Rock. Governor of.
Belhaven, Lord. Troop commander at Killiecrankie
Blackader, Rev John. Covenanting preacher, prisoner on The Bass.
Blackader, Lt John. Cameronian officer
Blackader, Dr William. Doctor to King William III. Brother to the
    above.
Blackwood, Lawrie of. Cameronian regimental agent.
Borthwick, Capt William. 5th Coy Cameronians.
Boyd, Rev William. Cameronian minister.
Brown, Rev John of Wamphray. Exiled Cameronian minister.
Brown, Lt Charles. Officer on the Bass Rock
Bruce of Earlshall. Royal commander at Airdsmoss .
Buntine, Maj Hugh. Muster-master General
Caldwell, Capt James. 6th Coy Cameronians
Cameron, Alan. Richard's father, prisoner in Edinburgh Tolbooth.
Cameron, Rev Richard. "The Lion of the Covenant".
Cameron, Michael. Richard's brother.

Campbell, Archibald. 9th Earl of Argyle.

Campbell, Capt John of Moy. 8th Coy Cameronians.

Campbell, Capt John Dhu, (the Elder). 7th Coy Cameronians.

Cardross, Lord. Covenanter exile, cavalry commander.

Cargill, Rev Donald. Covenanting preacher and martyr

Carsan, Mrs Elizabeth. Mother of James Renwick.

Carstares, Rev John. "Cardinal" Carstares, adviser to William of
    Orange

Cathcart, Lt William. 7th Coy Cameronians

Christie, Peter. Soldier in Cleland's company

Cleland, Lt-Col William. Commanding officer Cameronians.

Cleland (née Steel), Margaret. William's wife.

Cleland, Janet. William's sister

Cleland, James. William's brother

Cochrane, Sir John. Deputy leader Argyll Rebellion. Uncle of Lady
    Claverhouse.

Colyear, Adjutant-general to the Prince of Orange.

Cranston, Capt James of the Glen. 1st (Col's) Coy Cameronians.

Crawford, Earl of. Privy Council member 1689.

Dalrymple, Sir James. President Court of Session, later Earl of Stair.

Dalrymple, Sir John. Lord Advocate, Edinburgh. Son of Sir James

Dalzell, Gen.Thomas of the Binns. Royalist army commander.

Dalzell, Thomas, Lt. 18th Coy Cameronians, son of Gen Thomas.

de Bie, Mev. Mother-in-law to Hugh Mackay.

Denniston, Lt Andrew. 11th Coy Cameronians

Dixon, Rev John. Cellmate of Shields on the Bass and Edinburgh
    Tollbooth.

Douglas, James. Earl of Angus. Col Cameronians

Douglas, James. Marquess of Douglas. Father of above.

Douglas, Lord George. Commanding Officer of The Royals

Douglas, Rev Thomas. Covenanting preacher

Douglas-Hamilton, William, Duke of. President Convention of Estates.

Elliot, Surgeon Gideon. Medical officer Cameronians

Elphinstone, Col Dougie. Despatch rider extraordinaire

Elphinstone, Capt Bruce. Dougie's son, also despatch rider.

Fagal, Pensionary. An adviser to William of Orange.

Flint, James. Divinity student at Groenigen
Fordyce, Francis, episcopalian curate in Cumnock.
Gordon, Duke of. Governor of Edinburgh Castle.
**Gordon, Sir Alexander of Earlston. United Societies' emissary &
prisoner**
Gordon, Lady of Earlston. Alexander's wife
Graham, Capt. Commander Edinburgh Town Guard.
Graham, John of Claverhouse, Viscount Dundee. Jacobite leader.
Graham (née Cochrane) Lady Jean. Wife to above.
Haddow, (née Cleland), Anne. Wife of John.
Haddow, Capt John. Cleland's brother-in-law. 11th company
Cameronians.
Hall, Henry. Covenanting leader, captured at Queesnferry..
Hamilton, Sir Robert, of Preston. Leader of Cameronian extremists.
Henderson, Maj James. Second-in-command Cameronians.
Hackston, David. Covenanting leader and martyr
Hastings, Lt Col Fernando. Regimental commander Killiecrankie.
Hay, Capt Wm. 12th Coy Cameronians
Hodge, Capt. Master of brig, *Song of Queensferry*
Huie, Ensign John. 6th Coy Cameronians
Hume, Rev David. Petition bearer to Monmouth at Bothwell.
Hume, Sir Patrick of Polwarth, later Earl of Marchmont. Whig
statesman.
Hume, Capt Robert. 14th Coy Cameronians
Inglis, Andrew. Covenanter killed for reading a Bible
James Duke of York. Subsequently King James VII & II.
Jenner, Sir Thomas. Recorder at Alex Shields trial in London.
Johnston, Lt Nathaniel. 5th Coy Cameronians
Justice, Thomas. Exciseman who captured Renwick.
Ker, Capt Daniel of Kersland. "Rabbler of the curates", 15th Coy
Kid, Rev John. Covenanting preacher and martyr
King, Rev John. Covenanting preacher and martyr
Kirkland, Ensign John. 16th Coy Cameronians
Lanier, Maj-Gen Sir James. Second-in-command to Mackay.
Lauder, Lt- Col. Advance guard commander at Killiecrankie
Law, Captain James. Landed Cleland in Northumberland, 1685

Learmont, James, Major. Covenanting officer and prisoner on The Bass
Learmont, Mrs. Wife of James.
Leven, Earl of. Exile, soldier and statesman
Lindsay, Capt James. 16th Coy Cameronians
Lining, Rev Thomas. Cameronian minister.
Livingstone, Sir Thomas. Cavalry oficer for King William.
Lockhart, Sir Bruce. Privy Council member.
Lockhart, Ensign Allan. 2nd (Lt Col's) Coy Cameronians.
Lyon, Sgt Thomas. 1st (Col's) Coy Cameronians
Mackay, (née de Bie), Clara. Wife of Hugh.
Mackay, Maj-Gen Hugh of Scourie. Cmdr Dutch-Scots Brigade and C-in-C Scotland.
Mackenzie, Sir George. Lord Advocate in Edinburgh.
M'Ward, Rev Robert. Exiled Cameronian minister
Middleton. Governor of Blackness Castle
Monmouth, Duke of. Variously royal and rebel commander.
Morton, John. Covenanter killed at Drumclog.
Monroe, Capt George. 18th Coy Cameronians.
Murray, Trooper. Cut off Richard Cameron's head after he was killed.
Orange-Nassau, William, Prince of Orange, subsequently King William III & II.
Orr, Thomas. Soldier in Cleland's company.
Paterson, Sir William. Clerk to the Privy Council. Former lecturer of A Shields.
Perth, Earl of. Lord Chancellor for Scotland
Quartermaster. The Royals.
Queensberry, Marquess of. King James' High Commissioner for Scotland.
Ramsay, Col. Army commander at Perth.
Ramsey, David. Royalist second-in-command at Airdsmoss.
Renwick, Rev James. Cameronian minister and martyr.
Russell, Andrew. Benefactor of Scots exiles in Rotterdam.
Ross, Lord William. Cavalry officer, Claverhouse's Best Man.
Rothes, Duke of. Lord Chancellor, judge at Cargill's trial.
Sandilands, Willie. Cadet Cameronians.

Scot, James. Married Janet Cleland.

Semple, Davie. Picquet commander, Mackay's servant at Killiecrankie

Semple, Effie. Housewife in Hamilton, cousin to Gavin.

Semple, Gavin. Covenanter at Bothwell Brig

Semple, Jimmy. Servant of Hugh Mackay and a boarding house keeper

Semple, Marette. Servant of Mev de Bie and wife of Jimmy.

Shields, Rev Alexander. Chaplain to the Cameronian Regiment.

Shields, Michael. Scribe to the United Societies.

Shields, Mrs. Mother of Alex and Michael.

Smith, Walter. Cameronian intellectual. Executed with Cargill.

Spence, Sgt William. 16th Coy Cameronians

Steel, Capt Ninian. 19th Coy Cameronians.

Steel, John. Margaret Cleland's father.

Steel, Thomas. Chamberlain of Jedforest. Margaret Clelands's brother.

Stuart, Lt Henry. 3rd Coy Cameronians

Stewart, Lt John. Sold into slavery, subsequently 2nd (Lt Col's) Coy.

Tarbet, Viscount George. Lord Chancellor, Edinburgh

Ure, James of Shargaton. Covenanting soldier.

Van Deventer, Capt. Master of barque which Renwick and A Shields sailed on

Veitch, Rev William. Spy with Wm Cleland in 1685

Walker, Patrick. Cameronian writer.

Waus. Keeper of Edinburgh Tolbooth.

Welch, John, Rev. Covenanting preacher, leader of moderates.

Young, Scribbie. Tavern keeper in Strathaven.